Buzzard Bait

Secessionists, Drones, & Serial Killers:
Nowhere Else But Texas

Nick Sibelius Series, Book 3

by R.W.Hacker

Buzzard Bait

R. W. Hacker

ISBN-13: 978-0-9982030-2-7

Buzzard Bait

R. W. Hacker

Acknowledgments

These novels have been a way to say goodbye to Texas after moving to Seattle a few years ago. Several decades of my life and some of the most important events happened there: meeting and marrying the woman I have loved from the moment I met her, becoming a father, and learning to fly. I am indebted to family and friends, as well as the many people whose paths I've crossed while living in the state. And I'd be remiss if I didn't' thank my friend, Chip Locklear for his careful edit of the final manuscript.

Buzzard Bait

R. W. Hacker

Table of Contents

R. W. Hacker

Buzzard Bait

Buzzard Bait

Lake Hazard

Nick leaned back in the cockpit of a rental sailboat, admiring a very fine, bikini-clad ass. Death wasn't on Nick's mind. Theresa, his partner in business and, over the last few months, in life, made her way across their boat's sparse deck. With line in one hand, she fed loops until only a few feet remained, then twirled it around the center of her coil to make a neat package. Nick kept them sailing generally on course, but he found the small gold bracelet on her left ankle, the tuck of white bikini panties between those round, muscular butt cheeks, and her dark, straight hair tumbling down her back, to be quite distracting. When a wake from a bass boat racing past at high speed slammed into their sloop, he initially admired Theresa's athletic form flipping gracefully overboard. Then she hit the warm water of Lake Travis with a ferocious smack.

He yelled over the roar of three hundred Evinrude horses. "What the hell! Slow down!" The boat, lost in its own engine spray, sped away like some giant buzzing water insect.

"Theresa!"

Having focused on the offending boat, Nick had kept sailing on, which meant Theresa was somewhere behind him. He searched the water, making out her head fifty yards away.

"I'm coming around!"

Nick tacked and the sails fell limp, then gathered air, flapping loudly. Theresa, who learned to sail as a young girl, had talked him into going out today. Nick's entire sailing career consisted of a single outing on a twelve foot Sunfish at camp in high school. Sailing a twenty-eight foot sloop with a mainsail and whatever they call that triangular sail in the front, left him with a steep learning curve. Not the optimum conditions for saving your girlfriend from drowning.

As he turned, he kept an eye on Theresa, then watched in disbelief as another bass boat raced toward her. Frantically waving, he yelled at the boat. "Stop. Turn away! Stop!" It missed her by only a few feet, then passed Nick, its wake leaving him grasping for a firm hold.

"Theresa!" *I can't see her. Did I hit her? Oh, God.* "Theresa!" He saw a flash of white. Her bikini. Screw this. Nick dropped the sails and dove in, swimming in the direction he last saw her. He stopped, treading water to scan the lake.

"Theresa!"

A splatter of water to his right.

He raced toward it, each stroke an explosive splash. Part of her head rose above the surface. He closed the fifteen feet between them, slipped an arm around her chest, and rested her back on his hip.

"You're okay. I've got you."

"Nick." She gasped, coughing. "What...happened?"

"Let's get back first."

He got them to the boat's stern, slipped a life preserver on her, and with some effort, hauled her aboard. Blood dribbled down her forehead.

"Goddamn fishermen. Jesus." Nick pressed a cloth to her head, already imagining the terror and anguish those fishermen would experience from his vengeance.

Theresa smiled, placing a hand on Nick's. "My own fault."

"Your fault? You've got to be kidding me. Those assholes came through here at a hundred miles an hour."

"Yeah, but I should have been wearing a life vest. Anyway, I think I hit my head on the boat as I went overboard."

1

"Maybe you should be in a life vest, but those guys shouldn't be racing through here like hell on a hydroplane either. When we get back to the marina, I'm going find those bastards."

"Nick."

"What?"

She smiled, then winced. "Thanks."

He touched her cheek, leaning in to kiss her. "I believe rescue is part of my job description with you." They never talked about Izzy Zydeco impaling her with spikes to a wall or Nick fighting a blood match against a huge adversary to free her while Izzy made his escape, but the pain of those experiences left an imprint on both of them.

She pulled herself up, pausing as if to realign her senses, then stepped down into the hold.

"What are you doing?"

"Ice."

"Let me get it for you."

She turned, only her head visible. Swollen and bruised skin surrounded the gash on her forehead, still seeping blood. "I've got it, Nick. Just make sure we don't get run over by a cigarette boat or something."

A mixture of relief and anger swirled inside Nick's gut. If she'd been killed... How could he let his guard down, after all she'd been through? And the jerks on those boats. Clearly they didn't care about anyone but themselves. *Well, I'll make sure they remember this day.*

"Hey, move over."

Nick, lost in his thoughts, hadn't noticed Theresa back on deck. "You doing okay? Maybe you should let me get us back to the marina."

She pressed a plastic bag wrapped in a towel to her head, taking the tiller from him. "I'm fine, Nick. How about if I steer and you follow my every command."

Given he didn't know what to do with the sails, her plan did make sense. However... "Or I could fire up the outboard and you could kick back with your ice pack."

2

"We came out here to sail. I'll be damned if I'm going to let a couple of fishermen mess up my day. Now get ready to come about."

They sailed up the lake, then tacked back to the marina. Theresa expertly maneuvered the boat into a slip. The marina office, a small wood building on a floating dock, held an assortment of fishing, boating, and skiing gear. Stuffed striped bass, blue gill, and crappie hung on walls, each posed to celebrate the epic struggle of man versus fish.

A gray-haired man in his late sixties, wearing a green gimme cap emblazoned with a large mouth bass leaping out of blue water, sat behind a glass counter filled with reels. "How can I help you, young man?"

Nick laid the boat keys down on the counter. "Just turning in our boat. By the way, we had bass fishermen flying around us like they were at NASCAR. Knocked my girlfriend right out of the boat and then almost ran her down."

He let out a sigh. "Yeah. Striped bass."

"What do you mean?"

"We've got a big striped bass tournament goin' on this weekend." He laughed, shaking his head. "Some of these folks will kill their kin to get a lunker. So I'm not surprised. Those ol' boys put some big engines on the back of them bass boats. Crazy fast, tryin' to beat each other to the best spots." He paused, concern etched on his face. "They didn't damage my boat, did they?"

"Well, no, but like I said, my girlfriend took quite a fall."

He relaxed, leaning back in his chair. "That's good. Not good about your girlfriend, mind you. But good about the boat."

"They were moving so fast I didn't get a registration number, otherwise I'd call it in."

The man took the keys, chained to a bright yellow float, and hung them on a board crowded with other boat keys.

"Well, the tournament's being held at the Mansfield Dam Park. I'll bet if you remember what the boat looked

3

like, then you'll find the guy there. He's got to bring his catch in if he wants to win."

"I tell you what. If I find 'em, that will be the last damned fish he'll catch for years to come."

~ * ~

Nick climbed back into his pickup. Theresa, now in cut-offs and a tee, along with a clean bandage on her forehead, pulled a brush through her hair. She smiled at Nick.

"Don't let the bandage put you off there, cowboy. I can think of quite a few things we can do that don't involve my head."

Nick glanced at her and put the truck in reverse. "Glad you're feeling better. I'll definitely take you up on the offer, if you're sure about your head."

"But?"

He shifted into first, pulling away from the marina parking lot. "We have one stop to make, then we'll head on home."

Theresa looked out the window, then back to him. "Nick, I know what you're thinking."

"You don't know what I'm thinking."

"You want to find the bass fisherman who bounced me off the boat. And let me guess—you want to kick the crap out of him. Am I close?"

Damn. Bullseye. He kept his focus on the road, not wanting to give her the satisfaction. "No, I just want to talk to him. Help him gain a deeper appreciation of water safety."

He could feel her eyes rolling. "Right. Mr. Coast Guard's going to school him. Nick, leave it."

"I'm not a dog, Theresa."

"Leave it alone. Look, neither one of us saw a registration and we definitely didn't see a face. How do you think you're going to identify the guy?"

"I'll know."

"Nick."

4

He looked over at a slight pink tinge staining a portion of her bandage. "I'm not going to let someone hurt you."

"You mean, hurt me again, don't you?"

Nick gripped the steering wheel so tightly his knuckles turned white.

"That's what you mean, Nick. You still think it's your fault about what that psycho Izzy did to me."

He reached for her hand, feeling the ridges of scars left by the stake Izzy had driven through her palm. He should have been there. He should have protected her.

"Nick, you came for me. You saved me from that bastard."

"I know." She didn't get it. She couldn't. He had failed to keep his Houston PD partner alive, he'd let his buddy Quen almost get blown up, and he barely got Theresa out in one piece. Nick had sworn to himself he'd never let anyone take the people he loved away from him, ever again. "I know, Theresa. I just wish I could have gotten there sooner."

"You got there soon enough." She squeezed his hand, but he kept on driving to Mansfield Dam Park. Some good old boy with a rubber worm was about to wish he had never been born.

~ * ~

Nick expected to find a few guys in lawn chairs drinking Shiners by an awning for the weigh-ins. Instead he found a bustling crowd gathered at the park, country music from a local FM station blaring, food venders lined up selling turkey legs, tacos, beer, and funnel cakes dusted in confectioner's sugar, a stage for the weigh-ins and photos, a mobile fishing trailer charging five bucks for kids to catch perch with bamboo poles, and an assortment of vendors selling everything from folding camp chairs to lures to fishing vests and gimme caps. At the center of activity sat a gleaming new eighteen-foot bass boat painted metallic red with a sign proclaiming the boat came with the latest in fish-finding technology, ergonomic seats, and huge outboard engines complete with electronic ignition.

Walking through the crowd with the smell of hot dogs and funnel cakes wafting in the air, Nick made his way to the information table. A volunteer in a Texas Bass Roundup tee shirt smiled up at him, but his eyes focused on the armadillo struggling to haul in a big bass across the woman's well-endowed chest. A perky ponytail of blonde hair stuck out of a hole in the back of her Roundup ball cap.

"Howdy. How can I help you?"

"I'm looking for one of the competitors."

"Sure. What's the name?"

"Uh, that's the thing, I don't know the name. Just saw him pass by."

She chuckled knowingly. "A fan, eh? Well, they do all come back here to weigh their catches. So, I imagine if you stick around, you're bound to find him."

"You don't do any GPS tracking or anything like that?" Nick tried to keep his eyes up, but the armadillo was having quite a battle reeling in the bass on her chest.

"Are you kidding? Some of these guys would kill for their precious fishing spots, honey. They sure as hell aren't going to let us track 'em with a GPS. You fish?"

"Yeah, some." Nick looked around the park, feeling a bit defensive. "But not like this."

"Well, take your normal fisherman. By normal, I mean a guy who likes to drink beer and sits waiting for a fish that may or may not ever strike. When he catches one, he does a little jig, has another beer, then sits in a boat waiting for another fish that may or may not ever strike. When he runs out of bait or fuel or, worst case scenario, beer, he comes to shore with his catch and at least one tall tale about the fish that—"

"That got away?"

She dismissed the notion with a wave of her hand. "Oh, hell no, honey. They got away in the old days. Now the biggest fish in the pond is the very one, for the sake of the environment, he caught and released. So you take this normal fisherman and you give him a financial incentive, carbon fiber rods, and a 350-horsepower engine. Do you know what you've got?" She stood, hands on hips, waiting for his response, the armadillo still in the fight of its life with the bass on her chest.

"No ma'am, I'm afraid I don't have clue."

"A damn psychofishinlunatic. That's what you got."

"I don't understand. If you feel that way about fishing, then why are you here?"

She teared up. "'Cause my husband, well, my ex-husband, Harlan, died from his addiction to fishing. I guess I do this to honor his memory. He lived to fish, but my Harlan, he was a good man. Besides, my current husband's in the tournament."

Through the tears, the ponytail, the ball cap, and makeup, Nick now recognized Harlan Jones's ex-wife, Dolores. He'd interviewed her after Harlan turned up missing, then floating dead in Junior Pendleton's pond. "Dolores. Ms. Jones, I didn't recognize you."

"Sorry?"

"Nick Sibelius. I spoke with you after your ex…after Harlan, was reported missing."

She cocked her head, taking him in. "Oh, yeah. I remember you. Nick. I guess I should be thanking you for putting Junior in prison, but knowing the two of them, I can't help but figure it was some sort of weird accident."

"Yeah, you've got a point. But Junior's in prison for quite a few more things than drowning Harlan."

"I suppose he is. Well, if you're looking for one of the competitors, like I said, he's bound to show up here, so stick around."

Gubernatorial Jacuzzi

Governor Francis Adamson nestled down into the hot waters of a rooftop Jacuzzi, watching sporadic snowflakes dance in a cold Colorado mountain breeze before plummeting to their deaths like so many fairy kamikazes. Only her head protruded above the bubbling surface, her short red hair damp from steam and snow melt, the rest of her naked body luxuriating in warmth and the gentle massage of strategically placed jets. Closing her eyes, she transported herself into the embrace of past lovers. A development entrepreneur who did this wonderful thing with her toes. The college-aged daughter of a well-known state senator, whose tongue, during the last legislative session, worked a magic this Jacuzzi could never emulate. And her personal pilot, who took her up into the clouds even when they weren't in her gubernatorial King Air.

If only sex, her third favorite thing after power and money, helped her career. Instead, it always seemed to muck things up. She lost her first bid for President, mostly because her stupid bastard of a son, Izzy Zydeco, decided to become some kind of domestic terrorist in the middle of the political silly season.

Izzy. Now there was one for the books. She had actually loved the guy who helped create Izzy, a fellow law student at the University of Texas. The sex wasn't outstanding, but this was love, not pay for performance. After knocking her up, he convinced her to keep the kid, then left a month before the birth because a child would "slow him down." No shit.

8

Throughout her youth she dreamt of becoming a state senator, a governor, and yes, President of the United States. But at the age of twenty-three, even she knew having a child out of wedlock, which was nice talk for saying your kid's a bastard, would torpedo her political quest before she got out of the gate. As soon as Izzy took his first breath when she birthed him in her apartment, alone with no witnesses, she made sure to distance herself from him. She drove to New Mexico, called social services, and told them she found an infant seat resting on the hood of her car when she went into the local Albuquerque Walmart to buy Slim Jims and tampons. Using a fake ID with a false name and address in Little Rock to misdirect the authorities, she drove I-10 east toward Austin, never looking back.

Opening her eyes, foaming water tickling her nose, she lifted a leg up until her deep red French painted toenails splayed against the bare chest of her most recent lover, Bruce Reynolds. She smiled as he took her size six foot in his warm hands, nibbling her arch in his mouth. Not as good as her developer toe-sucking lover, but not bad.

She had known him for several years as a financial donor to her campaigns. He started small. A few hundred thousand here, a few hundred thousand there. So she decided he needed a more personal reason to fund her campaign.

Sex wouldn't do it. She had already tried campaign fucking earlier in her career. Men had an annoying ability to compartmentalize their bank accounts from their dicks. In her case, she endured six months of boring sex with a man old enough to be her father, but he had financial resources she hoped to capitalize during a run for state representative. Not only did she have to fake her orgasms, but she learned too late his desire for his "sugar pie" didn't directly link to his offshore accounts. No, experience had taught her she needed to target a guy where he lived, which with money guys and politicians had everything to do with power and surprisingly little to do with sex.

Bruce Reynolds, a lawyer by training, had purchased two hospitals in Abilene with family money, fired everyone in both facilities, closed one up, and rehired a staff from the laid-off pool of past employees. Declaring his new hospital the flagship of an emerging empire in healthcare, he also bought some office space downtown, slapping up a big sign. The Mesquite Ridge Healthcare Corporation had been born. Since then, he had spread east to Dallas, Oklahoma City, Little Rock, Birmingham on down to Tampa and Miami like some terrible, great wildfire consuming every healthcare facility in its path. In short, the man was loaded and she planned on relieving him of a large chunk of wealth. She couldn't offer up hospitals since he had already ravaged most of those in the state, but her research revealed a unique interest. He not only believed strongly in the for-profit healthcare model, he also fervently hoped for the resurrection of what he considered to be the state's God-ordained destiny—returning to its glory as the independent and sovereign Republic of Texas.

At first she couldn't believe anybody felt strongly about Texas becoming its own nation. Sure, she railed against federal money and intervention, but that was politics. If Texas left the Union, it would be surely and irrevocably fucked. During her presidential bid, she took the opportunity to offer up some conservative candy, calling for the secession of Texas from the Union. Yes, it was over the top. No, it wasn't taken seriously by anyone but the late night comics and a few nutters in her right-wing base. But if Bruce was a rabid rebel of the Republic, a call by a standing governor for secession would give him an erection Viagra would never be able to match.

To her delight, he called within twenty-four hours. The lovemaking, damn. She should have called for secession earlier.

10

"Did you mean it, Fran? Are you serious about the Republic?"

She straddled him, her hips pulsing in rhythm with his, hoping for her third orgasm, but who was counting. "Absolutely. But I can't succeed without your help." She dug her nails into his chest.

"Anything, Frannie. Anything."

Exactly what she wanted to hear.

The first few months of their new relationship had gone according to plan. His desire to see a Republic come to fruition was so strong, he even set up, in the event of his death, an offshore account. He kept the passcode in a safe deposit box at the Cattleman's Bank in Houston. Of course, she planned on having access to his wealth well before any of it flowed to the Caymans. However, she soon realized a dyed-in-the-wool revolutionary, especially a capitalist like Reynolds, would expect results. She wasn't about to let him have his Republic, but he had to think she would. In discussing the necessary elements of a successful military, they had landed on the notion of air power as the key. No matter what they did, if the new Republic's leadership didn't control the skies above Texas, they'd never be able to hold off the Americans, or the Mexicans, for that matter.

Air power. How perfect. She figured Bruce would spend years trying to figure out how to acquire and hide aircraft and weapons. Long enough for her second well-financed campaign for President. Then she would, in a noble act of patriotism, bring Homeland Security down on her traitorous longtime friend like the wrath of God. This was the stuff of made-for-television movies and second-term Presidents.

"But if you're President, Frannie, why would you allow Texas to break away?"

"Oh, but that's the beauty of our plan, Bruce. Imagine the President of the United States calling for the independence of Texas. We'd both get what we want the most."

11

Buzzard Bait

She came back to the present when Bruce slipped her graceful arch slowly from his lips, his feet adroitly exploring her nether parts. "I have news for you, my dear."

She looked up into a dark sky. The snow had stopped falling. "Another hospital acquisition?"

"Nothing so mundane. No, I'm putting the first step of our strategic plan into place."

Crap. This was supposed to take six years, not six months. "You've put an air force together in six months? How could you possibly have enough aircraft and resources in place in this short a period of time?"

"You sound angry. I thought you'd be pleased. You're not having second thoughts, are you?"

She pulled her foot, cold in the night air, back under water. "No second thoughts. I just want to be sure we have what we need to be successful."

"Maybe a demonstration."

Great. He wants to have Republic of Texas F-16s fire missiles at a refinery? Maybe the capital? "No demonstrations, Bruce. We don't want to give away our one strategic advantage. Right now, no one knows about our movement. We need to keep it that way until we're ready to strike."

He moved toward her, squatting to keep his shoulders under the water. "I don't know. Maybe it's time to raise the Republic's flag. A demonstration might help some of the naysayers shift into our court."

"No demonstrations. Not as long as I'm governor. We go when I say we're ready to go."

He ducked under the surface, barely visible in the bubbling water. His lips circled around her right nipple, doing the little nibbling thing he did. Her heart beat faster, her body prickling with desire. She placed her hands on his head, shoving him down, past her stomach, between her legs. Even though he stood over six feet tall, she knew the strength of her thighs, tempered by distance running, swimming, and cycling. She could easily hold him under and end this little game. Her legs tightened around him. He

12

strained to pull his head away, his hands struggling for leverage to part her thighs. If she killed him, the police would be involved and Bruce had an annoying ability to capture a win from the jaws of defeat. She could see the headline. Governor Adamson's Pubic Hair Found In Dead Healthcare Executive's Mouth.

Spreading her legs, she let him pop to the surface, gasping. "What the hell, Frannie?"

She rushed to him, a hand stroking his face. "I'm so sorry. You're just so...incredible. I forgot you were under water."

He continued panting, but a slight smile parted his lips. "It's okay. I understand."

How have men been in power all these centuries when they all lead with their dicks? "No demonstrations, right?" She kissed him, then hugged him, making sure her breasts had full contact with his chest.

"No demonstrations. I'll just have to remember the scuba gear for next time."

She ran her nails down his back. "Mmmm. Tanks, hoses, masks. I love it."

Bobbi Shank

Bobbi Shank's life had spiraled out of control until she had a breakthrough in therapy. She had been seeing Amanda Wesson, PhD, for several years after she got out of grad school and started her accounting business. For all the success coming her way, her past still haunted her, waking her up late at night in a panic.

It was her old man. Her quote unquote father. Asshole. From the time her mom died in a car wreck and breasts blossomed on her chest, her dad, Lenny Shank, started his nighttime visits. At first he told her he wanted to snuggle and though it seemed a little weird, she would fall asleep with him spooned behind her. By her sophomore year his hands were down her panties and worse. Three years of hell, endured in silence. Who could she tell? Her mom sat in an urn at Memorial Park Cemetery. She didn't have any siblings and the only friends she had were boys wanting to grope her. She couldn't go to any of the adults at school. They were the enemy, considering they were all friends and colleagues of the Fighting Tiger's band director, her father, Lenny.

By her senior year, she'd had enough of his night time visits and embarked on a plan to rid herself and the world of the asshole forever. Over two months she used her shop class skills to fashion an instrument of death. She sharpened the end of a flute to a circular razor's edge, then engineered a spike fitting neatly inside, locked in place by a trigger cleverly disguised as a key, a powerful spring straining to thrust the spike out with tremendous force.

14

Once it was complete, she impaled a watermelon, a wood fence, and in the most definitive test of her weapon's efficiency, a stack of steaks. Months of effort now prepared her to finally end the nightmare. Only the son of a bitch never came home. During a rehearsal for his beloved marching band, he fell from his directing tower to the grassy field below. The doctor couldn't say if he died of a massive heart attack or if he broke his neck before his heart completely imploded.

Bobbi should have felt relieved, but for years after his death she still woke up late at night, imagining shadows lurking at her door. She got through high school and on her father's insurance money went to undergraduate and graduate school, culminating in setting up an accounting firm. Yet she couldn't shake his dark shadow in her life. Dr. Wesson had helped her peel back layers of pain and shame over several years. Then one day last year, the waters parted and Bobbi could see her path. With Dr. Wesson's help, she realized the only way to get peace was to find what the doctor called closure. The Reagan High School band director who hired her to do his taxes didn't look anything like her dad, but he did have one thing going for him—he did conduct a band. However, completing her therapy in Austin, the place she lived and worked, could be tricky. So she decided to find a director in another town.

Attending a marching band contest in Houston, she found her mark. Carl Hines, the director of the Marching Lions. She stalked him for a few days, making note of the pattern of his life. Bobbi discovered he always stayed late in the band hall on Sundays to go through the tape of the band's performance during the previous week's football game. At 9:30 on a Sunday night, she slipped into the hall. Carl sat in his office, a pad on his desk, making notes, his eyes transfixed on a television sitting on a brown metal AV stand in the corner. He didn't notice her step into his office. He didn't notice when she stood behind him, as he leaned back, crossing his legs. He did notice when, with the killer

15

flute in both hands, she raised her instrument over her head, then plunged it into his chest. The sharpened tube sliced flesh to the bone, painful, but survivable. He didn't get much of a chance to ponder these facts, however, once Bobbi pressed the key trigger and a stainless-steel spike drove through his chest and into the back of his chair.

Bobbi felt an exhilaration, a freedom, like a skydiver making the leap into space. *My God, why did I wait so long for closure?* Her heart raced and she giggled like a little girl, while Carl gurgled, then went still. Closure.

The feeling stayed with her for weeks as she read stories in the Houston Chronicle of the police's inability to find the poor band director's murderer. The latest suspect was a band parent who had screamed obscenities at Carl when his son didn't pass his tuba sectional, only to be relegated to the flag team. Soon, though, the old haunting returned. She needed more closure. A West Texas band director turned up missing, then was discovered after a wretched stench led the substitute teacher to remove a drum head from one of their large kettle drums. Inside, Warren Crumbly lay beaten to death with a dinged-up trumpet found with the body. When authorities and the press made the connection between the two murders, the "Musi-Killogist" was born.

Bobbi had to admit, she kind of liked the title. However, she didn't have long to bask in her new celebrity. Her third murder got her in the mess she now found herself in. Watching a thriller on HBO, she got the idea of stuffing a clarinet with C4 to off her next victim. She smiled, thinking about how the forensics team would be picking through bits of Franklin Jones, her next victim, along with thousands of little clarinet toothpicks. A black-market connection with some pseudo-militaristic yahoo named Tex hooked her up with a small quantity of the stuff. She rigged Franklin's clarinet to blow when he pressed down on the reed of his mouthpiece. Bobbi had second thoughts when she considered he might decide to play his clarinet in class, killing a bunch of kids in the process. To her relief, Franklin

16

liked to play late at night in his ranch-style home in a quiet suburban neighborhood. Sitting in the dark a block away, she couldn't believe the explosion her little bit of C4 made. The next morning, only the driveway and part of one wall of his house still remained. Franklin would no longer play the clarinet in this life. Closure.

She enjoyed her usual rush, the press abuzz with the frantic hunt for the Musi-Killogist. Bobbi couldn't have been happier. Then the walls of her life came crumbling in on her. She still remembered the moment she knew her perfect life would no longer be viable.

One day, completely out of the blue, Bobbi got a call from the personal assistant to the biggest name in healthcare in the South, Bruce Reynolds. He needed an accountant and had heard some wonderful things about her. Bobbi couldn't believe word of her accounting work had reached someone like Reynolds. She'd have to find out which of her clients recommended her and give them a discount for their next tax return.

Arriving at Reynolds's office, she sat across from him in a tasteful black business skirt and jacket. Reynolds looked his part in a tailored suit, white linen shirt and silk tie. Gold cufflinks peeked out of his jacket sleeves.

"Ms. Shank. Thank you for coming by. I've heard a great deal about you."

"I don't know who to thank, but I'm glad they let you know the quality of my services."

He leaned back in his chair, his fingertips touching. "Yes, the spiked flute was both creative and beautifully engineered."

A moment of silence separated them as she let his words sink in.

"Excuse me?" Bobbi couldn't believe what she just heard.

"Now, Ms. Shank—or may I call you Bobbi?"

She nodded, her grip tightening on the armrests of her chair, wondering if she could escape before the police arrived.

"Bobbi. Let's be honest with each other. Beating a man to death with a trumpet is a bit uncivilized, but the kettle drum thing did make me chuckle."

She wanted to flee, to run away, but Reynolds's sudden disclosure caught her like a deer in headlights. "I don't know what you're talking about."

"Bobbi, there's no reason to deny it. Did you come up with the Musi-Killogist label or did the press do that for you?"

She sat frozen, unsure what to do or say.

"Don't be alarmed. I don't think the police are onto you yet. Usually takes a serial killer eight or ten victims before law enforcement gathers sufficient clues to figure it out."

Bobbi wondered how he figured it out.

"I see from your expression, you're wondering how I know about your...proclivities. Tex. Remember the fellow who hooked you up with the C4? Nice job, by the way. Well, when a beautiful young woman comes to him looking for high grade explosives, he thought correctly that I'd want to know who I'm selling to."

"It was your C4?"

"I dabble. What can I say. Anyway, one thing led to another and soon I realized I had sold explosives to a serial killer. You can imagine my dismay."

"If you were worried I'd use it, why did you sell it to me?"

"You misunderstand. My dismay wasn't over selling you the C4, it was not having you on my team."

"Your team?" Her eyes narrowed as she tried to discern what Reynolds meant.

"Yes. Clearly you've got skills. And the accounting business gives you some good cover. Besides, if you get caught, they'd be arresting a serial killer, not my hit woman. I could use someone like you to handle...situations."

"I'm not a killer for hire."

He laughed, then rose and walked around his desk until he stood behind her. She felt his hands rest on her shoulders.

"I wouldn't be so crude. No, you're an accountant for hire. You're a killer when I tell you to be."

Her shoulders stiffened at his touch, but his grasp tightened.

"I don't take orders from anyone."

"Oh, you'll take orders from me, Bobbi." He let go, stepped in front of her, then sat on the edge of his desk. "If you don't, the police will discover your secret. With my help, of course."

Her eyes went to a letter opener by his side. She rose, intending to stab him in his throat as many times as possible. He had a Glock 9mm pointed at her before she could reach for the dagger-like weapon.

He smiled, shaking his head. "Bobbi, Bobbi. Is this really the way you want to start our working relationship? Sit down." His face went killer cold. "Now."

Bobbi sank back into her chair. He had her. Reynolds wasn't sneaking into a young girl's room at night to have his way with her, but he had her all the same. *Goddammit. It's Lenny all over again.*

~ * ~

A few weeks into her working relationship with Reynolds, he gave her a first assignment—to kill the CEO of a hospital in El Paso who was talking to the feds about an illegal Medicare transaction. She took him out. What choice did she have? But the joy, the orgasmic exultation of her killings as the Musi-Killogist, did not accompany the murder of the CEO. Two bullets to the head. Cold. Empty of meaning. She vowed to find a way out of Reynolds's hold on her. Then she discovered his crazy plan to create a new Republic of Texas. The dumb fuck left the blueprints of his revolution on a conference table when he went to take a leak, so confident in the righteousness of his cause. With

19

her phone she took photos of the documents, including some crazy-ass attack plan using drones.

He may have had the upper hand, but she had proof of a conspiracy to take over the state and use armed aircraft to destroy various military and infrastructure targets. All she had to do was get this information into the right hands anonymously. Once Homeland Security had a bead on Reynolds, he could go on day and night about the Musi-Killogist and no one would believe him. And once she handled Reynolds, maybe she'd consider giving the Musi-Killogist a prolonged vacation. Let the Demon of Executive Death take over.

R. W. Hacker

A Kick in the Pants

Andy Sullivan looked in the rearview mirror of his Dodge Caravan. He saw a man with a plan for his future. He also noticed he'd need a new pair of rear shocks, because clearly the woman stowed neatly away in his trunk weighted his back end precariously low to the ground. He'd met the woman at Julie's Pancake House off 290 near Brenham. She had dirty blonde hair and wore skintight leathers, like some biker chick. Under her jacket, which she had taken off and draped on the back of her chair, she wore a spaghetti strap tee, giving Andy a great view of a tattoo of thorns wrapped around her upper arm. The only seat left at the counter had been right by her. She'd turned, smiling, when he sat.

A waitress poured coffee into his cup, setting a menu in front of him. "Would you like any cream or sugar?"

"Yes, please."

The woman, probably in her thirties, said, "You're welcome to mine. Don't use the stuff."

That's all he needed. "Thanks." He nodded at her half-eaten breakfast. "How are the pancakes here?"

"Pretty good. I'd recommend the blueberry."

He closed his menu. "Blueberry it is. So, where you heading?" He had learned from experience not to suggest a direction or location for his own travels, since he would go in whatever direction his victims were going.

"I'm waiting for a bus to Austin. Had a couple of hours to kill so I thought I'd grab some breakfast."

"Austin? You don't say. I'm going that way, too."

Their waitress walked past. "Know what you want, honey?"

21

Buzzard Bait

Andy loved flirting with waitresses. "Yes, I believe I'll have the blueberry pancakes, darling. A short stack."

"Coming up."

He turned back to the dirty blonde. "So, where you from?"

"I was born in San Antonio, but live in Austin now."

"You ride a motorcycle or something?"

"Yeah. My ride had some issues, so I'm leaving it at a shop."

"Motorcycle. Wow. Bet that's lots of fun. By the way, my name's Frank." He extended his hand, which she took in her own.

"Bobbi."

He went on to talk about his career as an Indy race car driver (best to avoid NASCAR in case she followed the sport—she was a biker chick, after all) and his work on the latest hydrogen fuel cell car. All lies, of course, but she didn't have a clue, beguiled by his innate trustworthiness.

She jumped off her chair before he had a chance to expound on his fake trip last year to Paris and his pretend love of tattoo art. The universe, however, supported him.

"I'll be right back. Just need to pop into the ladies room."

"No problem. I'll hold your spot."

He watched her walk away, already imagining what she would look like naked, tied up, and terrified.

Back in prison, he pretty much went by the name Bitch. On his release, he vowed if he ever found himself behind bars again, it would be for horrific, violent crimes so unspeakable the inmates would cower in fear, begging to be his bitch. While he had gone to a penitentiary for a sex crime, he knew he had to up the ante from statutory rape to at least murder. Then last month, like a freight train slamming into a '57 Chevy pickup, the idea hit him. Serial killer. Nobody screwed with a psycho serial killer. All he had to do was

#1: Make sure he offed every one of his victims.

#2: Bury them somewhere imaginative.

22

#3: Lead a perfectly normal life.

So far he had one and a half out of three. Starting at the bottom...

#3: He led a perfectly normal life. An inspiration to kids, a pillar of the community. Hell, he won best yard in his neighborhood last year. If the cops ever arrested him, the neighbors would all go on TV saying things like, "Andy's the last person I'd ever suspect of such a heinous crime."

#2: He sort of had this one under control. He hadn't buried anyone yet, but he did have a spot all picked out. In the excitement of concentrating as hard as he could on thinking and doing whatever it was psychos did, he'd pulled up the laminate in his back bedroom, exposing cold, hard concrete. He had been so intent on burying victims under floorboards he forgot the house had been built on a concrete slab. Deciding Plan A had been the floorboard thing, he shifted to Plan B, a rose garden. He wasted an entire weekend laboring to dig up caliche and stone, denting his shovel and leaving him with back spasms for a week. However, the following weekend, Plan B fell into place when he constructed a raised garden. He'd bury his victims in its loamy soil, then plant roses, maybe enter them into fairs. Andy chuckled to himself, imagining some old lady asking how he got such wonderful blooms.

#1: In order to meet his requirement in the serial killer trifecta, he needed to start killing women, which to date had been a bit of a problem.

He'd driven I-35 north of Austin hoping to find some woman in need of assistance or alone at a rest stop. For a week he drove up and down between Austin and Waco without any luck. Then one Saturday night at a deserted rest stop, he found a woman crying at a picnic table. She looked to be about forty, older than his profile, but she was female, alone, and available. After introductions, he discovered she had just left her boyfriend, the cheating bastard, and then her car, an old El Camino, had quit on her. Andy put an arm around her, offering comfort. He'd give her a ride up to

Waco so she could get a tow truck. Things went smoothly until a guy in the very same El Camino ran him off the road.

His passenger kept cool under pressure. "Do you have a gun, mister? Looks like he's getting out of his car."

Of course he had a gun. What self-respecting serial killer wouldn't have a gun? He reached across her lap to the glovebox, which, besides the woman's knee smashing into his face, was the last thing he remembered. He came to in a field about twenty yards from his car. No cell phone, no wallet, no gun (a brand new Smith & Wesson .38, goddammit), no car stereo, no pants, and no boots. It's one thing to get rolled for your wallet, but stealing a pair of ostrich Noconas? What kind of sick mind would come up with something like that?

After his first potential victim turned on him, he decided a change was in order, figuring the I-35 crowd to be too urban and dangerous for a novice serial killer. He went east which, it turned out, had lots of potential. In fact, the very first place he stopped this weekend, Julie's Pancake House, appeared to be reaping great rewards.

Waiting for Bobbi to return from the restroom, he'd reached into his pocket, taking out a small vial and popping open its lid, then dropping its clear liquid contents into her coffee. A few minutes later his victim returned and they resumed their conversation through the remainder of breakfast.

The drug, coursing through her system, made her much more susceptible to his suggestions. He paid their bills, left a reasonable tip, then guided her out to his car. He'd be happy to give her a lift to Austin and she was happy for him to give her a ride. He stopped once he got off the main road to put her in a bag and dump her in the back of his van. Driving another twenty miles, he banged a fist into his forehead. Newbie mistake.

"What are you doing? The bag is for after I whack her."

Andy stopped once again, lifting her out of the back, pulling off the bag while copping a feel, then grabbing under her arms to drag his victim around to the passenger side door. Leaning her against the van, he pressed one hand on her chest, getting a good feel of a breast while opening the door. Finally, he muscled her into the passenger seat, securing her with a seat belt. Andy Sullivan, aka Frank, was a dangerous serial killer, meticulous in every detail and brutal beyond belief. This woman was about to enter the gates of hell.

Instead of continuing to Austin, he took a Farm to Market Road south from Giddings into mesquite and scrub hills. The gallon of coffee he consumed made its way to his bladder, so he pulled to the shoulder to relieve himself. The woman looked completely out of it. He figured he had a good two hours before the drugs would begin to wear off. Andy stepped to the rear of the van, his back to the road, sending an arc of piss into scrub grass. He felt a little nervous, having never killed anyone before. Could he get away with a head shot, quick and to the point? Or for the sake of his image as a crazed serial killer, did he need to slice her open and strangle her with her own intestines? Tough call.

Finishing up, he zipped his fly and went back to the driver's seat. His captive leaned against her door, eyes closed, drooling on his interior. He'd have to remember towels for the next one. He let an oil rig truck go by, then accelerated onto the two-lane road. A click came from the passenger seat. He glanced over to be sure she wasn't screwing with the lock or something when he came eye to muzzle with his own recently replaced Smith and Wesson .38.

"What the hell?"

"Drive, Frank, if that's your name."

"Aw, not again." She must have faked drinking the coffee or he hadn't put enough G in it. One thing was for sure—she didn't look too interested in being one of his victims right now.

She growled at him. "What do you mean, again?"

25

Andy slapped his steering wheel. "What's with women nowadays? How's a man supposed to take advantage if you all keep being so damned aggressive? You answer me that."

"Frank." She poked him in his ribs. "What's your real name?"

"Andy. I go by Andy."

"When you're not Frank. Are you sure you're just an asshole or do you have multiple personalities?"

He swallowed, his throat dry with fear. "Look, little lady, you need to be careful with that gun. You ever shot one before?"

The explosion almost made Andy crap his pants, not to mention set off a ringing in his ears, as a bullet shattered the window next to him.

"Yeah. Nice trigger action, Andy."

"Shit. Come on. Take what you want."

"Thank you, Andy. I believe I will."

She directed him down a dirt road in the middle of nowhere, then had him get out of the van. Soon he found himself bent over a wood fence railing, his pants down to his ankles, reliving his prison days. Bobbi, if that was her name, stepped up beside him.

"You put something in my coffee back at the cafe, didn't you?"

"No, ma'am." Swack. Something like a tree branch whipped across his bare ass, his flesh exploding in a hot, searing pain. "Ow, hell. What'd you do that for?"

"Lying to me, Andy. You're going to tell me the truth. You owe me."

"Okay. Yes, I put something in your coffee. Just to relax you a bit. I didn't mean any harm." Swack. "Crap!"

"The truth, Andy."

"All right. Just don't hit me again. I, I drugged you 'cause I'm a dangerous serial killer."

He couldn't see her, but he heard her laughing. A beginning chuckle evolved into a full body roaring, pee in

26

your pants, fall on the floor, howling. Andy didn't think his chosen profession was all that funny.

"You've got to be kidding me. A serial killer? Who have you killed?"

"Well, no one to date, but I intend to do so in the near future."

He heard her steps rustle grass close to him.

"Here's the thing, Andy."

Something very cold and very hard poked between his butt cheeks.

"You don't want to do this, Bobbi. You're not that kind of girl. Don't let my life of crime lead you astray."

She shoved the .38 in deep.

"Holy mother..."

"Andy, you listening to me?"

He squirmed against the sharp pain twisting inside him. "Yes, ma'am, I'm listenin'. I'm listenin'."

"If I ever find out you killed some poor girl and buried her in a shallow grave, I will find you, shove this gun up your ass as I am currently doing, and pull the trigger until I'm out of bullets. Do you believe me, Andy?"

"Yes. Yes, ma'am, I do."

"Good."

Mercifully she dislodged the .38 from his rear end.

"Now you're going to deliver me to Austin without incident. Give me trouble and we'll find ourselves another fence." She slapped open the .38's cylinder, ejecting the cartridges which she slung into the brush. "And here's your gun. You might think about cleaning it sometime soon."

In that moment he came to the conclusion the universe simply didn't support his desire to be a serial killer. He would have to find a new gig.

~ * ~

About a month after Andy's encounter with Bobbi, he stopped at a south-side dive where no one in Pflugerville would see him. Dejected, depressed, and he hoped, very soon drunk, he sat at the bar, a shot of tequila in hand, when a biker chick with a thorn tattoo wrapping around her upper arm sat down beside him.

"Oh Lord. I haven't killed nobody. I swear."

Bobbi put a hand on his arm. "It's okay, Andy. We're just having a friendly conversation."

He looked around for something he had never sought before. Law enforcement. But scanning the room of alcoholics, mean-ass looking guys, and women who had not only been around the block, they built the damned thing, Andy knew he was completely on his own. "I think we got off on the wrong foot before."

"Ya think?"

"Yeah. My bad. Entirely my fault and you were absolutely in the right."

She stared at him, then downed a shot of tequila.

"So let's begin again. Hi, my name is Andy." He extended his hand to her.

She downed another shot, smiled, then shook his hand. "Good to meet you, Andy."

As the night progressed Andy developed good feelings about Bobbi, even if she had assaulted him with his own Smith & Wesson. In fact, the more Bobbi drank, the more they hit it off. When the bouncer threw them out and Bobbi passed out drunk in his back seat, Andy's criminal genius kicked in. He took her home, stripped off her clothes, then set up his video camera. He contented himself with simple shots of her naked, but in the middle of his shoot, she came to life, performing all kinds of sex acts with him and various pieces of furniture.

Man, was she hot. But more to the point, his video gave him some protection from her threats. If she decided to tighten the screws, he'd threaten to post their little tryst online. He may be a loser serial killer, but he definitely had social networking skills.

The next morning he woke up with Bobbi snoring in bed beside him. He moved ever so slightly toward the edge of his bed, hoping to get out before she awoke.

"Andy?" She let out a long sigh. "Hell."

Damn. "Good morning, Bobbi."

She sat up in bed holding the sheet around her. "Did we?"

"Yes, we did. Multiple times. And I've got to say, you were a raging fire."

Bobbi rested her head in one hand, keeping the sheet up with the other. "Unbelievable."

"Breakfast?"

Andy went into the kitchen, starting a pot of coffee and frying up some bacon. About the time he cracked eggs in the skillet, Bobbi came into his kitchen in panties and her tee. She sat down at the kitchen table where Andy had placed a steaming cup of coffee. Finishing up the eggs, he set a plate down before her, sitting in the chair opposite. They ate without speaking, only the ding of stainless against ceramic and the occasional grackle squawk breaking the silence.

Her plate empty, she took a sip of coffee, put the cup down, and looked straight at Andy. "Did you say you did prison time?"

In the heat of the moment, he had bragged a bit about his jail time, mostly because it seemed to turn her on. His fictionalized version of his internment emphasized his violent nature and how he ran the place with an iron fist. "I might have mentioned something."

She tapped a fork on the table. "Normally, I wouldn't bring this up, but given our history I think you might be the right guy for the job."

"Job? I've got a job."

"A criminal job, dumb shit."

"Oh. Right. What kind of job do you have in mind?"

"I have a little problem I need handled. A guy took something from me and I can't afford to have him talking about what he might have seen."

"So you want me to put the fear of death into him. Beat the hell out of him, that sort of thing?"

"No, Andy. I want you to kill him. Straight up, kill him."

They stared at each other for a time, Andy taking a sip of coffee, then swallowing the brew and her proposal. He had planned on blackmailing her with the sex tape to get something from her—like money. Now he might have to use it keep her from making him kill a guy.

"Why don't you do it yourself? I mean, from what I've seen, you're plenty capable of taking somebody out."

"If this goes wrong, I need to have some distance."

"What about me?"

"Well, Andy, I thought you were a serial killer. Besides, if you don't do it, you know you've got an appointment with a fence railing. Right?"

She smiled in this creepy way that made him feel like she truly hoped he'd say no. However, he still held out hope he'd be able to save the tape for financial gain. "Is this some scary bad dude?"

"I don't understand why it would matter, but no. He's a backwater fisherman." She put two fingers to her head. "Two in the head and you're done."

He hesitated, just to show he wasn't afraid, but not long enough to piss her off, then agreed to the job. "Five thousand dollars."

"One thousand and if you screw it up, I'll only fire twice when I shove a gun up your ass."

Twice sounded much better than shooting every round in the gun, even though one thousand dollars was a steal. Like he had a choice. "Sure. One thousand it is."

Not big bucks, but from Andy's perspective the gig would allow him to make a clean break with serial killing for the more lucrative murder-for-hire business. And he'd still be able to bleed her for cash, and other favors, with the sex tape. Bobbi's methods were crude and painful, but Andy had to admit, sometimes a guy just needed a kick in the pants.

30

Dillon

Despite Theresa's protestations to Nick, they waited at the bass competition grounds. While Theresa ate roasted corn and shopped the vendors, Nick kept an eye on the boat ramp. Trailers met each competitor as they rumbled in, then silently glided onto their respective trailer's supports. After several grimaced head-waggings from Theresa across the grounds, each clearly communicating her disapproval of his desire for vengeance, Nick decided to pack it in. Then a blue boat, the blue boat guilty of speeding across Lake Travis and putting Theresa's life in danger, floated in. A man in his early forties with a slight beer paunch, wearing jeans and a polo shirt proclaiming the local Fetch n' Buy convenience store as his sponsor, leapt off his boat into knee deep water before it reached the trailer. He looked around nervously, as if he sensed Nick's intention to beat him to a pulp. Dolores, who had backed the trailer down the ramp and now stood by water's edge, yelled at him.

"Dillon. What in the hell are you doing?"

"Forget the boat. We gotta go. Now."

"Dillon. If you think I'm leaving a twenty-thousand dollar bass boat floating in the water, you've got another think coming."

He grabbed Dolores's arm, pulling her toward their matching blue double dually pickup with a Fetch n' Buy magnetic sign on the door.

"Goddammit, Dillon. What's wrong with you?"

"Dolores, I'm not messin' around here. Get in the damn truck. No time to explain."

Nick walked up to the arguing couple, so absorbed in their duel they didn't notice his approach. "Excuse me."

Dolores yanked her arm away. "Dillon, people are looking at us. You can't just drag me to the truck like some damn caveman."

Nick spoke louder. "Excuse me."

"Well, if I gotta be a damn caveman to get you to do what I ask, then so be it. Now, woman, either you get in the truck, or so help me God…"

Dolores, five foot six and a hundred and forty pounds, somehow became larger and more menacing than Nick thought possible. "So help you God what, Dillon?" She shoved him. Hard. Then kept coming. "So help you God, what? Come on, Dillon. If we're going to do this, goddammit, then let's do it."

Dillon spat to one side, his face red with rage. He moved to answer her assault, but before he could make contact, Nick had him in a bear hug from behind, his arms pinned to his side. Dillon squirmed in Nick's grasp.

"I said, excuse me. Now are you going to have a conversation with me or do I have to beat you into the ground first?"

Dolores stopped inches from Dillon, hands on her hips, the barest hint of a smile creasing across her face. "I say beat him first."

Dillon pleaded, "Now hold on there, Dolores."

Nick squeezed tighter. "If you say so, ma'am."

"Wait, wait, goddammit." Dillon squirmed in Nick's grasp. "Who the hell're you?"

Dolores, with a satisfied smirk, looked over Dillon's shoulder at Nick. "That's Nick Sibelius. He's the investigator that put ol' Junior away for good."

"Really? Well, mighty good to meet you, Nick. Hey, you think you could ease off on the bear hug so's I can shake your hand?"

Nick eyed Dolores who nodded assent, then released his quarry. Dillon turned to face him, hand extended.

32

"Like I say, good to meet you. Now me and her gotta get on down the road. Hope you don't mind." He turned to leave.

"Slow down there."

"Yeah, look, mister, I gotta go."

"What you've gotta do is explain to me why you almost killed my girlfriend."

"What? You must mean why that ol' boy almost kill't me. And I'm sure it was a guy. Jesus, hell bent for leather chasing my ass down the lake. Good thing I know where the low spots are, cause I scooted right past 'em. Man, that ol' boy's boat turned to kindlin'." Dillon looked past Nick toward the lake. "Look, I gotta go. If there's smoke there's fire. Know what I mean?"

Nick had no idea at all what he meant, but he'd had enough of this two-bit fish chaser. "What are you talking about? Are you trying to deny you almost ran our boat down?"

"I'm just saying I gotta go." He stepped away, but Nick grabbed his arm, turning him back, his fist connecting with Dillon's face, sending the fisherman to the ground.

"And I'm saying, be a man and take responsibility." He stood over Dillon, fists clenched. "Now get up."

Nick leaned over and grabbed Dillon by his sponsor patches, intent on pummeling this wayward fisherman. However, Theresa, who dropped her turkey leg upon hearing Nick's angry voice, and Dolores, who Nick figured had shifted from wanting Dillon taught a lesson to not wanting her health insurance premiums to go up even more, both stepped in.

Theresa shouted from across the grounds, "Nick, stop. Dammit. There's no call for this."

Dolores placed herself between Nick, his fists up, ready to brawl, and her dazed husband who sat in the dirt rubbing his chin. "You leave my husband alone. If anybody's going to beat him senseless, it's going to me."

Nick wished Dillon would stand up so he could put him down again. A hard shove left him hopping on one leg. Theresa.

"Nick, what the hell? Now, stop. Just stop. I don't want you beating up some stupid fisherman for me. Stop."

Dolores turned her attention to Theresa. "Stupid? Who's calling who stupid? Your boy there assaulted my husband in front of a hundred witnesses." She crossed her arms, looking around the crowd gathering to watch a good dust up. "Now that's stupid."

Theresa followed Dolores's gaze, then looked to Nick, shaking her head. "Aw, Nick."

Dillon, still on the ground, spoke up. "It's not his fault. I probably deserved it. Not sure why in this particular instance, but I usually deserve it." He stood up, brushing dust off his jeans. "Okay, folks. It's over. Everybody back to the fishing. Okay?"

The crowd, bored with the lack of World Wrestling action, melted away. Dillon gave Dolores a hug. "Baby doll. We do have to go. Someone's trying to kill me. We've got to leave now."

"What? Why didn't you say that before?" She cupped his face in her hands. "Who would want to do a thing like that to you?"

"I don't know. We just have to get outta here."

Dolores kissed him on the cheek, then looked over his shoulder at Nick, who had overheard the conversation. "Just hold on a sec more there, honey."

Impatience pulled at Dillon's voice. "Dolores."

She walked past Dillon, directly to Nick. "You still in the investigation business?"

"Yeah." Nick didn't like where this was going.

"Well, I've got some investigating for you to do. You heard him. Someone's trying to kill him."

"Yeah, kill me dead. Almost had me, too. That's why I gotta go. A guy like that always has a backup, you know, like in the movies."

Nick did not want to get tangled up in whatever twisted craziness Dillon had gotten himself into. But Dolores stood with pleading eyes, while Theresa, hands on hips, made clear her agitation at his single-minded focus on avenging any perceived threat to her well-being. Dillon looked a bit like a Lab retriever—all good intention and absolutely no common sense.

Before prudence kept his mouth shut, Nick let the investigator within him speak. "Slow down, Dillon. You keep saying someone's after you and something about someone dying. When did this happen?"

"Just now. I was trying to tell you, this guy chased me across the lake, shootin' at me. Hell, I'm sure I've got holes in the boat. Hope it's not too expensive to fix. Don't know if my sponsor would be all too happy—"

Dolores interrupted. "Dillon, will you stay on point? You were saying this man was after you, taking shots and you were trying to get away."

"Yeah, that's it. Then I went down the lake a bit by my inlet."

"Your inlet?" Nick shifted his weight, wondering what a man does with an inlet.

Dolores interpreted. "He don't mean he owns it. He means it's his secret fishing spot."

Dillon nodded. "Yeah, that's right. So, I go past my inlet, knowing there's shallow spots and rocks, hoping to Jesus this guy don't know the lake. Then BAM! He hits some rocks doing a hundred miles an hour and his goddamn boat broke up all to hell."

"You're saying he's dead?"

"Whatever's left of that ol' boy is seriously dead. So I hauled my ass here as fast as I could go, knowing if there's one trying to kill me, there's probably another." He cocked his head slightly, as if attempting to read Nick's mind. "So you can help me?"

"I don't know, Dillon. Sounds like a tragic accident, not a murder attempt."

"Accident? You come on over here. I'll show you an accident."

He pulled Nick over to his boat, wading out into the water. Nick could see bullet holes in the windscreen from the shore.

"Does that look like an accident to you?"

Sirens wailed in the distance while the local FM promo truck blared a country singer's despair over the loss of his pickup when a train ran over his ex. Dillon stood knee deep in water looking something like a small animal who knows a hawk is about to pluck him out of the lake and eat him alive. He splashed up on shore. "Let's go, Dolores!"

Nick caught him by the arm, Dillon flailing in a panic. "Please, Jesus, let me go. They's comin' for me, man."

"Running makes you look guilty. I thought you didn't kill him."

"Like they're goin' to believe that. Come on, man. I gotta get outta here."

Dolores chimed in. "Maybe we should go, Nick. I don't want Dillon hauled off to jail."

He grabbed Dillon by the shoulders. "Listen to me, Dillon. You listening?"

"Yeah, yeah I'm listenin'. Just make it fast."

"Given the circumstances, the police will want a statement."

"What?"

"If you run, you'll only raise more suspicion. You need to give them a statement."

"But—"

Dolores held onto her man. "You've got to help him, Nick. You're our only hope."

Nick looked to Dolores. Her eyes teared up for the man she loved because he was the brother of the man she loved. Theresa had the look folks get at a free puppy giveaway. And Nick knew in that moment, he was coming home with a puppy, whether he liked it or not. *How did I get myself into this?*

Dillon pleaded, "Yeah, you gotta help me, Nick."

He released his grip on Dillon, now that the fishermen appeared to not be doing a runner. "And why is that, Dillon?"

"I figure this situation is just like Babe Ruth used to say. We all hang together or we all hang separately."

Dillon must have skipped history class. "You're thinking of Benjamin Franklin."

"Franklin? What team did he play for? Must've been double A ball."

While Dillon seemed pretty worked up and in all probability there was a dead body floating in Lake Travis, the case looked small and low profile. Nick took solace in knowing at least he wasn't facing some neo-Nazi or a terrorist this time. Small and low profile had become his mantra in the last few months. He let out a long sigh. "Okay, I'll look into it. I promise."

Dolores threw her arms around him. "Thank you, Nick." Releasing him, she poked a finger into Dillon's chest. "Now you do what he says, Dillon. For me. You hear? You die on me like Harlan and I swear to God, I'll kill you."

~ * ~

After two Sheriff Deputies pulled Dillon aside for a statement, Nick and Theresa drove home to Pflugerville. They sat in silence in his truck, gliding along rolling hills west of Austin towards the Blackland Prairie to the east. Billowing cumulus clouds hung in the sky, looking something like bolls of cotton pinned to a blue bulletin board. Theresa let out a deep sigh. Nick looked over at her, slender, athletic, a Latina Olympian slash sex goddess. He didn't feel the love he had for MaryLou, that deep, pained yearning, but he felt responsible for Theresa, like holding an infant in his arms. Was that love or something else?

She sighed again.

"You okay, Theresa?"

He could feel her eyes scanning him. "It's always about the same thing, you know."

37

"What's always about what?"

"Am I okay? Am I hurt, do I feel any pain, am I safe?"

"What, is something the matter?"

"There you go again." She rolled her eyes, shaking her head.

"What?"

"Nothing's the matter, Nick. I'm fine. I'm a big girl."

"Oh, like today when I pulled you out of the water."

"Before you came along I did take care of myself just fine."

"Really? That's not how I remember it." *Hell, why did I say that?*

"Yes, Nick. Izzy Zydeco, the sick fuck, probably would have killed me if you hadn't saved me. Is that what you want to hear?"

"No, look, I didn't—"

"No, it's okay. Without you, without the great Nick Sibelius, well, hell, I'd be dead. I'm just barely hanging on as it is without you standing guard over me twenty-four seven."

"Theresa."

"What, Nick? You say you love me, but I think I'm more like a project to you."

"I never—"

"Wait, what am I talking about?" She put a hand to her head. "You've actually never said you love me. That's just me. Poor, pathetic, helpless little me hoping you love me."

"Theresa, stop. Just shut up for a second. Why are you doing this?"

"You assaulted that man, dammit. Don't you get it?"

Nick had no idea what she meant. Well, he did know what she meant, but he had no intention of letting himself know. "Get what, Theresa?"

"You still blame yourself for Zydeco driving spikes through my hands."

He thought about what he should have done differently every time he held her hand, felt the scars, every time they made love or sat across a table. If only...

"It wasn't your fault, Nick. I'm a professional doing a job just like you."

Nick glanced at her, then back to the road. "He used you to get to me."

"He was a prick. And if we're going to have a chance, you've got to let it go."

"What do you mean, have a chance?"

"I'm not spending my life with a man who thinks I'm a fragile little bird requiring his protection. It's not going to happen."

He didn't know what to say, what to feel. Nick hadn't considered spending life with Theresa, or with any woman for that matter. After a cheating ex-wife and a super-agent ex-girlfriend, his heart only had room for one day at a time. However, he did feel an obligation, a sense of duty to Theresa. Couldn't that be love? And when did wanting to protect the woman you loved become a bad thing? She didn't understand how responsible he felt when he saw her nailed against a wall, blood streaming down her arms. He would never let someone hurt her again. Ever.

Theresa's voice broke through his thoughts. "So that's it. You've got nothing to say?"

"It's been a pretty emotional day. Maybe we better talk about this when we're both in a better place."

"Nick, the conversation isn't going to change."

"Humor me. Let's talk about this tonight over a bottle of wine. Besides, it looks like I've got a client. I'll drop you off, then I'm going to swing by Quentin's and see if I can get a look at the evidence from the accident today."

"Okay, we'll talk tonight. But we've got to sort this out."

"Tonight. I promise."

~ * ~

Walking across El Rincón's parking lot, Nick considered he probably should have changed out of his shorts and t-shirt for this visit, but the idea of giving Theresa more time to probe their relationship while he slipped into some jeans just didn't sound appealing. After the Bluebonnet Cafe got blown to bits in a failed attempt to keep him from stopping a psychotic dentist's killing spree, Nick had doubled down on the Mexican restaurant he had relied on for caldero and beef enchiladas. Now he found himself addicted to their huevos con chorizo.

Stepping inside, Nick found his friend, Sergeant Quentin Matthews, at a table watching a telenovela, a big bowl of menudo steaming in front of him. Seeing Nick, he stood his full six foot four-inch frame, extending a hand which Nick shook firmly. "Look at you, man. Casual Friday, I see. You PI types have it easy."

"Yeah, I was floating in my pool eating bon bons and thought I'd come out to watch a real professional police officer work. Very impressive."

"Touché. Have you eaten?" They both sat down at the small table.

"Got a favor to ask."

"Of course. Our friendship is grounded in me doing favors for you. How could I possibly say no?"

"Did I or did I not spend all last weekend with you putting your motorcycle back together?"

Quentin raised his hands in mock surrender. "Okay, okay. Jeez, you're getting touchy in your old age. So, what can I do you for?"

"Theresa and I were out at Lake Travis today."

"How's that going, by the way?"

"It's fine. Well, I'm not sure."

Quentin frowned, folding a tortilla in his hand.

Nick absently tapped the table. "I don't know."

"Don't screw this up, Nick. She's good for you."

"Look, can we focus on the subject at hand?"

"Which is?"

"A boating accident. I need to see if the sheriff's department gathered any evidence from the wreckage."

"What are you looking for?"

"Don't know. Just think it might not be a simple accident and I'm hoping to find a lead. Think you can get me in with the sheriff?"

"On one condition. Don't screw up what you have with Theresa."

"I don't know." Quentin stared with a straight face. He meant it. "Okay. I'll do my best. All right? Now, how about if you get out of my love life and into my need for evidence?

"Done."

~ * ~

Quentin had a buddy with the sheriff's department, so getting Nick in to view the little evidence gathered was easy. Unfortunately, the deceased had slammed with tremendous force against a rock embankment in a fiery explosion. The corpse, which the coroner was "pretty sure" had been a man, had the look of a marshmallow left in a campfire a bit too long. In other words, he was a charred lump, along with everything else in the boat at the moment of impact. However, an energetic deputy had found a bag tossed clear of the wreckage on shore. The bag, University of Texas burnt orange with a white longhorn emblem on the side, sat before Nick on a table in one of the interview rooms at the department. A label hanging from the bag's handle said the owner was Harry Crenshaw.

Nick looked at Quentin's friend, Deputy Bill Simmons. "Know anything about this Harry Crenshaw guy?"

"Yeah. Done some time in Huntsville for armed robbery. But he was mostly a two-bit con man, we think doing some enforcement work for a drug ring, and a bit of gun nut."

"Is he the kind of guy someone might hire for a hit?"

"Harry? Not my first choice, but I suppose he'd be available for that sort of work. Probably at a bargain price, too. I think he was more interested in mayhem than in money."

41

Buzzard Bait

Nick unzipped Harry's bag. A pair of black leather gloves, a hunting knife, a Beretta M&P 9mm semi-automatic, and an Uzi machine pistol. Definitely, not the guns of a deer hunter. He was about to call it a day, not finding anything of importance to be of help to Dillon. Lifting the Uzi out of the bag, Nick's eye caught the edge of a piece of paper peeking from under the bottom lining. He pulled out a business card adorned with a fierce aardvark. Beside its bared snarling teeth were the words,

Andy Sullivan
Band Director
Ingersson High School
Home of the Fighting Aardvarks
Pflugerville, Texas

Nick handed the card to Quentin. "Why would a failed felon have a high school band director's business card in his bag full of guns and knives?"

"Maybe his kid plays in the band."

"You really think Harry has a kid?"

"Or Andy is his target."

"I'd agree with you, except Harry managed to put several bullet holes in Dillon's boat before he launched himself into the afterlife. Andy might have more going on than marching band practice."

Quentin crossed his arms, pondering Nick's words. "So a band director hires a two-bit felon to kill a competitive bass fisherman. You live in a very strange world, my friend."

"You have a better theory?"

"Simplest is usually the best. How about Dillon pissed off Harry, so he tried to end him at the lake."

"And the card?"

"His kid's in the band. Andy's a drug dealer. They met at the Optimist Club, the gun range, a church..."

"Church?"

42

"Okay, that's a stretch. But saying this band director hires killers just because the killer has his business card seems a bit of a stretch, too."

"Well, there's only one way to find out." Nick stood, tapping the card on the table.

Quentin put out his hand. "Hey, no stealing from the evidence room. That is, if you want to be able to come back."

Nick set Andy's card in his friend's open palm. "Thanks for your help, Quen. I owe you."

"Yes, you do and don't ever forget it."

Ingersson Aardvarks

Harry should have called by now. Andy Sullivan took a drag of weed. Thick smoke filled his lungs, calming his nerves. He needed to calm his nerves. He had agreed to do the killing, but the more he thought about it, the less he wanted to be intimately involved in the act. Something about bending over a fence, with a Smith and Wesson in the last place you want one, put him off the whole killing thing. Then he remembered a guy he knew in prison, his cellmate for a few months, who used to brag all the time about killing people. Harry Crenshaw. Lucky for Andy, the wheels of justice wobble all over the damn place, so Harry had managed to get paroled. They had only gotten him on manslaughter anyway. Although Andy never could figure out how embedding a guy in the concrete foundation of a split level in Maple Hills counted as manslaughter. He heard Harry had hit the streets a month ago, so he gave him a call. They agreed to meet in a state government parking garage near the capital to do the deal.

"You sure you can handle this, Harry?"

"Handle it? Charlie, I can do this shit in my sleep. The guy's a bass fisherman, for crissake. Back in Jersey, I whacked guys like him for breakfast."

"Don't call me Charlie."

Harry looked around the empty parking garage. "Who's listening? You fuckin' Deep Throat or some shit?"

"It's Andy. Better you call me Andy all the time than make a mistake in public."

44

Harry chuckled, shaking his head. "Jesus, Charl...Andy. You're turning into a real pain in the ass for a five-hundred dollar gig."

"Just call me as soon as you get it done."

Harry walked away, his steps echoing off concrete walls. "You got it, boss."

Apparently, Harry didn't get it. Here he was on a Monday morning and no word from his ex-cellmate. Andy chewed his nails to the quick waiting for a call. He went into the bathroom, setting his joint on the counter. The guy in the mirror looked like shit. Successful hit or not, he had band practice and a pretty damned good shot at Regionals, maybe even State. He splashed cold water on his face, flushed the joint down the toilet and drove to work.

~ * ~

Football season wouldn't officially begin until September, but two-a-days had begun for the Ingersson Aardvarks in July. The football team practiced drills and plays on the field, while the band learned their complex marching configurations in the parking lot while blaring out the theme from Star Wars. Nick stood at a chain link fence, the band members in shorts, earnest and precise. He could hear commands lofting out of a metal framework towering over them. A trim man in his thirties with thick brown hair stood atop a tower, megaphone in hand.

"Tubas, pay attention out there. You're looking sloppy. And percussion, someone's missing the downbeat. Fix it. Or we'll be out here until you do."

A groan rose from the lot, but the director shouted out like a taunting drill sergeant, "I can't hear you."

A unified chorus of surprising volume responded with, "Be. Aardvark. Strong!"

"Okay, take ten. We'll run through the show and if it's flawless, we're done for the day."

The perfect lines of band members fell into chaos as kids clustered together or jogged across the lot for a drink from two large ice chests. Nick stood at the bottom of the tower ladder as the man descended.

"Mr. Sullivan? Andy Sullivan?"

"Yeah, I'm Andy Sullivan. You with the press?"

"Ah, no. Something else entirely."

"Look, I'm in the middle of practice and as I'm sure you know, we only have a few more weeks before the first game, not to mention contest. Is this something we can talk about later?"

"I'll only take a moment of your time, Andy. It's about a friend of yours."

Andy looked concerned, as if preparing himself for some news about a friend who had a car accident. "Really?"

"Yeah, it's about Harry Crenshaw."

He shifted from anticipated grief to nervous denial. "Harry? Sorry, don't know anybody by that name. Look, I really need to—"

"You don't know Harry? That's funny because he seems to know you."

"He told you he knew me? Son of a..." Andy smiled nervously, his eyes darting away from Nick's gaze. "Harry. Yeah, okay. I remember him. We met at church."

"You met Harry Crenshaw, the felon with a record as long as this tower is tall, at your church."

Andy took a step back, his eyes conveying panic, his voice mimicking shock. "I had no idea he had a record. Seemed like a nice enough guy. I guess you just don't know about people, do you? Look, I'm pretty busy with my kids here. Anything else?"

"I suppose we never know everything about each other. Although he spoke highly of you."

Andy blinked, his voice held to a whisper. "He said that? Are you, well, you know..."

"I don't know, Andy. Am I what?"

"Who are you? What do you want?"

"I'm Nick Sibelius. And I just want some peace and quiet. But you see, Harry, your pew mate Harry? His boat exploded all over Lake Travis and poor Harry, well, he looks like a piece of charcoal. So I'm wondering why a piece of charcoal has your business card, Andy. Got any ideas?"

Andy gazed past Nick, as if planning his escape. "I want a lawyer."

"Okay. I want the Rangers to make it to the Series. Now, how about Harry?"

"You're a cop. I know my rights. I get to have a lawyer."

Nick stepped closer. "I'm not a cop, I'm glad you know your rights, and I don't have to get you diddly squat." Nick moved into the band director, trapping him against the tower's metal grid work. "So, you were telling me about Harry."

"I don't know him, man. Really. Never heard of him."

"I thought you went to church together."

"Look, I didn't know who was asking. Okay?" He smiled nervously. "So I made up the church thing."

"Really. But you're telling me the truth now?"

Andy's left eye twitched. "Absolutely. I don't know a guy named Harry."

"I hope you're telling me the truth, Andy. I really don't take kindly to prevaricators. When I'm around a liar, the little hairs on the back of my neck stand up."

"I'm not lying, mister. Honest to God."

Nick could usually tell when someone lied to him and Andy proved to be an open book. "I don't know, Andy. I'm not getting a good feeling here." Nick sensed a crowd gathering. He leaned in, whispering in the man's ear. "You don't want me for an enemy."

He followed Andy's eyes to see about fifty band members in a semi-circle around them, watching him intimidate their beloved band director. Maybe Andy was simply a band director and Harry Crenshaw stole a bag from one his students. However, his intuition told him otherwise. He'd let Andy stew awhile then try again.

Nick stepped back, smiling broadly, then slapped Andy playfully on the shoulder. "Great job, Mr. Sullivan. I'll tell our fund raising committee all about it." He turned to the crowd. "And these guys. Talented. Very talented."

Andy rubbed his shoulder, but played along with Nick. "Yeah, they're the best. And, uh, thanks for dropping by."

"My pleasure, Andy. If you have any other ideas you want to share with me, give me a call."

~ * ~

Andy gave his kids a surprise unlike anything he had ever done. He gave them the rest of the day off because they were doing such a wonderful job. Leaving the final details of the day to his assistant, Andy jumped in his Dodge Caravan and pulled out a cell phone.

A woman answered. "Yes."

"It's Andy. Andy Sullivan."

"I know who it is. No names, remember?"

"Sorry Miss, uh, yeah, sorry."

"What do you want? You know this line is only for emergencies." She sounded pretty pissed.

"We need to talk. Now. It's important."

"The southeast parking lot by Pflugerville Lake in fifteen."

He glanced at his dash. A needle hovered below the E on his gas gauge. "Sure. Uh, I need to run by the gas station. Can we make it thirty minutes?"

Silence. She had hung up.

~ * ~

Andy scanned for Bobbie Shank's car as he rolled up to a small parking lot near Lake Pflugerville dam. He figured on an Audi or a BMW. A weird thing happened once he agreed to kill the guy with her phone. She got all up in his grill, crazy like their first meeting. Then he'd remembered his tape, comforting himself with the knowledge that if she pushed too hard, he'd get the last laugh. He'd go to the cops with her murder for hire scheme, then distribute his homemade porno tape to his sources and make some fast money off her while destroying any reputation she had left. The woman was downloadable gold.

48

The loud rumble of a big Harley thundered into the lot, pulling alongside him. A very sexy-looking woman in a full-face black helmet and black, skin-tight leathers highlighting all of her curves pulled up beside him. Even though he knew Bobbi lived inside the helmet, he still felt stirrings of desire. Yeah, she was one crazy bitch from hell, but what a fine piece of ass. Watching her, he wondered what it would be like to tame the beast when she wasn't drunk and semiconscious. She pulled off her helmet, dirty blond hair cascading down her shoulders. Andy jumped out of his Caravan, a bit self-conscious of his ride compared to the curvaceous lines of her cruiser.

"Bobbi. Good to see you."

She looked up from her low rider perch, glaring. "Cut the crap, Andy. What's so fucking urgent?"

She mouthed off more than she used to. They were going to need a come to Jesus soon. "Well, I, uh, I had a visit today by this guy asking questions." He swallowed, his heart pounding in his throat.

"Yes?"

"You know you asked me to take out the fisherman? Well, I kind of delegated." He wished she would scream or slap him or something. Instead she stood there, her eyes burning holes right through his body. "It's okay. I made sure to get a professional."

"So why are we talking if you've got a professional on the job?"

"Well, my guy, Harry Crenshaw—"

"Names again. Do I need to beat your head in with that stupid megaphone of yours?"

"Now don't be that way, Bobbi. It's just I guess he didn't get the job done to the standards you expect."

"This is a binary problem."

"What?"

"He's either alive or dead. So which is it?"

"This guy came around asking lots of questions."

"What guy?"

"You said no names."

She reached up, a cobra striking its prey, grabbing him by his shirt and pulling him close. "What's his fucking name, Andy?"

He couldn't put his finger on it, but something about Bobbi felt increasingly intimidating. "Sibelius. Nick Sibelius. He said Harry, our guy, died in an explosion on Lake Travis."

"What about the job you asked him to do. Did he get it done?"

"I think maybe not. Given his boat blew up."

She shoved him away. "God, I should've known better. This is your fault, Andy. You were supposed to kill him, but instead you bring in an amateur. Couldn't bring in a real professional because you wanted to skim the fee. Am I right?"

She was dead on. "No way, baby. I'd never do that to you. No, I got the best."

"Andy, the best doesn't let a bass fisherman get the drop on him. And now you've attracted attention to yourself. Is this Sibelius a cop?"

"I don't think so. He's some kind of investigator. Maybe insurance or something."

He shifted back and forth nervously while Bobbi stared across the lake. Andy waited anxiously, but when she kept silent, he finally stated what he considered to be the obvious solution. A solution which would make her more indebted to him. Maybe he'd set up a threesome for the next shoot. "I'll get another guy, one of the best. He'll clean this up for you. Of course, guys like him aren't free."

She leaned back on her bike, offering Andy a smile. "I'm sure he's quite expensive, but you've got a way for me to lower the payments. Am I right?"

"Yeah, baby."

"Well, Frank, I'm not sure I can trust you to get it done."

God, he hated it when people used the wrong assumed name. "It's no problem, really. I guarantee my man will get it done in the next forty-eight hours."

"A guarantee, huh?"

He relaxed. Maybe he just thought he heard her say Frank. "I'm a man of my word."

"I'm sure you are. So try this truth on for size, Franky. You're a fuck up. So you're officially on the bubble. One more failure and you're done."

Andy dug deep. He would not let some biker chick poser run over him. "Hassle me and my video goes viral."

"What video?"

"The one I've got of you fornicating with every door knob, leather chair, and appliance in my house. That's what video." He had her right where he wanted her. Time to bend her over a fence. Yessir.

"Charles—it is Charles, the child rapist from Michigan, right?"

His heart caught in his throat. How did she know? The conniving little bitch was sixteen, dressed like a hooker, and knew more about sex than he did, which, as he thought about it, probably said more about him. All the other girls before her had kept quiet, but she had to go whining to her school counselor. Clearly he was the victim, entrapped by that minx. However, the damn judge didn't see it his way. Nobody in Pflugerville knew he had done time. He made sure when he got out of the pen to bury Charles Dudley, his real name, and bring Andy Sullivan, band director extraordinaire, to life. He even paid another of his cellmates, who had some serious hacking skills, to create college and employment records. Somehow Bobbi found out about him.

"How do you know?"

"Well, Charles. You didn't think I'd let a little prick like you blackmail me and get away with it, did you?"

"I still have the video."

She looked at him like a hunter might look at a stupid, untrained dog. "You're going to destroy every copy."

He laughed nervously, still not quite certain what was happening. "Don't mess with me. The last thing you want is for it to get posted online. Sounds to me like you don't understand the value of my videography. We're talking about my livelihood here."

"What are you talking about, Charles?"

"The name's Andy. And if you want all the copies of the video it'll cost you one hundred thousand dollars."

"One hundred K."

He shrugged, feeling a bit more in control. "I'm an artist who deserves to be paid for the quality of his work. And if I can't be paid by a slutty Harley riding poser, then I'll have to go to my public who, thanks to the internet, appreciates my work."

"Let me offer you an alternative, Charles." She stepped into him, grabbing his balls so hard he thought one would pop out and shoot across the parking lot. "You will hire a professional to kill Dillon." Her grip on his manhood tightened with each word. "You will hire this professional at your own expense."

Andy tried to squirm away, nausea rising in his throat, but his back was to the van and his voice pitched up higher than he had wanted. "Wh-why w-would I d-do that?"

"If you fail to kill Dillon, I will kill you. Do we understand each other?"

He looked at the woman he thought he had domesticated, but the whacked out crazy psychopathic bitch had returned full force. She said she'd kill him. He'd seen eyes like hers only one other time—in prison when Diego told Rivens he'd be dead by morning. Sure as shit, guards found Rivens sliced up in his cell at breakfast. The new Bobbi Shank scared him to his core.

"Yeah. Ah. Okay." Released from her iron grasp, he bent over, his hands between his legs. He managed to get a few words out. "What...about...Sibelius?"

52

"I'll take care of him. You just be sure Dillon dies."

"Yes, ma'am. I'll take care of it. Promise." He wasn't sure why he called her ma'am. It seemed the thing to say to a woman who crushed your testicles.

"Do not disappoint me."

Gaining some composure, he rose to a partial standing position. "Like I tell my band kids, integrity is the cornerstone of excellence."

She gave him a smirk, then shoved him. His head banged against his van. Holding one hand to the newly formed lump on his scalp while his other hand still nursed his crotch, he watched her fire up her Harley, pull out of the lot, and rumble down the road.

Andy drove away from his meeting with Bobbi shaken. Not so much by her threat, which definitely packed a punch, but also from the knowledge she had him by the cojones. Literally. He took pride in his ability to manipulate and use people, not the reverse. His courage, however, increased with each mile he put between himself and Bobbi.

The bitch might think she's got the upper hand, but she doesn't know who she's messing with. No sir.

He'd take care of Dillon himself. Save on hit fees. Then he'd teach Bobbi Shanks a lesson she wouldn't live to forget. His newly minted serial killer instincts resurfaced. He spoke to the killer staring at him in his rear view mirror. Wincing, he shifted to soothe his swollen, bruised nuts.

"When Charles Dudley's got your number, it's lights out."

His Caravan sputtered, then stalled as he rolled to a stop on the side of the road. Charles Dudley, aka Frank, aka Andy Sullivan, had run out of gas.

RC Flyer

Nick dropped by to see Dillon, but discovered from Dolores he had gone to an RC airfield to fly his radio-controlled model airplane. Apparently, Dillon loved RC planes as much as he loved fishing. Nick took the drive north past Georgetown, down county roads and then a dirt road to the Georgetown Aero Modelers Association airfield. Pulling up to two long covered hangar-like workspaces, he parked beside a familiar double dually pickup. He stepped out of his truck into a one hundred degree, dead calm day and the high-pitched drone of an RC airplane buzzing overhead. Dillon stood near a miniaturized asphalt runway, manipulating a little black box complete with antenna, a small red flag on its end. A silver Mustang P-51 descended from his left, flying twenty feet above the tarmac. Midfield, the plane rolled, then the nose pointed up, the aircraft shooting skyward into a loop.

Nick meant to interrupt Dillon's joy flight, but found himself mesmerized by the graceful beauty of his model in the sky. After ten minutes, Dillon lined up the aircraft with the runway, landed her, and taxied the plane back to a halt a few feet away. He was kneeling to pick up his plane when Nick approached from behind.

"Nice day for a flight."

Dillon startled, then seeing it was Nick, relaxed. "Yeah. You fly?"

"The full-size version. Not one of those. A Cessna. I started lessons, but haven't gotten around to finishing yet. Kind of expensive hobby."

Dillon stood up, holding what looked like a perfect replica of a P-51. "You should get into RC. You get to fly on the cheap. Of course, you've gotta like to fiddle with these babies." He walked toward an open air shed, setting his plane on a wood rest. "I just need to refuel. If you want, I'll let you take a spin."

Nick sat at a picnic table beyond the work shed while Dillon attached a fuel hose to the plane's tank. "I got back from Ingersson High a few hours ago." He waited for some response, but Dillon stayed focused on his work. "Saw Andy Sullivan. You know Andy?"

"Andy? Hell, Nick. I barely made it out of high school and it was twenty years ago."

"So you've never heard of Andy Sullivan, the high school band director?"

Finished refueling, he picked up his airplane. "I don't have a kid, at least one I know about, or play an instrument. So why would I know a band director?"

"Remember the fellow you told me was trying to kill you?"

"Sure."

"He's dead."

Dillon nodded with a shrug. "Figures. That was one hell of a crash. Well, better him than me." He walked past Nick toward the runway, then stopped. "But what does a band director have to do with it?"

Nick stood up. "That's the thing, Dillon. Your killer had Andy's business card in his bag of guns."

"Shit. He had a bag of guns?"

"A bag of guns with Andy's business card. Now why would a two-bit felon want to kill you and also have a high school band director's card?"

Dillon turned back to the field, setting his plane on the ground. He moved silver sticks on his transmitter, checking ailerons and rudder control. "I don't have a clue."

"Dillon, folks don't typically try to kill you for nothing."

Buzzard Bait

Dillon leaned down, attaching a battery wire to the engine's glow plug. "Do I look like the kind of guy who'd be a threat to anybody? Hell, I'm just a good ol' boy fisherman who drinks beer for breakfast, smokes a little weed, and flies a mean-ass model plane." He gave the small plane's prop a quick flick and the engine fired to life, buzzing like some giant bee. He taxied it onto the runway then pushed his throttle control forward. The scale model P-51 accelerated down the tarmac, quickly taking to the air.

~ * ~

Andy pulled his Caravan off to the side of a county road behind a line of trees. He had been following a small blue dot on his cell phone map which stopped moving about thirty minutes ago in a field on the other side of the trees. He scurried out to look for his target. Dillon stood about a hundred yards away in the middle of a field. *What is he doing?* He had a black box in his hand with a little red flag. Then Andy heard the buzz of a model plane. *Perfection.* He'd be able to take the shot with his Bushmaster rifle and show Bobbi how a man takes care of business.

He made his way back to the van, careful to stay behind cover. After shoving a loaded thirty-round clip into his rifle, he took his position once again at the tree line. What's this? Another man stood beside Dillon. *Damn, I wish I had bought a scope for this thing.* Andy had never hunted with this rifle, or with any rifle, for that matter. Crawling around in the bushes to shoot Bambi didn't interest him. He bought the assault-style rifle to hang in his pickup as part of his new tough guy, serial killer persona. But when he went to the Ford dealer to buy the truck, his credit score destroyed any chance of financing and the sales manager wouldn't give him squat for the Caravan. At least today he'd found a good use for the gun.

Andy pulled out a small set of binoculars. As the fuzzy image came into focus, he smiled. "Nick Sibelius. I think I've got me a two-fer." He settled into position, controlling his breathing. A killing machine poised to strike.

~ * ~

Dillon's plane flew away from him, turning gracefully back toward the field. "Nick, I really don't know why somebody would be tryin' to kill me. Really. Here, you want to give this a go?"

Before Nick could refuse, Dillon handed him the transmitter. Nick grasped the box, hoping some instructions followed.

"If you want to go up, just push this lever up."

Nick pushed the lever. The plane's nose shot straight for the sky.

"Whoa, there. Just a bit." Dillon reached over, bringing the craft back under control. "Steady. Now if you want to go left, you move this stick left and you move it right, if you want to go right. No need to worry about the landing gear. I'll be landing her."

Nick concentrated on his fast-moving aircraft, making turns, Dillon reaching over occasionally to save him from disaster.

"You're doing good there, Nick. A natural."

"Thanks." He hadn't intended to spend his time with Dillon flying RC airplanes, but he found some joy in having control over something for a change.

"You better pass her back to me. She's a bit tricky to land and I'm guessing you've never landed an RC plane before."

As Nick handed the black transmitter box over to Dillon, a movement caught his eye. Distracted, he dropped the box in the dirt before Dillon had a chance to grab it.

"Hey, be careful."

Dillon bent down to pick it up just as something pinged off a corrugated steel shed behind them, followed swiftly by a boom. A gun shot.

Nick shouted, "Down!"

He dove on top of Dillon, splaying him out in the dirt. The gunman had a clear shot from the tree line across a plowed field and the asphalt runway. A puff of dirt exploded in front of them, followed again by a boom.

Buzzard Bait

~ * ~

"Damn!" Andy couldn't believe he missed his first shot. And then the second went off all on its own. *Man, this thing's got a hair trigger.* He looked down the sights, but his targets failed to be as cooperative as before, both now sprawled on the ground. He took in a deep breath to settle himself, taking aim at one of the heads in the distance. *Just squeeze the trigger, Andy.* With a deafening blast, his rifle slammed into his shoulder. He had forgotten ear plugs. A puff of dirt kicked into the air several feet from from his target. *Damn. I keep missing.*

~ * ~

Nick scanned around them. "We've got to get out of here. Stay on your stomach and don't move an inch. Got it?"

"Sure. What's happening?"

"I'll be right back." He hoped. After a third shot, Nick rose, running to a wood table. It wouldn't stop the bullets, but at least the shooter wouldn't be able to see them. He flipped it on its side, then pushed it toward Dillon. A fourth shot rang out.

"Damn, that was close, Nick."

Optimally, he'd wait for the next shot before he urged Dillon to move, but it sounded like the shooter had dialed in on his position. "Dillon, run as fast as you can to me. Now. Go!"

He heard Dillon grunt, then footfalls on dirt, another blast which exploded through the overturned table just as Dillon crashed to the ground beside him. Nick had positioned the table to block their shooter's view of a gap in chain link fencing. "Crawl straight back to the parking lot. Don't look back. Don't get up. Just crawl."

Fear etched across his face, Dillon did as he was told. Nick followed close behind, as a burst of gunfire pounded the table.

58

Once in the parking lot, they crawled behind Nick's pickup. The shooter had lost them, still firing rounds into the overturned table.

"Get in the truck and keep your head down."

"But what about my stuff?"

Between the shots being fired in their direction, the drone of Dillon's plane faded in the distance. "I think you may have lost her."

"Well, we've gotta find it. I put too much time into building that plane to just walk away."

"You've got someone with a high-powered rifle working hard to kill you and all you want to do is find your damn toy plane?"

"It's not a toy." He frowned. "But I see your point."

"Dillon, get in the truck. You can look for your plane later when someone isn't trying to shoot you. Sound reasonable?"

"Yeah, I suppose."

"On three, run to the passenger side, get in and get low. Got it?"

"Yessir."

"One, two, three!" They both ran to the truck's cab, flinging open the doors, then diving in.

Dillon folded himself down below the dash while Nick prayed his truck would start on the first go—not always a given. His engine roared to life. He threw his pickup into reverse, enveloping the truck in a cloud of dust, then skidded rear tires on dirt and gravel, accelerating away from the airfield. A ping let him know the shooter still tracked him, but Nick hoped being in motion would make them a more difficult target.

~ * ~

As his targets drove away, Andy lay prone on the ground in complete disbelief. Everything had been going to plan until the damned table got in his way. He had fired again and again, frustration building with each round. Memories of Bobbi shoving a gun in his nether parts haunted him.

Buzzard Bait

I had 'em. They were right in my sights.

A raging fire erupted across his left ankle, as if someone had poured lighter fluid on him and lit a match. "What the—"

Fire ants.

He tossed his rifle aside, frantically slapping a swarm of ants off his leg. Yanking off his shoe and his sock, he swept the last attacker away only to be left with red and swollen bites around his ankle and foot. His gaze shifted from his leg back to the road. No truck. They had gotten away. He sighed, looking up to a clear blue Texas sky which, from his personal experience, was completely devoid of a God who gave a crap about him. Limping back to his van, rifle in one hand, he pondered his situation. He'd have to come up with a plan B and pretty damn soon, or he'd have Bobbi all over his ass.

Literally.

~ * ~

Once off the dirt track, Nick drove onto a paved county road, fishtailing then regaining control. In a field to their left, a P-51 flew a twisting loop, dove for the ground, pulled up, climbing straight until she stalled, then plummeted down, striking hard ground with a thud and a cloud of dust. Dillon shook his head. "My plane. Dammit. You know how much time I spent building that thing? We need to go back so I can at least get the engine out of it."

Nick stared straight ahead.

"Aw, come on, Nick. That engine set me back five hundred bucks."

Nick let a couple miles go, while Dillon sighed and moaned, before he plunged ahead for the truth about what just happened. "Who's after you, Dillon? I can't help you if you're not going to be straight with me."

Dillon shook his head, gazing out his window. "I have no idea. I loved that plane. Best one I ever built."

"You can build another, but you've got to be alive to do it. So why don't you tell me what's really going on?"

"I have no idea. One day I'm happy as a pig in shit, and the next day I've got people trying to kill me dead." Dillon punched his door with a fist. "You tell me. Why is this happening?"

"Calm down. Beating my truck isn't going to help anything."

"What *is* going to help?"

"Let's think about this. Was the lake the first time someone tried to kill you?"

"Yeah." Dillon rubbed his chin, then hesitated. "You know, I've been thinking about it. Competitive fishing is pretty cutthroat these days. I didn't think it was possible, but maybe someone got intimidated by my fishing skills."

Nick watched several telephone poles go by. "Really? You think some good ol' boy's gunning for you because you caught a bigger fish?"

"It's possible. That's all I'm saying."

"So, we're talking about a fisherman who shoots high-powered rifles."

"This is Texas. Fishin' and huntin' go together. Hell, I used to take a case of beer and my thirty-aught-six to the lake with a couple of buddies."

"To hunt deer from the water?"

"Hell no. To shoot fish. If you miss, you gotta down one." He chuckled at the memory. "Man, we'd get so plastered."

"Well, we're not talking about a fellow fishing competitor. The guy who tried to kill you on the lake wasn't fishing. In fact, I don't think he ever fished in his life. So, a felon you don't know tries to kill you during a fishing tournament and then someone else tries to shoot you while you're flying your model airplane. Whoever it is seems to know your location."

"I know. It's crazy. How could they possibly know—"

"You have a phone by any chance?"

"Sure."

"Let's see it." Nick held out his hand.

61

Dillon fished his cell phone from his jeans pocket, passing it to Nick. "I don't see what my phone has to do with anything."

An iPhone. "Do you have this set up for Find My Phone?"

"Sure. If some sonofabitch steals my phone for my secret fishing locations, then all I gotta do is hit erase and snap, the phone's wiped clean."

Nick shook his head, pulling to the shoulder.

"I'm not as stupid as you think, am I, Nick?"

"What's your password?"

Dillon laughed. "Yeah, like I'm going to tell you."

"What's the damn password?"

"Just kiddin', dude. I suppose if I'm trusting you with my life, I can trust you with my fishing spots."

"Good thinking. Now what's the password?"

"Dillon."

"No, not your name, your password."

"It's Dillon. My name is my password."

Nick looked up from the phone. Dillon must have grown up by a lead mine. It was the only explanation for his complete lack of sense. "Don't you think Dillon is a bit obvious...Dillon?"

"Well, yeah. But if I used some fancy spy name or something, I'd forget it and then I'd be screwed."

"Yeah, instead of someone knowing your fishing spots, they'd just be able to track your every move and kill you whenever they damned well pleased."

"Got a point there, Nick."

Nick went into the phone's settings, turned off the finder function, then handed it back to Dillon. "I've turned it off. Do not, under any circumstances, turn the finder on again. Not while someone's trying to kill you. Can you do that for me?"

Dillon tucked his phone in a pocket. "Sure, Nick. Whatever you say."

Nick pulled back onto the road. "And I want you to leave town today. Take Dolores with you. Do you have someplace to go?"

"I suppose we could go to Indiana. I've got a cousin who's been dogging me to come visit for months."

"Good. Take him up on the offer. Just don't tell anyone where you're going. All right?"

"Yeah. Sure."

Up until yesterday no one had been after Dillon. Now suddenly hit men were coming out of the woodwork. Something must have happened in the last week or two, something Lead Mine Dillon, the flyboy fisherman, had no clue about.

"Dillon, tell me. What have you been up to, say, in the last couple of weeks?"

"Nothing special."

"Humor me. Tell me exactly what has happened and don't leave out anything. The smallest detail might be the thing keeping you alive."

Dillon's Last Two Weeks

Dillon loved fishing and flying model planes. But he also had a soft spot for guns. The perfect scenario in his mind would be shooting at his dead buddy's RC airplane—may Harlan rest in peace—with a line in a nearby water tank waiting on a strike. Harlan would be zigging and zagging evasively. Then some big ol' bass would strike his bait just as he pulled up a shotgun to blast Harlan's plane, probably a Messerschmitt (take that, you damn Nazi). He'd drop the gun, the plane spiraling down in flames, then turn to reel in a lunker of prize winner proportions. He'd be on the front page of the Austin American Statesman, named in Texas Monthly's Encyclopedia Texanica, probably an interview in Playboy, and for certain, he'd do a reenactment on the late-night talk shows. Hell, he'd never have to buy his own beer again with fans crowding around him wherever he'd go.

His ultimate fantasy floating in his mind, he pulled into the Will Rogers Memorial Coliseum parking lot for the annual Fort Worth Gun Show. He hoped to find a good assault rifle he could use to shoot coyotes and grackles. Instead, he found the woman of his dreams.

She drove into the parking lot on a big Harley, in skin tight leathers. While he appreciated the view and the sexual fantasy playing in his head beyond his control, he didn't figure her for a Dillon kind of woman. Sure enough, she looked right through him as if he was the invisible man. At least he had a ticket to the gun show.

After a day spent looking at guns, ammo, and just about anything that went bang, he got back in his truck, deciding to stop off at a little dive called The Eight Ball. One for the road. To his surprise, the same woman from the morning, the hot one in black leathers, sat at the bar nursing a whiskey. He sat next to her, ordered a beer and a shot, and "one for the lady," then tipped his gimme cap to her. If Dolores found out he was flirting with biker chicks she'd beat him senseless with a cast iron skillet. But two hundred miles separated Fort Worth and Austin, so he figured he'd be okay. It wasn't like he was having what the do-gooders called indiscriminate sex, although, good God, he sure wouldn't mind some if it came his way. She smiled back.

Encouraged, he decided to make some small talk. "You here for the show?"

Her helmet had covered long, blonde hair flowing down her shoulders. Five foot seven, trim as an athlete but with bumps in all the right places, early thirties, nice tits, long neck, and he figured a pretty good ass.

"Sure am." She put a hand on his arm. "This was my first. I guess you could say I'm a virgin."

Fortunately, the bartender had placed a beer at hand because he almost choked on the word virgin.

"I could have really used someone, a man, who knows his guns, to show me around today." She looked up to him, her blue eyes piercing the extremely thin armor keeping Dillon from acting on his thoughts.

"Yeah. Well, maybe I can help you..." He searched for a word.

She offered, "Debrief?"

Yeah, he'd certainly like to 'de-brief' her. "Yeah. Debrief. Happy to help a pretty thing like you out." He knew he had just crossed a critical line. Turning on the charm would either get him some more time with a leather clad goddess or a punch in the face. He flinched unconsciously.

She raised her glass. "Here's to debriefing." They drained their whiskeys, ordering another round and then another. Dillon felt his devotion to Dolores melting away with each drink. His bar mate's speech slurred, but there was something sexy about a tipsy blonde in black leather.

"I seeyou'reamember of the AMA."

"What?" His mind raced from her naked form bent over her motorcycle to the emblem embroidered on his hat. "Oh, right. Yeah. Academy of Model Aeronautics."

"Wow, youmuzbe pretty good... with your hands."

"I suppose so."

"I...like a man whozgood...withizands."

He thought he was about to do something embarrassing in the middle of the bar, but fortunately, she grabbed his arm, dragging him out the door. The drive was a bit of a blur, but he did recall ending up at the Texas Love Shack Motel and Diner, as well as a night of crazy sex he would not easily forget. All the while, he did stuff Dolores would never consider, especially the part with the duct tape and a jar of honey. Bobbi kept screaming, "Do me guapo, do me!" Damn, the woman could multitask. Upside down and sideways, he could have sworn he was having sex with identical twins, maybe even triplets. As luck would have it, he carried a few Viagra in his bag, leftover from a trip with Dolores to Corpus Christi last Spring. He wasn't about to stop an incredible night of hot sex he figured he'd never have a chance to repeat as long as he lived. At the first hint of fatigue, he dashed into the bathroom for a double dose. Do me guapo, do me!

By morning, he lay naked and spent, his nether parts aching with fatigue. He considered taking Bobbi out to breakfast, expressing his undying love and proving it by calling Dolores and telling her she never gave it up the way Bobbi did. Then he noticed the quiet. No footsteps, no tinkling like women do in the toilet, no shower. He raised his weary head. Bobbi's black leathers, which had been tossed askew on the floor of their cheap motel room, were nowhere to be seen. All that was left of Bobbi was her black phone with a pink skull and crossbones emblazoned on its case. He lay in bed until housekeeping banged on his door. Almost noon. The pinnacle of his sexual experience to date had up and gone.

A week went by and all he had of Bobbi was the fantasy he played over and over again in his head. The two times he had sex with Dolores after the Love Shack, he pretended she was Bobbi, just to liven things up a bit. When he accidentally shouted out Bobbi's name, Dolores accused him of wanting a gay lover, which pretty much put the kibosh on any affection between them.

He still had Bobbi's phone, intending to give it back to her if he ever saw her again. She had photos of a cat, plates of food, shots of naked body parts, all of them looking very much as Dillon remembered her, and a pretty raw video of her in some kind of S-M porn flick. Dolores might not be as adventurous, but sex with Dolores felt safe and comfortable. Bobbi was definitely into some crazy shit. He played some of her games. Most of them involved shooting at stuff, which was right up Dillon's ally. Then he noticed she had a password protected app for storing documents. He played around with it for a few hours, then a thought occurred to him. He tapped in d-o-m-e-g-u-a-p-o-d-o-m-e. To his surprise, it worked. He found himself looking at information about military bases and national guard movements across the state, ammunition suppliers, militia recruitment information, air traffic procedures, and many other bits of information he could hardly make any sense of. Then he realized she must be with Homeland Security and used the biker chick bit as a cover. *Damn. No wonder their encounter felt so dangerous. I had sex with an honest to God spy.*

Friday morning, he saw an ad for a gun show at the Travis County Expo that very weekend. He told Dolores he was checking fishing spots, but instead, made straight for the Expo center on Decker Lane, Bobbi's phone in his pocket, just in case lightning would strike twice.

He loitered in the parking lot for about an hour, hoping for a repeat of his Fort Worth rendezvous, but Bobbi didn't magically show up and come on to him in the parking lot. In fact, he got across the parking lot and through most of the show before he spotted her spotting him. Wearing the same leathers, she walked over to him. His night of ecstasy came rushing back. When she stepped in front of him he wanted to give her a hug, but he had a bag in one hand and a bottle of water in the other.

"Dillon. Good to see you."

"Really? I thought given how you left..."

"I'm just shy. The whole waking up in the morning thing. You know?"

No, he didn't. "Sure."

She asked him to walk her out to her Harley, which he did without question.

"Dillon, I've been meaning to ask you. Do you remember our night together?"

Dillon stopped in his tracks. "Do I remember? Darling, I'll never forget."

"Well, here's the thing. I think I left my phone in our room. You didn't happen to find it, did you?"

He could feel the tingle of hot sex lightning striking once again. Sex with Bobbi would be hot no matter what. But imagine a grateful Bobbi having sex. He reached into his back pocket, pulling out her phone. "I happen to have it right here. I was hoping I'd see you again."

"Thank God." She snapped it away from him.

"Yeah, thank God. Hey, I know a place we can go."

"What?"

Dillon nodded his head to one side. "You know. Go?"

"Not going to happen."

Dillon felt the blood rushing away from all his important bits.

"By the way, did you happen to use my phone for anything? I won't be mad. In fact, it'd be kind of sexy, if you did."

The tide rose back again. "Really? Well, yeah. Just a bit. But I'm a patriotic American, so no worries."

"Patriotic? What are you talking about?"

"All that super-secret spy stuff. You can count on me to keep my mouth shut. You know, loser lips sink shit."

She stared at him, unblinking. "The saying is loose lips sink ships."

"Really? Well, whatever. As a patriot, I want you to know your secret's safe with me."

"Show me what you're talking about."

She handed Dillon her phone. He obediently logged into her password protected e-wallet.

"Shit."

"Yeah. You probably want a better password. Or at least don't yell it out in the middle of stinkin' hot sex." He giggled before he could stop himself.

"Give me the phone, you idiot." She grabbed it back from him, using the device to poke him in the chest. "Dillon, you tell no one. Do you hear me? Not a damned soul. If I learn you've said a word, I swear to God the Department of Transportation will be scraping you off the highways of Texas for the next ten years. Are we clear?"

"You sure you don't want to get a room? You're like crazy hot when you're pissed."

She swung at him, but Dillon weaved away, then grabbed her in a bear hug, lifting her off the ground.

"Goddammit. Let me go."

"Calm down, calm down. I told you, your secret's safe. But you might want to work on your karate or whatever you spies use. You seem to be a bit rusty."

She stopped struggling. "Let me down. Please."

"Sure, honey. So, what do you say?"

She let out a deep sigh, straightening her leathers. "About what?"

"About us, of course."

She stepped back, her blue eyes glaring. "You're going to regret this, so help me God."

"I don't think so, darlin'. Wait, this isn't about the phone, is it? I saw this on Oprah. You're afraid of commitment."

She gave him a puzzled look, then turned on a heel, walking quickly away. Dillon shouted after her. "I won't let you slip away, Bobbi. Dolores will just have to understand

69

I've got someone else in my life. You and me. We'll go away."

But she kept on walking until she reached her bike. The Harley rumbled to life, then the bike and Bobbi rolled out of his life once again.

R. W. Hacker

Capital Campaign

Associated Press

Austin, TX—Business owners, shoppers, legislators, and university students looked up yesterday afternoon to thousands of fluttering miniature leaflets falling from the sky. The leaflets, the size of a chewing gum wrapper, were dropped from what witnesses described as drone airplanes in the downtown, capital and university areas of the city. The leaflets proclaim "Independence for the Sovereign Republic of Texas" on one side and "We Hang Together or We Hang Separately" on the other.

Asked about the leaflets, city residents gave a variety of opinions. UT undergraduate Alice Crumball, shopping on The Drag for a "cool pair of jeans" said, "I think it's good that in this country we can drop stuff from the sky to express our opinion, although I'm not in favor of communal suicide, especially by hanging." Joel Baskins, owner of Tequila Worm, a local bar on 6th street repeated what many on the street asked. "Aren't we already a sovereign state?"

Dr. Magdalena Ortega, University of Texas professor and expert on the Republic of Texas movement, met with state officials and Homeland Security. "I cannot divulge the content of our meeting," she said. "However, as an expert in the Republic of Texas operations across the state, I'd say dropping leaflets from drones must be viewed as a provocative act. The leaflets bear no resemblance to any form of communication the group has used in the past, but we all change, don't we?" The Governor's Office could not be reached for comment.

~ * ~

Buzzard Bait

"What the hell, Bruce?" Governor Fran Adamson held her phone so tight her knuckles ached.

"Frannie—"

"Don't Frannie me, Reynolds. Leaflets in my city?"

"I thought you'd be pleased. As we agreed, I have not attacked any of the state infrastructure."

"Attacked? Dammit, Bruce. You dropped thousands of your damned Republic leaflets across the city. People notice something like that."

"Of course they do. Which is why I did it. We're educating the people right now on the origins of our Republic. When the revolution comes, we want an educated Texian people on our side."

She closed her eyes, a pain forming between her eyebrows. She wanted his money. Hell, she needed his money. The last Presidential election required almost a billion dollars and you don't pick up that kind of change off a fifty-thousand-dollar-a-plate dinner. No, she had to have big donors like Bruce to have another shot at the White House.

"Fran, you there?"

"Yes, Bruce."

"We scored a victory for our cause, Frannie."

She had to get his money before he went off the deep end. "Yes, indeed. A great victory. Speaking of victories, have you given more thought to contributing to my Presidential campaign? Once the Republic comes into being, you'll need a friend in the White House."

"Yes, yes. Completely agree. There're a few things I want to have in place first. I'm sure you understand."

"A few things? What few things?"

"Best for you not to know, Frannie. Plausible deniability?"

"What few things, Bruce?"

"See you, sweetheart. Here's to the Republic."

"Bruce. Reynolds?" The line was dead. "Goddammit!" She threw her cell phone across the office, hitting solid oak paneling just underneath a buffalo she bagged on a ranch south of Johnson City. The phone hit with a thud, then bounced a few times on the floor, pieces flying this way and that. "Damn it." She yelled at her door. "Dennis. Dennis, get in here."

A clean-cut man of twenty-four in a gray business suit and red tie stepped into the office.

"I'm going to need another phone."

"Broke it again?"

She stayed seated behind her desk, but pressed her hands on the desktop as if she might leap across to slit his throat at any moment. "Yes, I broke it. Piece of crap. Do you think you can find me a phone that doesn't fall apart in my hand? That's all I'm asking here, Dennis. A phone that stays in one piece. Am I asking too much?"

"No, no, ma'am." He knelt, picking up her phone and several detached pieces. "I'll have something to you this afternoon." He turned to leave.

"And Dennis."

"Yes, ma'am?"

"Don't disappoint me. I've got too many people making promises then breaking them."

"I'll do my best."

"I don't want your best, Dennis. I want it done. Period."

As the door clicked shut behind her aide, Fran stood, pacing. Bruce Reynolds had moved from fun sex partner and big donor to an off-the-rails liability. His unpredictability presented a significant issue. She shook her head, reaching to touch the nose of her thirteen point deer hanging on one wall as she walked by. If she was honest with herself, and any great politician had be honest, at least with herself, the real issue with Bruce was his lack of respect for her command decisions. She asked him to lay low and instead she got leaflets dropping from the sky. What next?

She sat back down behind her desk, the trappings of her office all around her. Fran Adamson had worked too hard and too long to let a whack job like Bruce Reynolds get in

73

her way. She'd give him a week to come up with the money for her campaign. If he didn't come through, well, as they say in the hallowed halls of Congress, "Screw him."

R. W. Hacker

Screw and Skewer

Bobbi had just about had enough. Not trusting Charlie aka Andy to get it done, she had followed him. And sure enough, he managed to screw up what should have been an easy task. She admonished herself for ever thinking Andy could do a simple job for her. What was so difficult about killing a man, especially Dillon? The good ol' boy spent half his time floating on a lake looking for fish and the other half slamming down beer in anticipation of floating on a lake looking for fish. She would have done it herself, but she figured too many people had seen them together. *Why did I give Andy another chance? Bobbi, you can't turn a cow patty into a turd blossom.* She almost killed him right in the high school parking lot, moms with little kids in strollers be damned. Then she took a deep breath.

Andy could wait, but this Sibelius guy was another matter altogether. She could not have a cop or an investigator, or whatever he was, poking around her business, especially as the stakes were rising. Bobbi considered various ways of removing Sibelius from the equation. Obvious choices included planting explosives under his trailer or a simple bullet to the head. Both tried and true, but each had a downside. To blow up his Airstream she'd have to construct a bomb at least as powerful as her exploding clarinet, which would take a few days to pull together. No, this time-sensitive project required immediate action. Shooting him would be quick and easy. She had a gun and plenty of ammunition. Pressing a semi-automatic to someone's head required very little in the way of marksmanship. However, the last time she killed a man, she felt disappointed. Killing

75

him was like having an argument with someone who wouldn't fight back. Her partner sat there, tied to his chair denying he stole all the money they'd scammed off their mark, an old man millionaire. She knew he lied to her, which hurt more because she liked him as a partner in crime and in bed.

"Baby, I didn't take the money."

"Yes, you did, you lying son of a bitch!"

Her gun, pressed against his head, fired between 'son of' and 'a bitch', her finger carrying out her unconscious desire for him to be dead, dead, dead. Of course, she would have killed him eventually, but the point was, she acted rashly, losing those delicious tense moments of murderous foreplay. She apologized for her outburst, but with half of his head missing, it was hard for him to pay attention to his killer's good manners.

While a gun could fire prematurely, a knife might be the tool to help her exercise some restraint. She could soften him up with a little sex, then stab him in the heart in the throws of orgasm. She shuddered with pleasure, thinking about him inside her while she slipped a blade into his chest. First, she had to get him into bed and make sure he didn't change his mind or resist. But how? And then an idea with a kind of poetic symmetry came to her. She'd use Charlie's old trick, a little G in Sibelius's beer, so he'd be pliable and defenseless. They'd have some great sex, then she'd pick up her blade and end him, his blood spurting all over the sheets and her naked body.

She savored the image for a moment, then smacked her steering wheel. Restraint. Yes, a bloody orgasmic stabbing would be so hot, but she'd also be leaving enough evidence a rookie cop with ADD could nail her. No, she'd drug him, then take him outside to a nearby field and shove an ice pick in his brain. That's the business.

When she got to Nick's trailer, it sat empty, the surrounding field browned off from drought. She pulled her Porsche into the shade of a live oak, then waited for his

76

arrival. A little over an hour passed before he pulled up, taking time to put a sunscreen in his window in a feeble attempt to keep his truck's interior from frying in the heat. He seemed lost in his thoughts, since he hadn't noticed her Porsche yet. Bobbi, in a little black dress and heels, made sure she revealed the dark edge of her stockings as she emerged from the convertible. The man couldn't keep his eyes off her as she swayed her hips, flipped her blonde hair, and fixed her blue eyes on him.

Part of her regretted what would have to be done. He was a fine looking man. *Maybe I should bed him before putting him down.*

He spoke first. "Nice car."

She turned back as if the existence of her one hundred thousand dollar sports car surprised her. "Oh, thanks."

"Can I help you?"

"I know this is hard to believe, but I left my phone at home and my GPS isn't working. I think I'm a little lost. I just pulled in here hoping someone would be home and fortunately, you drove up."

He reached into his pocket, pulling out a cell phone. "Where are you going? I'm sure I can find it on my phone."

"Oh, would you? That'd be great. I'm trying to find the Pflugerville Herb Farm."

He tapped on his phone, looking up when he finished. "You'll have to take some back roads, so it's a little convoluted. Why don't I get a piece of paper? I can write it down for you.

He took several steps up through the Airstream door, Bobbi tagging closely behind. She stood in the doorway, her eyes following him as he searched for a pencil in the kitchen. Finally, he turned to her.

"Oh, well, yeah, come in. You thirsty?"

"I'd love a beer, but only if you'll have one."

"I think you talked me into it." He opened the refrigerator door, bending over to pull out two bottles. Bobbi examined his ass, imagining how firm and muscular he was under those jeans. He opened each brown bottle, handing her one. They tapped beers in a silent toast. Nick, his attention on his work, scrawled out directions to the herb farm, while Bobbi dropped some G into her beer. He put his bottle down on his right, so she stepped around him, leaning in to give him a good whiff of her scent, her left breast warm against his back, but also to peer over his arm while setting her bottle next to his. He paused, looking up, then re-focused on his work. She then reached over, picking up his bottle.

He straightened up, handing her the sheet of paper. "Here you go. Hopefully this will get you there."

A creaking from the door opening caught Bobbi's attention. A Latina about her age stepped in, stopping at the threshold. Nick spoke to her with a familiarity that said girlfriend. *Damn. How can I screw and skewer him now?*

"Hi, Theresa. I was just helping..." He turned to Bobbi. "I don't think I caught your name."

"Cindy."

The woman named Theresa stood, arms crossed, unimpressed. Bobbi needed to leave before things got too weird. Maybe blowing him up would be easier after all.

"You know, I should be going. Thanks for the directions. A real life saver."

"You're welcome."

She stepped past Nick, then paused as Theresa moved aside for her to pass. Bobbi heard the door shut behind her as she walked to her car. *Damn it.* She'd have to tie up loose ends with Andy, then come up with a better plan for Nick. Something with explosives. As long as he was dead and out of her way. The sooner, the better.

78

R. W. Hacker

Andy's Folly

After the airfield fiasco, Andy hid away at home, frantic for a way out of the inevitable confrontation with Bobbi. He couldn't believe he hadn't hit either of his targets. Bobbi would be pissed. He considered coming clean with her, but the new Bobbi scared him more than he'd admit in public. *What am I going to do?* He smoked a joint, then went into his bathroom, splashing cold water on his face. He lifted his eyes to the man staring at him with a sly smile in the mirror. *Of course.* He dashed out of his house, the Caravan failing to lay a trail of black rubber on his concrete driveway when he stamped on the accelerator.

Andy skidded to a stop in the school parking lot, jumping out of his van, running full speed to the band hall. It had come to him in his bathroom. His best route to survival lay in getting the hell out of there and disappearing again. He glanced around an empty band hall, then unlocked his office door. He had money and passports hidden in his office ceiling for just this sort of situation. *Thank God I know what the hell I'm doing.*

Andy closed the door, then twisted the lock, checking the knob to be certain. He turned, taking in Bobbi Shank in a short black dress sitting at his desk, her six inch spike heels on the desktop. Andy, to his shame, jumped, letting out a small, high-pitched cry.

"You squeal like a little girl, Charles."

He looked back to the door. "Please don't call me that around here. Jesus, Bobbi. You scared the hell out of me."

"Good. So, tell me, Charles, where did you bury Dillon?"

79

He stood frozen, his mind racing to find some way to get himself out of the trap he found himself squirming in. "What can I do you for, Bobbi?" He swallowed, his heart pounding.

She cocked her head, glaring silently at him, then spoke. "You didn't kill him, did you? Had a clear shot from a tree line across the field and you couldn't hit him for shit."

"You...you followed me?"

"What confused me is I thought I told you to hire someone who knew what the hell he was doing. Instead, I get a sad, creepy, child-molesting, serial killer wanna be. How did you manage to kill two people? Did you wait for them to commit suicide and then bury the bodies?"

How did she know about them? One was an accident involving a drunken Fourth of July party. The other could be called sort of a suicide. His neighbor, Alfonse, kind of fell off an apartment balcony when Charles punched him in the face. Is that murder or suicide? Besides, he wasn't a serial killer when Alfonse died. At least he didn't think he was.

"Charles." She'd gotten up, stepping around the desk while he was lost in thought.

"What?"

"You're done, Charles. Finished."

Something deep inside told him now was the time to bluff his way out of this predicament. "You know what I think? I think you don't know who you're talking to. I've been keeping you around for the sex, but you're wearing thin, Bobbi. You need to back off. I'm warning you."

She stood before him, hands behind her back, he hoped intimidated by his display of manly aggression. In his peripheral vision he noted something shaped like a brick accelerating toward his head. Pain erupted inside him, then nothing.

When he came to, he sat naked in the middle of his band hall on a cold metal folding chair. His arms, bound behind the seat back, ached. He flexed his legs, but hard metal dug into his ankles, which were taped fast to the chair's front legs. He labored to breathe, his blurred vision filled with shining brass. As his mind cleared, he realized he had a mouthpiece, as well as an entire attached tuba, duct taped to his flesh and the chair. He made out three music stands duct taped to the entire assembly, serving as a tripod for stability. Terror inched up his spine, but he forced it back down. *Nobody fucks with Charles Dudley.* He chuckled, as best he could with a tuba in his mouth. So this was her plan. As punishment, he'd be discovered by his students in all of his naked shame with a tuba taped to his mouth. *Like I care. Definitely better than the whole bent-over-a-fence-railing thing.* Bobbi could be intimidating, but she clearly didn't understand his unique and complex personality. Hell, he'd get one of his female students to make visits to his office each week to help him recover from this trauma.

He was fantasizing about Melinda, or maybe Donna, both quite mature for their ages, when a metallic clang interrupted his thoughts. He could see Bobbi's feet and what looked like a garden hose. What was she up to? Whipping with a hose? He'd gotten, and given, much worse. Footsteps moved away from him, a door opened, air and a little water puffed into his mouth. A bit startling, but manageable. The footsteps returned.

"So, Charlie. You're probably wondering why you've got a tuba taped to your mouth with a garden hose shoved inside."

Water gushed into his mouth. He choked, then fought to close off his throat from the sudden onslaught.

"You see, Charles, you've fucked me over one too many times. I don't like to be fucked over. And I especially don't like loose ends."

Frantic, he fought his bindings, holding his breath, his heart about to explode.

"I never considered you as the type to have an oversized instrument, Charlie. I know. A bit unexpected. I imagine you thought you'd be bent over a fence again. But I've got to say, Charles, the tuba really suits you."

81

Buzzard Bait

Her footsteps faded out the door as he squirmed in his chair. Unable to resist any longer, he gasped, water forcing its way down into his lungs and stomach. He lurched against his bindings, choking, frantic, water gushing over the tuba's lip, flooding the floor around him. With a final twitch, life slipped from his grasp.

R. W. Hacker

Tu Ba or Not Tu Ba

After the lost woman left, Nick and Theresa stood facing each other in the trailer. She wore lycra capris and a running shirt, her face flushed from a workout. God, she was beautiful. Of course he loved her. How could any guy not?

Theresa pulled off her running shoes and socks, dropping them by the door. "She was pretty."

"Not interested. Just gave her some directions to the herb farm."

She stepped over, picking up a nearly full beer on the counter, then took long swallows, emptying half the bottle. She liked a beer after a run. "Nick, we need to talk."

"She just wanted some directions."

Theresa took another swig from the beer, apparently not concerned at all Nick had a strange woman in the trailer. "Not about her. I want to talk about us."

Nick didn't want to go toward a conversation he dreaded. "We are talking."

"You know what I mean. About us."

He sighed, a little louder than he had intended.

"Nick, do you love me?"

Why did women always want to know if you loved them? You start talking about love and sooner or later, someone gets their feelings hurt and the whole thing turns to crap. "Of course I do."

She shook her head. "I want to believe you, Nick. I really do. But my intuition tells me you're confusing guilt with love."

"Come on, Theresa. Really? We're not going to plow this field again, are we? I feel bad about what happened with

83

Zydeco, but he has nothing to do with how I feel about you."

"So how do you feel about me?"

"I feel like we have a really good thing going here."

"A good thing, huh?"

"Yeah, a good thing. We like all the same things, we laugh and play together, we make love, really wonderful love."

"But what about your heart, Nick. In your heart, why are we together?"

"Are you breaking up with me? Is that what this is about? You finding a way to leave me?"

"Don't turn this around on me, Nick Sibelius. You know very well what I'm talking about. If we're going to do this relationship, then we're going to do it with our eyes open. So, other than the great sex, why are we together?"

Nick's insides went taut. How can a guy trade gunfire with mean-ass criminals, but be paralyzed by a woman wanting to know the truth about their relationship? He felt like a naked man walking through a mine field. He stepped up to her, slipping a hand behind her neck. She smelled of sweat, the nape of her neck damp. They looked into each other's eyes, then he felt Theresa pulling away. He couldn't let her slowly leave him. He wrapped his other arm around her, drawing her in. Her resistance melted away as they fell into each other's deep kiss.

Moving toward the bedroom, he took off her top and sports bra, kissing her neck, shoulder, then each breast as he stroked a finger down her spine. Laying her down on the bed he continued kissing her breasts and stomach, wrapping fingers into the top of her capris, bringing them past her hips, her knees, then completely off. She yielded before him, her legs parted, her eyes closed. They made love. Well, he made love. Motionless, she moaned softly. When he came inside her, all of the tension he felt between them melted away. He wasn't sure if he liked her so passive, but at least he knew they were still together. Maybe she understood him. Finally. He rolled over to let the air conditioning cool them both, Theresa resting her head on Nick's chest.

"I'm sorry, Theresa. I'm sorry for pushing you away." He ran his fingers through her hair. "You see, I'm afraid of losing you. I lost my wife, my partner, then I almost lost you. I know it's not rational that I blame myself for what Izzy did to you, but I guess I'm so scared of losing what I love, I think I have to always be there to protect you. It's not a bad thing, unless I get so overprotective you don't want to be around me. So I'm changing my ways today. Okay? Like you said, you're an adult who can take care of herself. So that's what I'm going to do. I'm going to back off and let you take care of yourself."

He heard her breathing, but nothing else. Had he let things go too long?

"I love you, Theresa. I do love you."

Her breathy voice confirmed what Nick needed to know. "You too."

Relief hit him. They were once again on the same page, loving each other. Nick pulled her close, wanting to be entwined with her soft warmth all night long.

~ * ~

His cell phone woke them up. Asleep at the Wheel belted out *Miles and Miles of Texas* in his pants, which were out of reach. He'd have to get up. Light filtering into the trailer told him it had to be morning.

"Don't go, Nick."

"I think it's Quen, probably about Dillon. I'll just be a minute." He stumbled off the bed, digging through his jeans pocket for the phone.

Theresa walked stiff legged and naked to the bathroom. "I'll make us some coffee in a sec."

Pulling out his phone, he hit the accept button. "Quen, what's up?"

"Did I wake you? It's eight in the morning. Man, the life of a civilian."

"Yeah, well, I had a pretty good night." He found his underwear, pulling them up while cradling the phone in his shoulder.

"You and Theresa make up? Awesome. Nothing better than make-up sex."

"Yeah. Uh, shut up, Quen. Why are you calling anyway?"

"Remember our band director from Harry's gun bag?"

He slipped on his jeans then looked for his shirt. "Yeah, I went by to talk to him. He's not a very good liar. Wanted me to think he was a dead end."

"More than you might think."

Slipping a shirt on, he sat down to pull on some socks and boots. "What do you mean?"

"He was found dead in the high school band hall."

"Heart attack?"

"Tuba."

Nick ended his call just as Theresa came out of the bathroom.

"You leaving? I feel like I haven't even seen you."

Nick smiled. She stood before him in all her beautiful naked glory. He loved her today and he wanted to be around to see her naked fifty years from now. "Haven't seen me, eh? You should open your eyes more when we make love."

"I'll open them if we'll make love sometime soon. It's been a week."

Nick laughed. "Right. Good one. Look, I've got to go, but I'll be back." He kissed her, letting his hands slip across her breasts.

She put a hand on his chest, sadness crossing her face. "When you get back, we do need to talk, Nick. It's important."

What was she talking about? They had talked. He bared his soul to her. "We did talk. Last night. Remember?"

"I remember you helped someone find the herb farm and then I guess I must have showered and passed out."

Nick couldn't believe what he heard. "You're kidding. Right?"

She reached for her robe from a hook on the door, wrapping it around her. "Kidding about what? Nick, I've been trying to get you to talk about us for days."

"No, we talked last night."

Her brow furrowed in confusion. "Well, you may have talked in your dreams, but in the real world we like to have actual conversations between two people." Anger rose up in her voice. "Talked. Do you take me for some kind of idiot? Look, I'm trying to save what we have, but if you're not interested just say so. Don't start making up crazy shit."

Nick didn't know what was happening. How could this morning be as if last night hadn't happened? He raised his hands in surrender to the moment. "We'll talk. I need to get over to a crime scene, but this evening, we'll talk. I promise."

Tears rolled down her cheeks, her arms crossed, shaking her head. "Just go, Nick. Go."

~ * ~

Driving to the high school, Nick distracted himself from the weird conversation he just had with Theresa by reviewing his meeting with Dillon. The experience of having someone take shots at him had loosened Dillon's tongue a bit. Nick had a new suspect. A woman named Bobbi. She sounded a bit like his Homeland Security operative and past lover, MaryLou. The significant difference, and one currently playing in Dillon's favor, was if MaryLou wanted you dead, you were dead. So, Bobbi either kept hiring the wrong people to do her dirty work or she was just a government wonk with some files on her phone, a secret S & M sex life, and an inability to hit the side of a barn with a shotgun.

Arriving at the high school, Nick drove back to the band hall entrance. Several police cars, as well as an ambulance, their lights flashing, parked helter-skelter across the parking lot. Quentin stood by his patrol car, radio mic in hand. Seeing Nick walk up, he raised a hand motioning him closer, then finished his call, dropping his mic on the front seat.

Buzzard Bait

"You're going to want to see this."

Nick had seen plenty of dead people, most of them murdered, so no, he didn't need to see this. "Why do you think I need to see a dead guy?"

"It's the way he was killed. Trust me, you've never seen this one before."

Quentin handed Nick a pair of black and yellow fireman boots with the Pflugerville Fire Department stenciled in white across one side.

"What are these for?"

"I'm guessing you don't want to ruin your Luccheses standing in a pool of water."

Nick couldn't imagine what Quentin was going on about, but he also didn't want to mess up his boots, so he took the offering.

Clad in their rubber boots, they walked into the band hall, which looked like all of the few band halls Nick had been in since junior high. Trophies stood in a glass case, and chairs, each with a black music stand, formed a semicircle around a raised podium. Posters with slogans about teamwork and sacrifice covered the walls. Yes, Andy Sullivan's band hall looked like every other band hall, with one exception. In this hall, Andy Sullivan's bloated naked body sat limp in a folding chair, a gleaming brass tuba and three music stands attached with multiple wraps of duct tape to his head and torso. His hands were bound behind the chair and his feet duct-taped to its legs. The tuba had a garden hose running out of the bell, across the room and out the door, where it attached to an outdoor faucet. They stood in several inches of water covering the entire floor. Andy Sullivan had been drowned by tuba.

"Christ."

"Yeah, I told you. Crazy."

Nick walked around the dead body-slash-large musical instrument drowning mechanism. "Somebody went to a lot of trouble."

"Think he pissed off some kid in the tuba section? They're always a little weird, you know."

Nick frowned. "I played tuba."

"Really? I knew you were a little off, but I didn't know you were a musician."

Nick leaned over, examining the killer's handiwork. "Didn't say I was, just that I played tuba. And we're not all weird."

Quentin chuckled, shaking his head. "Okay, whatever you say."

"I think someone is either sending a message, was extremely pissed, or both."

"You think this has something to do with Dillon and the guy at the lake?"

Nick followed the garden hose from the floor up into the tuba's bell. "Well, I did just talk to him. Maybe I struck a nerve, he panicked and talked. Instead of helping him, they just put him down."

"Putting down is a bullet in the brain, strangling, maybe drowning in a toilet. This however, feels like it's on another level altogether. We might have another Musi-Killogist murder."

"The string of band director murders? Yeah, could be. He does fit the victim profile, I suppose."

Quentin must have heard the doubt in his tone. "Okay, Sherlock. What do you think's going on?"

Nick stepped back, arms crossed, taking in the entire scene. "Someone took some shots at Dillon yesterday."

"Is he okay?"

"Oh, he's fine. Fortunately, our shooter couldn't hit the side of an aircraft carrier. But given our boy here has a link to the first hit man, I wonder if he had a connection with the second?"

"Think Andy served as a middleman and someone didn't take kindly to failure? So he gives our boy here a tuba lesson to make it look like the work of the Musi-Killogist."

"Could be. Whoever it is, he has serious anger issues."

Buzzard Bait

"What makes you think it's a man?"

"I don't know. A tuba strikes me as a man's kind of instrument. And there's lots of lifting involved in getting him attached to it."

"So if it was a woman, she'd use a flute?" Quentin had a smirk on his face, enjoying the moment.

"Very funny. Look, I'm just guessing. Okay? Jesus."

"Sensitive."

"Yes, I'm sensitive. Theresa's been on my case all week. Something about how I'm smothering her with protection. How do you smother someone with protection? I just want her to be safe. Is there anything wrong with wanting her to be safe?"

Quentin raised his hands in mock surrender. "Hey, Nick. Slow down, man. I'm on your side."

Nick waded across the band hall, studying a cheesy motivational poster declaring, 'There is no I in TEAM'. "I know. Sorry. You know she's pissed at me for saving her at the lake?"

"Really? Sure she's not pissed about something else?"

"What, you a shrink now?" He stepped into Andy's office, scanning his desk top. Someone, maybe Andy, maybe the killer, had wiped it down. He guessed forensics wouldn't find any prints other than that of Andy and his students.

"Just saying, most people prefer not drowning. So it's just possible she's pissed off about something else."

Nick stepped out of the office. "So I'm supposed to read her mind?"

"Talk to her."

Nick turned to Quentin. "You too? She put you up to this, didn't she?"

Quentin took a step back. "Ease off there, friend. She hasn't put me up to anything. In fact, you're the one who raised the issue. I'm your friend, remember. The guy who has your back?"

90

"Yeah, I know. Sorry." Nick scanned the band hall, wading over to the awards case. "I may have a lead for you."

"Great, what is it?"

"I need to check it out first. Could be nothing. But if it does come up hot, you'll be the first to know."

He had started with a bullet hole in a bass boat. Then someone tried to use him for target practice. Now he had a dead band director attached to a tuba. Sploshing out of the band hall, back into a bright Texas day, Nick recognized the familiar sinking feeling of a simple open and shut case turning into a shit fest right before his eyes.

~ * ~

Nick figured he should track down this Bobbi, the star of Dillon's woeful love story. She was either a crazy biker chick with a jealous lover, a government employee with a sex addiction, or some kind of whack-job militia leader. Again? How did these people keep stepping into his life?

Nick had a buddy from the Houston Police Department days, who he figured might have a line on Bobbi. An ex-cop, who owned a range just outside of Pflugerville called On Target. She taught shooting primarily to women and attended most of the gun shows across the state. As he pulled into a gravel lot, percussive bangs rang out from the other side of a long shed. He found ten women in pink camouflage taking turns firing at paper and steel targets. A perky redhead with sound-deadening headphones stood behind the current shooter, coaching her along. He could hear her familiar voice over a .38 revolver firing repeatedly at targets.

She caught sight of him. "Let's take five. Check your breach and guns down." A broad smile broke across her face. "Nicky. How the hell are you?"

They hugged. He noticed the firm bump of her abdomen. "Good. Well, okay. How about you?" He looked down to her waistline. "Anything I should know about, Chris?"

She put a hand to her stomach. "Oh, this? Yeah, Robert knocked me up. The sonofabitch." She laughed, her eyes alive. She and Robert got married five years ago and Nick knew she had wanted to start a family.

"When?"

"Four more months. But I'm feeling good."

"You look happy."

"Thanks. From what I've seen on the news you've been a busy boy yourself."

"Yeah, I set up a little investigation business. I keep getting these high-profile cases. Frankly, I wouldn't mind a little less excitement."

She slapped his arm. "You don't fool me, Nick Sibelius. You always seem to be in the middle of things. I think it's just the nature of your universe. Speaking of which, what brings you to my little piece of the world? Need some coaching to get your shooting back up to par?"

"I'll have you know, my shooting's just fine." He looked over her shoulder at the group of women standing around talking. "Looks like your business has taken off."

"Thanks. But I know you're not here to join my women's concealed weapon class. What's up?"

"Yeah, you're right. I'm looking for someone. I've got a first name, Bobbi. She's a woman, about five foot seven, dirty blonde, blue eyes, rides a Harley, wears black leathers. I understand she's a bit of a looker. I know you attend lots of gun shows, so I thought I'd take a shot and see if you've ever run across her."

She put a hand on his chest, moving him away from her class. "Damn. When you said you were looking for someone, I was about to say there's no way. Thousands of people go to those shows."

"But?"

She looked to the ground, shifting nervously. "I might be able to help you. Only you've got to promise what I'm about to tell you will never be shared with another living soul, especially Robert."

92

"Jesus, Chris. Lighten up."

"I mean it, dammit. You've got to promise."

"Okay, okay. I promise."

"You promise?"

"Yes, I promise."

"Because you know who always beat you on the range, right?"

"Yeah, you did. I don't—"

"So if I ever hear you breathed a word of this, I swear to God, I'll—"

"Chris. I'm your friend. If I promise you something, you can bank on it. I think you know that."

She looked around, as if he had a colleague hidden in the brush. "Yeah. I'm sorry. It's just, well, if Rob found out, it would break his heart. And I'm not going to let his heart be broken."

"I take it you know Bobbi?"

"I met her at a show a few months ago. Before I knew I was pregnant."

"Tell me about her."

"She's a tequila drinking chick who if you ever get a chance to bed, you should."

"Why's that?"

"Because, whatever bar you have for good sex, she'll blow it completely away."

"Sounds like, well—"

"The voice of experience? Yeah. But she's also crazy in the head, so I wouldn't want her, even as a friend. But oh my God, the woman knows her way around the human body."

"I didn't know you were—"

"I'm not. We were having some drinks, one thing led to another. Next thing I know I'm having an out of body experience. The woman's insatiable. Kind of like sitting in a Formula One race car. You're grateful for the ride, but it scares the holy shit out of you and you'd never be able to use it for your daily commute."

"Did she talk to you about radio controlled planes when you two were, you know, together?"

Chris chuckled, then broke into a laugh consuming her whole body. She had to hold onto Nick to keep from falling to the ground. "God, I almost peed myself." She shook her head.

"What's so funny?"

"Model planes, Nick. Trust me. Neither one of us was thinking about model airplanes. Is that what boys think about?"

"Got a last name?"

"She went into the bathroom to freshen up and I guess once a cop always a cop."

Nick smiled. "You went through her purse."

"Damn straight. But she was clean. No drugs, no gun, valid driver's license. Her name is Bobbi Shank. Don't recall the address, but she does live in Austin."

"Bobbi Shank. Thanks, Chris."

She let out a sigh. "I'm a bad person. How could I cheat on Rob? He's always been good to me. You probably think I don't love him."

"I know you love him, Chris. Don't talk crazy. It's one night in the past. You two have made a baby and the best years lie ahead of you. Besides, I hear Bobbi Shank is like crack to an addict. Very hard to resist."

"But I should have resisted. You would have, wouldn't you?"

There was a time when he would have answered her question with confidence. But lately he felt unhinged. He couldn't even decide if he really loved Theresa or if his affections reflected his need to protect her. "I don't know. Look, it's in the past. You and Rob have a great marriage and you're both going to be great parents. I'd focus on the good stuff."

"Yeah, you're right." She put a hand on his arm. "Remember, you promised."

He kissed her on the cheek. "Yes, I did. And I'm a man of my word. Take care of that baby."

"I will, Nick. And you be careful around Bobbi. I have a feeling she's got some scary demons going on."

Tex

Tex Sawyer had a love-hate relationship with all things aviation. As a boy, he'd watch airliners trace blue skies with contrails, imagining he held the yoke of a large multi-engine behemoth in his hands, hundreds of lives depending on his ability and skill. After school, he'd often go to the local airport, watching student pilots circle the field, then land, some letting their tires gracefully touch tarmac, while others bounced in, like big ungainly birds. His daddy, a plumber by profession and an alcoholic by training, spent most of the family's income on liquor and smokes, so flight lessons were a distant dream. At sixteen, Tex, sick of waiting, stole a bottle of vodka, drinking to build up his courage. During most of his swerving path to the airport, he wondered how he'd get through the gate to the airplanes beyond. Fortunately, not seeing the gate in time, he crashed right through with his truck. Problem solved.

Having already staked out the flight school, he smashed a window, doing a quick grab of keys on a board behind the owner's desk. He walked out to the airplanes, tied down as if they could take off on their own accord. Tex found his plane. A Piper Tomahawk, one of six in a line. He had stolen a pilot handbook for the plane a month before, just because he wanted to know how to fly. Now he stood in the dark, a Tomahawk before him, keys in hand and the certain knowledge the handbook gave him. After some initial confusion, he put the pieces together. Choke out, a little throttle, turn ignition. The plane roared to life. He let his toes off the brakes, increasing the engine's rpm, but nothing happened. *Crap. Forgot to untie the lines.* He idled back the engine, untying the left wing, then the right and finally the tail. The plane began moving away from him. He ran, his feet slipping on wet grass, then falling flat on his face. He saw his beloved Tomahawk pulling away from him. Getting back to his feet, he ran alongside the plane as it crossed a grass strip, then the asphalt of a taxiway. It bounced up onto a wide grass skirt lined with other planes. He hurled himself across the left wing, dragging his feet up until he sat on it. Then with some effort he opened the door, dropping into the small plane's cockpit. A rush of relief swept over him.

The sound of a propeller slicing through the side of another aircraft's fuselage, leaving gaping slices in aluminum, is a loud and horrifying thing. Tex knew this firsthand. The roar of his engine and the scream of tearing metal still haunted him. The drunken destruction of several parked aircraft with a stolen plane does not put a young man in a very good position to ever get a pilot's certificate from the FAA.

After completing his time in juvie and unable to ever fly, he looked for alternatives. In his early twenties, he tried the Civil Air Patrol, learning search and rescue lingo, finally riding shotgun in a Cessna 172 on a training mission. For some reason the pilot got all bent out of shape when Tex tried to commandeer the plane, resulting in a busted landing gear and the Civil Air Patrol banning him for life from their ranks.

Then in his thirties he thought he found a home in the AMA. The Academy of Model Aeronautics took him in, along with his money for annual dues, as a legitimate pilot. He didn't get to be inside the aircraft in flight, but at least he could pilot something flying in the sky. He started with a basic model, but quickly advanced to faster and more agile aircraft. Then one day a guy cut him off with his stupid little toy plane, so Tex showed him what a real pilot could do. His opponent lost two fingers and his plane when Tex slammed his bird into the fool. He might have retained his membership in the club if he had at least come to the man's

97

aid. Instead, he strode across the field to find and then stomp the fellow's already broken plane into a hundred little bits, while his victim lay bleeding and screaming on the ground.

With the FAA, the CAP and the AMA all against him, Tex decided he needed a new model for life, turning to the greatest military men of history—John Wayne, Sylvester Stallone, and Tom Cruise. He studied their films, a monk in the monastery of malevolence. The message of his idols was clear. He needed to arm himself. And so he went on a buying spree of weaponry. Pretty much anything with a clip holding more than ten cartridges or having the word automatic somewhere in the description. But no matter how many cans, bottles, varmints, or traffic signs he shot up, he couldn't forget his love for flying.

With renewed fervor, he threw himself into aviation, determining to combine his two favorite things, guns and planes, into an awesome and really cool killer radio controlled airplane. Something neither the FAA nor the AMA would ever sanction. By the time Bruce Reynolds contacted him, Tex had several prototypes capable of delivering a payload to, or firing on, a target.

He fondly remembered the warm autumn day Reynolds drove up to his house in a black BMW while Tex labored in his garage.

"Mister Sawyer? Tex Sawyer?"

"Who's asking?" He touched a Smith & Wesson 9mm Shield in its concealed holster at his side.

A fancy GQ looking man in a tailored suit and Italian loafers stepped into his garage. "Bruce Reynolds. Eddie Lavine sent me."

Tex looked up from his work, careful to keep his strong hand free in case he needed to go for the gun. Eddie, a buddy from juvie days, supplied stuff you couldn't pick up at a Walmart, like explosive materials light enough to fly in a drone.

"Yeah, Eddie's an old friend of mine." He seemed legit. Tex placed a .177 barrel, for a miniature machine gun of his own design, on his workbench. "How can I help you?"

"Maybe the better question, Tex, is how can I help you?"

"You foxtrottin' me?" Tex had noticed his trinity of military virtue didn't use many dirty words, so he made a concerted effort to eliminate such language from his vocabulary. However, finding it almost impossible to speak without cursing, he instituted what he figured was a good compromise and which gave a nod of the head to his love for all things military and aviation.

Reynolds looked confused. "Dancing with you?"

"Fucking with me. Ah, golf delta." He'd have to add ten push-ups to his nightly routine for that fuck up. "Foxtrotting."

"Oh, foxtrotting. No, I'm not foxtrotting with you."

Tex wiped his hands on a cloth. "So how can you help me?"

Reynolds stepped further into the garage, scanning Tex's workbench. A small, partially constructed helicopter sat on a stand in a corner. A larger fixed wing aircraft hung from lines attached to the rafters. He picked up the barrel.

"You mind? I spent a lot of time machining that part to perfection."

Reynolds hefted the barrel in his hand. "Pretty heavy. Sure this will work on one of your birds?"

Tex did not like strangers handling his private parts or questioning his engineering. Made him nervous. "Weight's a bit of a liability, but I'll manage."

"What if you make it out of titanium? Much better strength to weight ratio."

"Do I look like a JAFO to you? Titanium is delta expensive, not to mention the tooling required."

"Jaffo?"

Definitely, a civilian. "Juliet, Alpha, Foxtrot, Oscar. Just Another Fuckin' Observer." *Goddamit. Ten more push-ups.*

99

Reynolds, to Tex's relief, put the barrel down. "Ah, see, that's what I'm talking about. What if I could obtain as much titanium as you need? Actually, what if I fund your entire operation?"

Tex felt around for a stool, needing to sit down from the sudden rush of potential wealth. "Is this some kinda joke? You foxtrottin' me?"

"Again with the dancing. No. This is not a joke, nor am I asking you to dance. I'm telling you I will fund your entire operation."

"Why? What do you get outta this?"

"I get the fruits of your labor. I'm very interested in your work. You're a Mozart, a da Vinci of your time, misunderstood by those bastards in the FAA."

"Don't forget the CAP and the AMA."

"American Medical Association?"

"Academy of Model Aeronautics."

"Oh, yes. Those bastards in the AMA."

"And none of this is illegal, right? I've got enough grief from the Man, without raining down more sierra on me."

"Sierra? Oh, you mean shit. Yes, of course. No, everything you do will be sanctioned by the Republic."

His heart sank. He could use the money, but not if he was arming some drug running banana zone cartel. "Republic? What Republic?"

Reynolds smiled, putting a hand on Tex's shoulder. "Just my word for our sovereign land of Texas. But I imagine a man named Tex has an abiding love for Texas, just like me."

"I suppose I do." He took a deep breath, the excitement returning. This guy didn't look like a government type, but the old adage about not looking a gift horse in the mouth came to mind. A smile crossed his lips. Arming the state with my drones will show those Texas National Guard pussies a thing or two. "So when do we start?"

"Send me a list of materials and equipment you need and I'll put you in business right away. We'll put a hangar next door, get you out of this garage."

"That'd be great."

"Do you have any commercial clients?"

"Excuse me?"

"Commercial clients. Do you sell your planes to anyone?"

"Not to date."

"Let's start selling them. I'll have my marketing person get with you to develop a business plan and get a salesperson started. You need to have a thriving business in addition to what you're doing for me. It's a good cover." He turned to leave.

"Wait a second. Why are you doing this?"

Reynolds paused, his back turned. "We're going to do great things together, Tex. And when we're done, you'll have your own FAA and CAP."

"And AMA?"

"Of course. You'll be telling them to jump and how far. Sound good?"

"Yeah. Sounds pretty damned good."

"Delta, Tex. Sounds delta good. Right?"

"Ah, sierra." Tex shook his head in disgust at himself. "Yeah, sorry."

After Reynolds left, Tex sat on a stool in his garage, surrounded by his planes and tools and parts. Careful to have his back turned to Tom Cruise giving him the thumbs up as top gun pilot, Maverick, he let tears roll down his cheeks. After all his struggles, his dreams were coming to fruition. He'd go to the honky-tonk down the road tonight, kick up some dust, maybe get lucky. Tex wiped away the tears, knocking his stool over on the way out, a renewed swagger to his step.

Colt Texas Paterson

Nick now had a name and a city. If he could find Bobbi Shank, maybe he'd be able to get to the bottom of this mystery. He turned down a black ribbon of county road to his trailer as the sun set behind him. They never discussed it, but he imagined Theresa followed Izzy's story in the news, haunted by a fear he could return in all his crazy violent glory. If Izzy Zydeco went free, Nick vowed to do whatever it took to keep Theresa safe, no matter the cost. Fool me once, shame on you. Fool me twice...

Stepping into the silver trailer he caught sight of Theresa sitting at the fold down table, nursing a whiskey. Her long, straight black hair flowed down bare shoulders covered only with the spaghetti straps of her blouse. She gave him a sad smile, her eyes determined. Nick knew, before he said a word, this was not going to be a relaxing evening.

"How you doing, Theresa? Good day?"

She took a sip of whiskey, then set down her glass. "You mean did I have a great time hanging around the edges of our business because you're keeping case information from me?"

She had been going on about how he kept cutting her out of investigations for the last month. He couldn't get her to understand he was trying to protect her. "Maybe working with me isn't what you need right now, Theresa. Why don't you look for a job in town? Didn't you get your undergraduate degree in English? Maybe you could be a teacher."

"A teacher. Nick, I got my masters in criminology and trained to be a cop. I need to be working. My kind of work."

"We've talked about this. I know you want to get back out there, but I just don't think you're ready."

"Because you've lost a partner and you know how hard it is to come back."

"Yeah. I do."

"Have you considered maybe I'm not you, Nick? Playing your administrative assistant instead of doing investigative work isn't making things better. It's making it worse."

How did they end up in a fight this quickly? Did last night not count for anything? Trailer walls closed in around them.

"Look, Theresa, I only want what's best for you. And like I said last night—"

"Best for me?" She stepped around the table to stand in front of Nick. "I think you tell yourself you want what's best for me, but it's not what this is about."

"What are you talking about?"

"Nick, it's not your job to protect me. I can take care of myself."

"Really? How did that work out for you with Izzy?"

She took a step back, as if Nick had slapped her in the face. "Yes. Fine. You saved my ass with Izzy." Her tone turned facetious. "God, I'm so grateful to you for saving me when I was so helpless." She moved into him, angrily undoing his belt.

"What the hell are you doing?"

"I'm just so grateful to you, Nick. Let me show you. Please. I'm so helpless I need to show you how grateful I am."

She had his belt unbuckled and the top button of his jeans undone when he grabbed her hands. "Theresa, stop."

"Isn't this what you want? You can't love me and have me as a business partner, right? You want me all helpless and willing?"

He pushed her away, his hands shaking as he buttoned his jeans. "Jesus, what's wrong with you? Last night—"

"What was I thinking? I knew having a relationship with my business partner was a mistake. Hell, you don't really love me, do you, Nick? You care about me. You feel responsible. But you don't love me."

"But I do. And we are business partners. I told you last night."

Theresa screamed, throwing the remains of her whiskey past Nick, the glass shattering on the wall behind him. "Then let me live my goddamn life! And yeah, somebody might shoot me in the head or stab me in the heart, but it's my life to lose. Not yours. Mine."

"I just don't want you to get hurt."

"Guess what? I've been hurt and I'll be hurt again."

They stood, separated by history, in silence. Theresa raised her hands in surrender. "I didn't want to explode like that, it's just...I can't do this anymore. I know you care, but I can't have you hovering over me like I'm some frail little bird. It was a mistake moving in with you."

"Theresa."

"I need to go." She picked up a bag Nick hadn't noticed. Theresa had planned to leave all along. "I'm staying with a girlfriend."

She brushed past him then out the door. How did this happen? He had made things right last night, but it was as if she wanted them to implode. He thought of chasing after her, but somewhere deep inside, he realized she spoke the truth. His need to protect her had destroyed his chance of being her lover. He let her walk out the door.

~ * ~

Nick woke up the next morning with a Johnny Walker headache and the cramped heart rising to an empty bedroom gives a man. He forced down some granola, several aspirin, and a coffee chaser, then got in his pickup to get to the office. Even though his personal life continued to crumble around him, he at least had a case in front of him.

R. W. Hacker

The offices of Sibelius Investigations had been moved when the U.S. Government had taken possession of the land under his beat-up, rented office space. A significant amount of toxic chemicals had been dumped in the ground over the years, so a clean-up had been court ordered. He bid adieu to his drug dealing plumber neighbor and moved to a more upscale office in a strip center on Burnet Road. Weighing upsides and downsides, the lack of toxic waste and drug dealers was clearly offset by his proximity to a muffler shop, a car wash, two Chinese restaurants, a Mexican joint, a dollar store, and a convenience store. Plus, he had a parking lot instead of two parking spaces by the front door.

He opened the glass door to a reception area. Banging drew him to the storage-slash-break room. A woman over six feet tall with short, cropped brown hair, in black slacks and a white blouse, banged on a stainless-steel coffee machine.

"Come on. Work."

Nick could not help but smile. His transgendered office manager could never have a meaningful relationship with a coffee pot. It would be all hugs and kisses out of the box, but as soon as she plugged it in, everything would turn to shit—or at least it always tasted like it did.

"I didn't expect you back until next month. How was the Caribbean, Alice?" When Alice started with Nick she had been Al, a large, muscular Iraq vet. But in the last two years she had transformed into Alice, the woman Al always knew lived within her. A year ago, swept off her feet by an attorney, John Mathers of Smiley, Mathers and Pritchard, she went to the islands. He had several postcards of their adventures, the last one stating she would be coming back to work.

"Yes, I decided I needed get back here before you ran the business completely into the ground."

She was joking, sort of. While he limped along in her absence, he knew without her to handle the details of

105

running a business, Sibelius Investigations would slowly succumb to atrophy and die.

"Well, I am glad to see you, Alice." She threw her arms around him. Nick intellectually had made peace with Al becoming Alice, but for some reason, whenever she wanted to hug he found himself on uncertain ground and not too proud of feeling that way. She pulled away, giving him a kiss on the cheek.

"I could still be down in the Islands with Johnny, you know. I thought about it. But he spends so much time working. I don't know. I've sacrificed everything to be who I am. Should I settle for the first guy whose eye I turn, even if it's a guy like Johnny? I'd like to enjoy being an available girl, if you know what I mean. At least for a while before I settle down."

"He does have a lot of money. And from what I've seen, he's pretty taken with you."

She smiled, her red lipstick smeared from kissing him. "Yes, but what if I'm a novelty?"

"What if he's your true love?"

She gave him a playful slap on his shoulder. "You believe in true love, after everything you've been through?"

"Well, you're right. I wouldn't know from personal experience. But I sure hope there's someone out there for each of us. Maybe Mather's your man."

"Maybe so. If he is, he'll be back in six months. But enough about me. Tell me everything."

Nick filled her in on the Zydeco case, Marylou's reappearance and disappearance, and his current case with Dillon. He didn't mention Theresa.

"Dillon met a woman in Fort Worth and after a little drunken tryst, she left her phone."

"How sad." Alice's red lips pouted.

"Her encrypted phone."

Her lips shifted to a thoughtful pucker. "How interesting."

"Then someone tried to kill him."

She raised an eyebrow. "I'm entranced."

"Through some contacts, I now have a name and a city. Bobbi Shank in Austin. You think you can find her for me?"

Alice, her eyes sparkling at the intrigue of the hunt, nodded. "Just like old times. I love it."

Nick went into his office, bouncing a tennis ball rhythmically against a wall as he thought through the case to date. He took a sip of his now tepid coffee made borderline drinkable with copious amounts of cream and sugar. He spit it back in the cup, opening a drawer in the search for mints to cleanse the nasty taste in his mouth.

An hour later, Alice called out his name. "Nick. Found something."

He got up from his desk and stood behind her as they both stared at her computer screen.

"Here's her website. Shank Accounting, Inc."

"Accounting? I thought she was some kind of biker chick."

Alice rolled her eyes. "Nick, my dentist is a biker chick. All of these professional types love dressing up in leather, hopping on their Harleys, and riding to Sturgis every year."

"Does she list her clients?"

"No, but I did a search and found a connection to this man."

Nick leaned over. A website came up in pastel colors, a mesquite tree in one corner with the words, Mesquite Ridge Healthcare Corporation. Alice clicked About Us then Bruce Reynolds, CEO, a man in his late forties with a dark full head of hair and a tailored suit, smiled at them.

Alice purred. "My, he's hot."

"Settle down, Alice."

"Just saying."

"She knows this guy. So what?"

"You mentioned Bobbi met Dillon at a gun show."

"Bruce likes guns?"

"Oh, much better." She opened the Austin American Statesman online, then pulled up a news story several months old about a Presidential campaign fundraiser for Governor Francis Adamson. A photograph of a woman identified as Bobbi Shank held a revolver purchased by Bruce Reynolds at an auction raising money for the Governor's campaign.

Nick studied the photo. "I know her. She came by my trailer looking for directions."

"Coincidence?"

"I doubt it. I'm a bit off the beaten path. I wonder what she's up to?" Nick looked closely at the gun. "Is that what I think it is? A Colt Texas Paterson?"

"Specifically, a .36 caliber 1839 Colt Texas Paterson revolver. A Texas Ranger owned this one. It sold for over nine hundred thousand dollars."

Nick knew the gun. Hell, anyone who had a serious interest in guns and lived in Texas knew about the first Colt revolver giving the Rangers the ability to maintain sustained firepower against charging Comanche warriors. But more to the point, he now had a woman who might have a reason for wanting to silence Dillon connected to a major contributor to Governor Adamson's campaign. Separately, the pieces seemed innocent enough. Together, they didn't add up to much either. However, he learned long ago to listen to his inner voice. Right now, his inner voice screamed like a monkey on crack.

"Alice, I think I'll pay the governor a visit."

"You sure that's wise? I mean, you did put her boy away for good."

"One thing I know for certain about Francis Adamson. She's like smoke. If the governor's around, there's a fire somewhere."

108

R. W. Hacker

Bruce Reynolds

The executive offices of Mesquite Ridge Healthcare Corporation were perched on a cliff with sweeping views of Lake Austin and the Hill Country. Nick pulled into a visitor spot in front of a steel and glass structure, xeriscaped with cacti, desert willows, and mesquite. Black buzzards circled an updraft from heat reflecting off a nearby rock quarry. His boots echoed on marble floors as he made his way to a circular desk of some exotic wood. The healthcare business must be booming.

A young woman in her early twenties, a wireless headset sticking out of one ear like Uhura on the Starship Enterprise, glanced his way. He thought about making a comment, then thought better when he realized she probably wouldn't know a 1960's TV sci-fi reference from the stone ages. It would fall in the same category of ancient history as pay phones and rabbit ear antennas.

She smiled, her doe eyes flirting with him. "May I help you?"

"Yes, I'd like to see Mr. Bruce Reynolds."

"Do you have an appointment?"

"Gosh, no. I met him at Governor Adamson's fund raiser a few months ago. You don't see a Texas Paterson in such good condition every day, I tell you."

"Is Mr. Paterson a football player?"

Nick offered a hearty, good natured laugh. Best to keep her off her game. "Football. Now that's a good one. How long you been working here?"

"About a year."

"No wonder Bruce spoke so highly of you." He paused to laugh a bit more. "Love a girl with a sense of humor." He scanned her from head to toe with as much lust in his eyes as he could muster. She fidgeted in her seat under his salacious gaze.

"I'll check with his assistant for you."

"Now darling, slow down a mite. See, like I say, he probably doesn't remember me, but let him know I've got a line on a 1910 Purdy shotgun. I think you won't have any trouble getting his attention."

"A pretty shotgun?"

"No, no darling. Purdy. Pee-Ewe-Arh-Dee-Why. Purdy. Got it?"

Nervous, she smiled with her lips, the rest of her face keeping firm against Nick's continued x-ray vision gaze.

"Yes, mister...?" She looked at him.

"Sibelius. Nick Sibelius." He thought of using an alias, but a guy like Reynolds would flush him out quickly. Better to confuse him with the truth.

After a few more minutes of negotiation, Reynolds's assistant, who could have just finished a shoot for the swimsuit edition of Sports Illustrated, walked across the reception area. She flashed a bright yet insincere smile his way.

"I understand you're a gun collector."

"Yes, I dabble a bit, here and there. That's how I know your boss."

"Bruce will be thrilled. He loves his guns."

She guided him onto the elevator, and then to Reynolds's corner office. Glass on two sides, it had a spectacular view of the Hill Country rolling away to a blue horizon in the distance. A painting of Texian and Mexican soldiers killing each other in hand to hand combat commanded attention to one side, while a series of flintlock rifles adorned the other wall. In between were staged photographs of Reynolds with Bush Sr., Bush Jr., Jeb Bush, McCain, Romney, as well as photos of him standing in a duck blind with Governor Bush Jr., holding up a lunker bass with Governor Rick Perry, and with a dead, many-pointed buck beside Governor Francis Adamson. Reynolds's assistant handed him a bottle of water, encouraging him to sit in one of the cowhide and horn chairs to await the arrival of her boss.

On cue, Reynolds strode into the room. His photograph did him no justice. Six foot four, with thick dark hair and chiseled features, he looked like a GQ model in his expensive tailored suit, gold cuff links and watch, right down to his pricey Italian shoes sans socks. How European.

"Mr. Sibelius, so good to see you again."

"Oh, you remember me."

"Well, yes, at the Paterson auction if I recall. Quite a night. How often do you get a chance to pick up a Texas Paterson?"

Nick, of course, hadn't been at the auction, but if Reynolds wanted to provide the cover, he would certainly take him up on it. "Yeah, I would have loved to have it, but the better man won."

"Oh, you were one of the bidders? Well, don't be too hard on yourself, Nick. It is Nick?"

Nick nodded.

"I don't tend to lose easily or with much grace. Drink?"

"Water's fine."

"Don't be shy. If we're talking guns, we're drinking whiskey."

"Can't argue with that."

Reynolds poured whiskey from a cut crystal container into two glasses, then handed one to Nick. "To liberty."

"Liberty." They clinked glasses.

"So, I understand you might have a gun of interest to me?"

Alice had found a story where Reynolds went on and on about wanting an early twentieth century Purdy. He tossed the bait toward him.

"I do indeed. A 1910 Purdy shotgun in exceptional condition."

Reynolds took a sip of whiskey, his poker face breaking ever so slightly. "Really? How much are you asking for it?"

"Here's the thing. I want to take it to auction. I was hoping you might be able to hook me up with that accountant of yours, what's her name?"

"Bobbi?"

"Yeah, that's it. I recall reading in the Statesman she managed the auction you put on for the governor."

"You sure you don't want to just sell it to me outright? Auctions can be tricky things."

"I've got the Purdy and several other guns in my collection. The wife wants to do one of those round the world cruises, so I need to liquidate a few things. I'd sell it to you, but the Purdy is the real prize. Can't catch a catfish without some stink bait, right?"

Reynolds drained his glass, reaching over to press a button on his phone. "Jasmine, would you ask Bobbi to come in, please?"

They passed the next few minutes discussing guns and the Cowboys, until the woman who had been waiting for him in her Porsche to get directions walked through the door. This was the woman who had drunk-fucked Dillon and bedded Chris. While Jasmine looked like a swimsuit model, the woman before them looked like the real deal. It was the difference between an exotic super car which rarely left the garage, purchased more to be viewed, and a Shelby Cobra, demanding to be driven...hard. He could feel her pull, a black hole of sexual desire and danger, from across the room.

"Bobbi, let me introduce Nick Sibelius. Nick, Bobbi."

They stepped toward each other, then Nick took her hand. Soft, yet strong. The last time he met a woman like this she was a Homeland Security agent with anger issues. And he loved every minute of her.

She kept hold of his hand, locking eyes with him. "Good to meet you. A friend of Bruce?"

Interesting. She didn't mention their previous meeting. "Of sorts. We're bound by a love for guns."

"Well, then." A wicked sparkle flitted across her eyes. "We're all bound together."

Nick struggled to get an image of a bound-up Bobbi out of his mind. "I, uh, I'm familiar with the services you provide, that is, in terms of managing auctions."

Reynolds sat on the edge of his desk. "Yes, Bobbi. Your good work on Frannie's campaign has gotten out. Nick wants to put an auction together for some guns in his collection."

She looked at Bruce. "Any friend of Bruce is a friend of mine. Sure, I'd be happy to help."

"Great." Nick glanced at Reynolds then Bobbi. "I'll have my assistant be in touch for us to discuss the details?"

She took his hand again, ushering him to the door. "I'll look forward to your call."

Bobbi handed him off to Jasmine who escorted him to the lobby. He hadn't learned much, but he'd know more soon enough.

~ * ~

After Nick left the office, Bruce started in on Bobbi. "What the fuck was that?"

"What are you talking about? It's just an auction. I thought you wanted me to do it."

"Not that. This." He tossed an eight by ten photo across his desk. Bobbi picked it up, her stomach sinking. In bold color Nick stood beside the idiot Dillon. Andy had babbled on about how he sent photos to Bruce before she shoved a tuba mouthpiece between his lips, taping it firmly to his head with duct tape. She thought he meant the sex tape. The sonofabitch managed to screw her in the end after all. *Crap.* "I don't know what to say."

"I'm sure you don't. Do you have any idea of the ramifications of having Nick Sibelius sniffing around?"

His name had sounded familiar when Andy mentioned him, but she never quite put it together. She must have looked a bit confused because Reynolds picked up on it like a hound dog on a scent.

"You don't know, do you?"

"Should I?"

"Remember when the Governor's bastard boy, Izzy Zydeco, tried to blow up Mansfield Dam?"

"Sure, it was in all the papers." How could she have missed it? Nick Sibelius, private investigator, instrumental in stopping Zydeco's twisted terrorist plot. *Shit.* "Right, Sibelius. I remember."

"Well, hooray for you. I'm not paying you to be a step behind, Miss Shank. I'm paying you to be out front of the game."

"And I am. I've just had a couple of missteps, but—"

"Missteps? You allowed some damn redneck fisherman to get ahold of your phone which had unauthorized top secret documents on its hard drive."

She didn't think he knew about her phone. *Damn.*

"You think I'm an idiot? Telling me this Dillon fellow wandered too close to our build site? Nice try, but once I had clear data," he tossed a sheet of paper listing all of the documents on her phone, "I knew you were lying to cover this up."

"Bruce."

"Shut up. I'm guessing you went on one of your little sex-a-thons and got sloppy. Now to your credit, you did try to clean up your mess. However, you failed miserably, not once, but twice."

"The first hit man died in a boating accident and the second, well, after his failure, I made sure he would never talk."

He banged his fist on the desk. "Goddammit, woman!" He shouted, spittle flying at her. "I don't give a rat's ass about your sorry excuses. We still have two people walking around who could scuttle our enterprise. And I hold you completely responsible."

"Yessir."

His scowl transitioned to a friendly smile, so quickly Bobbi felt a queasy pang of fear. "But no worries. Nick thinks I bought his story about meeting at an auction last year. At this point, he doesn't know much. Which is why you're going to help him with his little auction. Killing him outright would raise too much suspicion at a delicate moment in my strategic plan." He walked around his desk, his finger tapping its surface. "Unless you can make it look accidental." He stepped in close, whiskey on his breath, his eyes scanning down her blouse, then back to her eyes. "So keep eyes on him, kill him if the opportunity arises. Got it?"

"Yeah, right." She wanted to believe she had dodged his wrath, but Bobbi knew she'd better watch her back. Reynolds's cold, calculating heart would only keep her around if he saw her presence as a business advantage. "I won't let him out of my sight. And like you say, he doesn't know anything."

"You just stick close to Sibelius and everything will work itself out."

~ * ~

Bruce Reynolds watched Bobbi stride out of his office. Damn, she had a way in bed that made Jasmine look like a girl scout. But he learned long ago not to run his business with his cock. She might be a great lay, but she allowed Dillon and Nick Sibelius, of all people, to get way too close to his operation. Sibelius had a reputation for sniffing out trouble and snuffing out the source. Another time, he'd probably let it go, give Bobbi another chance. But too much rode on his every move. He had a destiny and he was not about to let anyone, even a hot sexy mess like Bobbi, screw things up for him.

He pulled his cell phone from an inside suit breast pocket. Tex's voice on speaker filled the office.

"AeroPflug Incorporated."

"It's BR. You're up, Tex."

"Sir? I...I'm still working out a few kinks. But I'm sure I'll have everything in place on the day."

Reynolds turned toward his wall of antique guns. "I don't give a damn about your problems. I recall you making a promise. You'd be operational this week with the entire project coming online at the beginning of the month."

"Well, yes sir, but..."

A flintlock rifle caught his eye. He stroked the Virginia musket's tiger wood stock, admiring the work of a craftsman who lived two hundred years ago.

"A man's word is all he has in this world, Tex. If you can't keep your word, well, you might as well be dead. Don't you agree?"

"I'm keeping my word. Yessir." The nervous voice chuckled. "Thought we were talking about the whole thing. But sure, I've got some of our resources ready and available."

"Good. Exactly what I wanted to hear. I need a black light on Bobbi Shank. ASAP. We've got a GPS on Bobbi, so she'll be easy to locate."

The voice on the other end of the line hesitated. "Bobbi?"

"You have a problem?"

"No sir. No problem. Black light on Bobbi Shank, ASAP. Roger that."

"Notify me when you've flipped the switch."

Reynolds heard Tex's voice groveling on the line, but he cut it off, pressing the END button.

Photo Op

Bobbi Shank left Reynolds's office with a gnawing pain in her gut. She wished she had the flu, but instead the pains were symptoms of Reynolds crawling up her ass. She hadn't seen him quite so pissed before and then go all friendly at the end. The whole encounter gave her the creeps, reminding her too much of Reynolds's Executive Performance Improvement Clinics. EPIC, for short.

EPIC consisted of Reynolds bringing in his bottom ten performing CEOs. Over sushi in the Executive Conference Room, he shouted and screamed at them, even pulled out one of those pump action water guns, soaking them like children. Building the humiliation to a crescendo, he pointed to a poor bastard with a soaked Italian suit, the executive's pride dripping on the carpet, firing him in front of the other nine. Yeah, this is what Jonah must have felt like swallowed whole by a whale. Although, Jonah had it easy. He just had the Almighty after his ass. While the guy had been at corporate for the week, Reynolds's hired-gun hackers zeroed out the ex-CEO's bank accounts and investments. To top it off, he had his victim's entire office packed and shipped to headquarters, the boxes, furnishings and framed certificates piled up in the parking lot, rain or shine. In the two years she had known Reynolds, two fired execs had officially committed suicide, one died in a car accident under dubious circumstances and four had died of heart attacks. He was the poison viper of healthcare.

She had to turn things around—like yesterday. You did not want to be perceived as the low performer, especially when it had to do with his destiny, which involved some

117

asinine plan to bring the Republic back in all its glory. Bobbi had cared less about his politics so long as he kept his mouth shut about her need for closure. The money was good and the sex stayed interesting. But now, because of a lapse in her concentration, she had to deal with Dillon and Sibelius. And this time she would not use the hired help. No, she would take care of business herself. She'd show Bruce who the real performers were on his team.

When she called, Nick agreed to be picked up outside El Rincón at eight in the morning. He'd bring the breakfast tacos, she'd bring a thermos of coffee. She gave him a line about how she liked to work walking on her property east of town. Bobbi smiled when she delivered the line about how her creativity exploded when she walked the fields. She wasn't so sure about her creativity, but she did know Nick would certainly explode when she guided him into a field laid with an old Claymore mine. Who says doing two Marines at once doesn't have any benefits?

She pulled up to a small fieldstone house belonging to a client she knew would be in Vegas for the next two days.

"Nice place."

"Thanks, Nick. My Dad, well, he left this for me when he died." An image flashed by of her bastard of a father gasping for his dying breath as his heart imploded. Not much of a payback for all those nights he crept into her room, but killing Andy had brought some momentary closure.

"He must have loved you."

"Yeah. Maybe too much. He just gave and gave. But I do love this place." She stepped out of her Porsche to scan the surrounding cotton fields. "All seventy-five acres of it."

"You do the farming?"

"Me? Heavens no. I've got a guy. Come on, let's walk."

Nick followed her along a path between two fields. In a couple of months, white cotton bolls would open, ready for harvest. Bobbi pulled a small camera out of her pocket.

"Nick, this is an odd request, but would you mind doing me a favor?"

"Sure."

She handed him the camera, giving her hair a teasing flip. "I've always wanted a picture of me standing in these fields. Would you mind?"

"No problem." He pushed a button and the lens extended out.

"Just walk out into the field there." *Yes, right where I laid the mine.*

Nick turned his back, walking over loose tilled soil. "You know, Dillon speaks very highly of you."

"Dillon? I don't think I know a Dillon."

He stopped, looking over his shoulder. "It's just you and me out here, Bobbi. I know you slept with him, left your phone and now, for some reason, you're trying to kill him."

"Keep on going. Just a bit further." Bobbi had rigged the photo app on her phone to not only snap a pic, but detonate the Claymore mine fifty yards away. She'd be in the kill zone, but the ditch between the path and the field, not to mention a strategically placed tractor, would provide cover.

"Doesn't bother you I just accused you of attempted murder?"

A buzz, pitched a bit too high for an airplane, hummed in the background. "I figured you were joking. Why on earth would I want to kill, what was his name again?"

Nick took a couple more steps. "This far enough? And his name is Dillon."

Something caught her attention behind him. An airplane? She looked at Nick. *Just one more step. One more.* "Just a bit further."

But Nick heard the sound, too. She watched him turn as a small gray plane with an eight or ten foot wingspan swooped down on them. He swung around, running with awkward steps over cotton plants back to Bobbi. She stood paralyzed, trying to take in the data her eyes and ears were sending her. A miniature airplane was flying right at her. Her concentration on the aircraft had become so complete, Nick's body tackle into a ditch took her by complete surprise. As the gray beast roared past overhead, they slammed hard into the dirt beside the tractor.

Nick lay on top of her. Any other time, she'd be fine with the arrangement, but with some flying thing buzzing after them, Bobbi wanted more freedom of movement.

"Will you get off me. Jesus, what was that?"

Nick rolled away, looking skyward. "It's coming around. We better make a run for it."

He jumped up, grabbing her hand to pull her to her feet, then dragged her into the field toward the Claymore.

"No!"

"What? Lady, we've got to go."

The aircraft homed in on them again.

"We can't."

"Why the hell not?"

She looked away, then back to him. "It's mined. Okay? We can't go in that field."

They sprinted down a path lined with trees toward the farmhouse. She hoped the trees would provide cover, but halfway to the house, the drone swooped down in front of them, barely three feet off the ground. They stopped, turning to run. The high pitched buzz of their attacker increased in volume as it bore down on them.

Nick, still holding Bobbi's hand, yanked her off the path. "Through the trees."

They jumped the ditch, then ran across a field of small green cotton plants, following the space between rows. The aircraft's engine whined behind them as it cleared the trees, then looped back towards them. The whine grew louder, cotton plants slapping the wings. Nick and Bobbi dove for the dirt just as the aircraft flew by only inches away.

Nick popped up, dragging Bobbi behind him. "Let's go!"

"We're not going to get away from this thing."

Nick stopped, watching the airplane make a graceful one hundred eighty degree turn. "You're right. Does your bomb have a remote?"

"What?"

Nick pulled his Glock. "You'd rather face a killer drone than run across the field, so I imagine there's a trip wire. If you also have a remote, tell me or let this bastard kill us. Your choice."

"Where's the camera?"

"I dropped it by the tractor when I tackled you to the ground."

She shrugged under his gaze. "Let's go."

They ran toward a green tractor, the drone making a lazy turn then coming back around on them. They could hear it closing in, the buzz louder and louder. When it seemed to be right on them, Nick threw Bobbi to the dirt, whirling around and firing his Glock as he fell backwards. They both lay stunned for a moment, then Nick jumped back to his feet, pulling Bobbi up with him. The drone turned in her peripheral vision, one hundred eighty degrees for another pass, just as they arrived at the tractor.

Nick plucked the small digital camera out of the dirt. "Where's the switch?"

A wry smile crossed her face. "Point and shoot. But I don't understand what you're doing."

The drone raced only feet off the ground, this time firing. Bullets? Two parallel lines of small puffs of dust raced toward them.

They crouched low behind the tractor's rear wheel. Nick poked his head out beyond the tire, pulled back, counted to three, then pressed the shutter release. A thunderous explosion shook the ground. A metallic *pop, pop, pop, ping,* pummeled the tractor. What seemed like millions of projectiles hit all around them. The tractor shuddered with a thunk like some great beast. *Crack. Swish.* Something gray catapulted by. *Tish. Tish. Tish.* Pieces flying through cotton plants. Then silence.

121

Bobbi lay in the dirt, her hands shaking, taking slow breaths in an attempt to settle herself. Nick stood, offering a hand for Bobbi to rise. She got to her feet. Parts of a small aircraft lay in pieces thirty yards away.

"I'd say somebody's decided to kill you, too, Ms. Shank."

Bruce. Goddammit. He didn't even give me a chance to make things right. Sent a damned drone to end me.

Nick grabbed her arm, his hand a vice-grip leading her toward the wreckage. "I think you and I have lots to talk about. Don't you?"

"What are you doing?"

He let go. *Damn, that's going to leave a bruise.* She almost liked this guy.

He pointed his gun in her direction. "Move and I'll put a 9mm hollow point in your leg. Won't kill you, but will hurt like hell and definitely leave a scar."

"You wouldn't."

He leveled his gray blue eyes at her, his mouth a thin, determined line. *Yes, he would. He would indeed.*

"Pick up the tail section and the engine over there." He motioned with his gun.

Bobbi, not really in a position to argue, did as she was told. Given he now knew she had planned on blowing him up, she didn't know what to make of the fact he hadn't put a bullet in her brain. As she worked, Nick leaned against her Porsche, Glock in hand. "Why are you trying to kill Dillon, anyway? He's about as harmless as they come."

"Don't know what you're talking about."

"I figure you wanted to protect the files you thought Dillon had seen on your phone. Who do those files belong to, by the way? Your buddy, Bruce Reynolds? The governor?"

Hands on her hips, she smiled. "Like I said. I don't know what you're going on about. Looks like we've got some crazed radio controlled airplane nut on the loose and you're talking about the governor."

Nick motioned her over to the car. "Give me your keys."

122

"Where are you going?"

"Nowhere. Just don't want to have to shoot you because you tried to drive off." He held out his hand. "The keys."

Bobbi handed him her keys. It didn't seem healthy to do otherwise. Nick pulled out his cell phone.

"Who are you calling?"

"The police."

"What? No, you can't call the police."

"I'm no lawyer, but I'm guessing they can charge you with conspiracy to commit murder, attempted murder, illegal possession of explosives, and drunk sex in a cheap motel."

"First of all, there's nothing illegal about drunk sex, no matter where you do it."

"If you hadn't tried to kill me, we might've gotten along—"

"Second, you won't find my fingerprints anywhere on whatever you blew up out in that field. Only your fingerprint on the button. Third, you've got nothing to connect me to murder or attempted murder. Why bother with the police? You might as well let me go." She offered a sultry gaze. "I'll make it worth your while to put that phone back in your pocket."

While Nick tapped out a number, she pulled her tee shirt up over her head, standing topless in jeans and cowboy boots. Nick paused, giving an approving nod. Bobbi never doubted the power of her breasts over the heart and soul of a man.

The man put the phone up to his ear. *Dammit.*

"Quen. Nick. Have something of a..." he looked her way, a crooked gotcha smile crossing his face. "Nutcase for you." He nodded. "Yeah. She likes long walks on the beach, hiring hit men, attempting to blow me up with a Claymore..." he paused, listening to this Quen person. "Yeah, a Claymore. Oh, and she's standing in front of me topless, I believe in an attempt to keep me from calling you."

123

Bobbi pulled her tee shirt back over her head. The arms twisted inside out, leaving her tangled in her shirt from the neck up. "What is wrong with you, Sibelius? Damn this shirt." Straightening her tee, once again covering what had always been her secret weapon, she looked at the man still holding a gun on her. "Are you gay or something?"

Nick held a hand up, motioning for her to wait until he finished his call. "We're just off 973 about a mile from Schmidt Lane. Thanks."

He slipped his phone in a pocket. "Are you done making a scene? Because if you're not, I'm going to have to stuff you in the trunk until Quen gets here."

"Making a scene? I give myself to you. Give. On a damn silver platter. I bare my breasts for you. And you act like nothing's happening. I bet even if you drank the beer I drugged you still wouldn't put out. You've got to be some kind of eunuch. Were you castrated in a farming accident? Or is this Quen your lover boy? That's it, isn't it?"

"What did you say?"

"I was wondering if your balls got whacked off in a farming accident."

"No, before that. Something about drugging a beer."

"Lot of good it did. Your girl, who I'm sure isn't getting any from you, should thank me." Bobbi smiled. "Did she take you for a ride after you drank it?"

"You drugged my beer? With what?"

"G."

"Say again?"

"You know Liquid E, Fantasy, Scoop, Salty Water, G-Riffick, Organic Quaalude?"

Nick's face turned crimson with rage. "Christ. Goddammit. A roofy?"

"Which one of you took it?" She wanted to hear the whole sordid story, but his visible misery tasted almost as good. She may not have killed him, but he had the look of a man who wished for death.

124

He walked to her, and for a moment she thought he might punch her in the face. "If I were you, I'd stay in prison the rest of my life."

"Yeah? Why?"

"If you ever get out, I'll be coming for you."

She laughed him off, but inside she knew Nick meant what he said. He rattled her to the point that, when a Pflugerville Police and County Sheriff's car followed by a bomb squad paneled van pulled up beside them, Bobbi felt nothing but relief. This was all her fault. She should have killed Sibelius right away. Stabbed him in the heart, stuck an ice pick in his brain, shot him in the head, then blown up his trailer to destroy the evidence. If Reynolds got wind of her arrest and residency in a Texas prison, every inmate in the system on his payroll would be sharpening shivs to slice her open.

Men. You can't live with 'em and they're so damned hard to kill.

Dust Devil

Back in his office Nick found Alice clicking away at her computer. Her time with Mathers had, among other things, greatly improved her fashion sense. Before leaving for the Caribbean she always looked like a cheap hooker on steroids at a clown convention. Now, he had to admit, she had a more refined, feminine sensibility. In a light blue dress and understated makeup, she gave off a composed, professional vibe.

Looking up, Alice caught Nick staring. "Like what you see?"

"Well, Alice, I've got to say, you're looking really good. Mathers is probably crying in his umbrella drink on a lonely white sand beach."

She smiled. "Wouldn't that be wonderful."

"I thought you liked the guy?"

"Oh, I do. But to think I could do that to a man..." She cocked her head, then frowned. "You're right. I don't want him to suffer." She offered a wicked grin. "But you think he might be suffering?"

"I'm sure of it." He stepped behind her desk to view the computer screen. "Did you get the pics I sent?"

"Sure did. Someone really sic a drone on you?"

"Yeah. Have you found out anything about it?"

She clicked through the photographs Nick had taken of the wreckage. "Well, it's not a government drone. Must be private sector."

"An armed, privately owned drone? Didn't know you could do that."

"Not sure about the armed part, but you can pilot a drone as long as you fly under four hundred feet and stay away from airports and populated areas. Of course, I have a feeling whoever built this could care less about the Federal Aviation Administration."

"How do you know so much about this?"

"Trained to fly helicopters for the Army."

"But you didn't fly for the Army. You were boots on the ground, weren't you?"

She looked up at Nick, and he could almost see the movie reel of death and mayhem running in her mind. "Got a special assignment. I couldn't do both, so I quit flying."

"Must have been a pretty cushy deal to be willing to let go of flying."

"Yeah, mountain air, plenty of insurgents and IEDs. A real paradise."

Alice stared off somewhere far away. Nick hadn't meant to pull up the darkness, but it happened so quickly. "Alice."

She took a deep breath.

"Alice, you okay?"

"What?" She offered a pained smile. "Sure. So, we were talking about a drone."

Nick figured staying focused on the work at hand would be best. "Yeah, what about the parts? Were they fabricated to build the aircraft or can you get this tech off the shelf?"

"Not sure. I called Dillon, since he's into this stuff. Figured he might know someone who leans toward building more commercial aircraft. He gave me a name. Tex Sawyer."

"Tex builds big model airplanes?"

"He builds UAVs for police and emergency services, pipeline inspection, that sort of thing."

"UAV?"

"Unmanned aerial vehicle. Lucky us, his company's in Pflugerville. AeroPflug, Inc. Dillon said he's been in business for five years, but it really took off this last year. From his website, it sounds like they've been building hovering craft for search and rescue and surveillance, as well

127

as fixed-wing aircraft for monitoring pipelines and aerial photography."

Nick scanned AeroPflug's home page. Little helicopters and small radio controlled airplanes seemed harmless enough. And he didn't see anything like the armed aircraft that almost punched his ticket.

"Maybe I can meet with this Tex at AeroPflug, see if he can identify who made the drone that attacked me."

"Dillon said one other thing about this guy, Nick. Apparently, the rumor mill in the RC community says Tex builds armed drones, which he sells to third world governments. Of course, it could all be wag and no bark."

"Sounds like the club members have active imaginations."

"Be careful. You didn't get attacked by a model airplane, you know."

Nick sat on the edge of Alice's desk, letting out a sigh. "I just wanted to run a little investigation business. A divorce here, a cheating business partner there. Somehow, I keep getting sucked into dust devils. I thought I'd be able to keep Dillon from getting shot by one of his crazy, irate fishing buddies. Instead I'm up to my ass in armed drones."

"Maybe the better play here is to gracefully bow out. If Dillon's right, we're talking about illegal international arms dealing. This can get very nasty, really fast."

"I wish I could, Alice. Without me, Dillon doesn't stand a chance. Besides, whoever's behind this drone has made a serious tactical error."

"They didn't kill you?" She crossed her arms, a smirk on her painted lips.

"Well, there's that. And they've pissed me off."

"Nick, you've dodged the bullet. Walk away. The police will protect Dillon. Homeland Security will sort out Tex Sawyer."

"Did you get me an appointment with the governor?"

"Yes, but do you think meeting her is a wise move here? You do realize she blames you for losing her presidential bid and for incarcerating her son?"

"If anyone knows if Tex is an international arms dealer, it will be the governor. Besides, I want to see how she reacts when I tell her about a connection between my client dodging bullets and her biggest campaign contributor."

~ * ~

Nick walked out of his office as Theresa drove up in her MG. He really didn't want to have another argument, but he wouldn't be able to avoid crossing paths with her. They were business partners, after all.

"Hi, Theresa. What are you doing here?"

Stepping out of her car, she put hands on her hips. "We're going to do this again? If I recall, before I lost my mind, we were partners in this business and as far as I know we still are, right?"

"Well, yeah."

"So, I'm doing what people do who own businesses. I'm working." She pursed her lips, staring at him. Nick knew she wanted more, an explanation, an apology, something. He couldn't find the words. "Okay."

"Okay. So that's what you've got to say. Okay?" She raised her hands in surrender. "Fine. I see you're heading out. Need me to go with you?"

"No, no. Not going anywhere important. Why don't you check-in with Alice? She's back, by the way. She can get you up-to-date on the business."

Nick got into his truck, closing the door and quickly starting his engine. Someone slapped his window. Theresa was dead set for a big confrontation. He rolled down the window. It was Alice.

"Nick, got you the appointment with the governor."

Theresa stormed toward them. "Governor? I thought you didn't have anything important going on."

Alice gave him a disappointed shake of her head. "You didn't tell her?"

129

Nick asked, "When's the appointment?"

"Noon. 360 overlook."

Theresa's fist banging on the truck's hood grabbed his attention. "Hey, cowboy. We're partners. What's this about the governor?"

"Got to go, Theresa. We'll talk later." Part of his brain warned him to stop his next words, but the winning chunk of his cerebellum blurted it out. "I thought we weren't partners anymore. So, which is it?"

He pulled away, watching her become smaller in his rearview mirror, Theresa swearing fire and damnation in his direction. He needed to get his head straight about her, at least Quen kept telling him he did, but he'd have to deal with his life later. First, he needed to find out why people possibly involved in murder and international arms dealing were palling around with Governor Francis Adamson.

~ * ~

Loop 360 cut a curve around the western side of Austin, slicing through limestone and over the Colorado River, or at least the dammed version of the river called Lake Austin. He pulled into an overlook, a small parking lot with a fieldstone retaining wall intended to keep visitors from falling down its steep incline. To the east, Austin lay before him, nestled in the rolling foothills of the Hill Country. A young couple stood at the wall, the boy wrapping an arm around his girl. They turned toward each other, the outside world a distant memory. The girl leaned in, the boy's hand sliding down from her waist to her rear end. They kissed long and tenderly. The boy opened his eyes, and a do-you-mind glare pulled Nick out of his voyeurism.

He turned away as a black limo drove up beside him. A darkened rear window rolled down silently, Governor Adamson peering out at him. Nick had imagined she'd be life-worn, wrinkled and gray, given her presidential bid had been torpedoed by her illegitimate son. A bastard would provide a challenge to any candidate. But a bastard nuclear terrorist psycho should have driven the last nail in her coffin. However, the governor looked as perky and engaged as always, her charisma flowing out her window, across the parking lot, and into the Wilderness Preserve.

"Nick, I said get in."

"What?"

A large man in a dark suit, white Stetson, and a military demeanor opened a door for him. Texas Ranger. "Please get in, Mr. Sibelius."

Nick stepped into her limo, the door closing with a muffled thunk. The governor wore a red dress suit, her lean, muscular yet pretty legs telling a story of miles running Hill Country roads.

"Good to see you, Governor."

"Bullshit. I'm the last person on the planet you want to see, so when I hear you want to talk to me, I have to wonder why. Have you seen the error of your ways and you're going to do everything in your power to get my boy out of prison?"

"Not going to happen."

She pressed a button on a central console between them. "Stop the car."

The Texas Ranger's deep voice responded. "We haven't left yet, Governor. Is there a problem?"

She turned to Nick, her eyes drilling holes through him. "You've got ten seconds to say something of interest to me or I will let Bernard know you're a threat. Bernard doesn't like threats. Takes them personally. You can visit the last threat at Brackenridge Hospital slurping liquefied spinach through a tube."

"Bernard? Really?"

She pressed her button again. "Officer."

"Wait. Wait. I just need to ask a few questions and I think you'll find my agenda is in your interest."

"I can't imagine what you could possibly say to me—"

"How about you've been connected to an international arms dealer?"

"What? That's ridiculous."

131

Buzzard Bait

Nick's door flew open. A cuff slapped across one wrist as another hand grasped him by the collar of his shirt and dragged him toward the parking lot.

"Wait, Bernard."

Texas Ranger Bernard kept one hand firmly on Nick's collar and the other around his wrist.

"Talk."

"How about if you get your action figure to let me go first?"

She pursed her lips then glared at Nick. "Don't disappoint me. It's very difficult to call him off the second time." She nodded to Bernard, who released Nick back to his seat by the governor.

"I have a case, a fisherman. Someone tried to kill him. I've got a possible suspect, a woman named Bobbi Shank."

"You're running out of time, Nick."

"Hold on. Bobbi organized a gun auction fund raiser for one of your key supporters. Bruce Reynolds."

She laughed. "You've got to be kidding me. You think Bruce is running guns?"

"I don't know what he's doing, but I do know he has an associate, Tex Sawyer. I think he might be building armed drones, then selling them on the international market."

"You think. You don't know."

"You tell me. Is Tex Sawyer an arms dealer?"

"How am I supposed to know?"

"You're the governor."

She turned, looking out her window, then sighed. "Goddamn you, Nick Sibelius. I swore to God I'd find a way to put you permanently in the ground for what you did to my boy. Then you come to me with a story accusing one of my best supporters with treason and worse. Do you have any idea what would happen if the press got wind my largest campaign contributor had an association with a gun runner? The important thing here is that this situation is contained without creating a big circus."

"What are you suggesting?"

132

"I'm suggesting you do what you do. Investigate. If you're right, contain it. If you're wrong, don't say another damned thing about it."

"He thinks I'm a potential buyer. I've got a meeting with him."

"And?"

"If you know something, now is the time to share. I think my fisherman may have been in the wrong place at the wrong time, maybe seen something he shouldn't have seen. I'd prefer to keep my client alive."

"Very noble of you, but you've got a more important client than this fisherman you keep talking about. Me." She reached for an inside pocket of her suit jacket, pulled out a business card, then handed it to Nick. "Memorize this number, then destroy the card. If you need anything, information, a SWAT team, the National Guard, call. Now get the hell out of my car."

Nick stepped out, still at the 360 lookout. They had never moved. As Governor Adamson's limo pulled away, Nick memorized the number, then slipped her card into his pocket. Frannie always had an agenda. He just needed to figure out what the hell it was before her agenda rolled right over him.

~ * ~

Fran's limo took her from the meeting with Nick to the downtown Four Seasons Hotel by Lady Bird Lake for a high-level briefing on healthcare policy. Her driver and bodyguard, Texas Ranger Bernard Stanton, pulled up to the valet station. He got out of the car, gave the uniformed valet instructions for the conveyance of her luggage, then opened the back door.

"Four Seasons, Governor."

She allowed him to offer a hand getting out of the limo, not because she needed the help, but she liked a man offering his hand to her as if she were a queen.

133

"Thank you, Bernard. I'll be in this policy session most of the day, probably into the evening. Treat yourself to dinner. I hear the cafe has a new chef."

"Yes, ma'am. I understand how some of these policy briefings go late into the night. Why don't I plan on picking you up in the morning?"

She put a hand on his arm. Bernard would not only take a bullet for her, but he had shown discretion over the six years he had been at her side. A twinge of sadness seeped into her consciousness. The only man she truly trusted had four kids and a twenty-six year marriage to a woman he worshipped.

She walked through the lobby, stepping onto an elevator to the penthouse suite where her meeting would take place. Fran liked the Four Seasons. It had a level of relaxed Texas elegance with cowhide chairs and trophy deer on the walls. Once at the suite, she slipped her passkey in the slot, and the lock clicked open. Before she could take hold of the doorknob, the door drew away from her.

Bruce stood barefoot in a terrycloth hotel robe, a martini in hand. "Darling, you made it."

Fran let the door close behind her, a sinking feeling in her stomach. She liked Bruce. He made her laugh and the sex was good. Hopefully, Nick's suspicions would not force her into choosing prematurely between this delicious man in terry cloth and her beloved state.

He leaned down, enveloping her in his arms. "Come in, Fran. We've got a lot of policy work ahead of us."

They laughed at their little deception. Both of them had been spending quite a bit of time on healthcare policy in the last few months.

"I do love our little talks, Bruce. Simply orgasmic."

They kissed, then he turned toward the sitting area of the suite. "Drink?"

"Perfect. How about a Sazerac?"

While Bruce made her cocktail, she went into the bedroom, slipping off her shoes, then unbuttoning her

134

blouse on the way to the bathroom. She stood before the large bathroom mirror in lace panties. At fifty-eight, Fran knew full well she no longer had her twenty-year-old body. More freckles, a mole here or there, a few skin tags. But her workout regimen kept her not only fit, but pretty ripped for her age. She ran a hand down her neck, between her breasts, then down to her side. Her abs rippled softly, and her breasts, while not as perky as they had been in her cheerleading days, were still firm and defined. Yeah, for fifty-eight, she looked pretty hot. She reached down past her panties, stroking herself, her pulse rising at her touch. She really needed a good policy briefing.

When she walked out of the bathroom wrapped in a towel, Bruce sat on the bed, still nursing his martini.

"Don't those things interfere with your Viagra?"

"I can do at least one of these before the CEO takes a siesta. Besides, we're celebrating."

She reached into the folds of her towel, slipping off her panties on the way to the bed. She picked up her Sazerac, took a sip, then set the glass on her nightstand.

"Mmm. If the healthcare business doesn't work out for you, I think I'd be able to find you a job as a bartender."

"We prefer to be called mixologists."

She dropped the towel, snuggling up to him. "What are we celebrating?"

"Remember when I told you I'd have an air force at your disposal soon?"

"Sure. How are things going? I imagine it must be difficult acquiring aircraft, not to mention the pilots."

"I've created something new, Fran. Something unexpected. I think you'll agree it will give us the edge we need."

She got that sinking feeling in her stomach again. Nick may have been right. "What are we talking about?"

"An Air Force. A drone Air Force." He watched her, waiting for a reaction. She wondered if she looked as stunned as she felt. "I know. Who would expect drones?"

135

He laughed. "We'll have the capability to use surgical precision while the U.S. Air Force struggles along with huge fighter jets and expensive Predators. It's brilliant. Isn't it?"

"You've got this drone force ready to go?"

"At your command, madam."

She couldn't believe this. Surely he didn't have these things armed. "We'll be able to use them for surveillance. Excellent."

"Surveillance, tactical maneuvers, defense. Of course."

"You mean to tell me these things are armed?"

"Yes. I know. I've gotta say, Tex is a genius. What he can do with drone aircraft on a budget."

"No." She stood up. Suddenly feeling extremely naked, she picked her towel off the floor, wrapping it around herself.

"What do you mean, no?"

"I mean we can't have a fleet of armed drones in my state. Are you crazy? What if Tex gets carried away and shoots at something?"

"Tex? You had me worried there for a moment. If it's Tex who concerns you, I've got it covered."

"How?"

"Every aspect of our operation has been siloed. If Tex goes against us, the traitor won't be able to destroy our movement. Trust me. I've got everything under control."

Her scheme to fleece this man of his wealth for her political ambitions transformed into a gigantic cluster fuck right before her eyes. She struggled to maintain her composure, not letting Bruce see her disdain for his crazy plan. No, to have any hope of controlling this potential apocalypse, he had to believe they were still partners in crime. "Sounds like you've got it all worked out. But remember, Bruce, nothing happens unless I say it happens."

"Absolutely, my love. Now why don't you come back to bed, sans towel, and let's get this high-level healthcare briefing under way."

She looked at Bruce, his Viagra having kicked in, his CEO standing proud. She needed this briefing. She needed to be briefed good and hard, but her situation with this man felt on the edge of chaos. She did have Sibelius investigating Tex and he'd hopefully be able to locate the drones and make sure she had control of the strings.

She smiled at her wayward lover, letting out a soft sigh. One of the things Fran learned about leadership early on was that you can't let the demands of the job impact your personal life. She dropped her towel.

"Let the briefing begin."

Playing Catsup

After banging around the office, letting off steam from her latest encounter with Nick, Theresa spent several hours catching up on the business in general. Then she picked Alice's brain about the current case, while Alice, tape rule in hand, measured a reception area wall for some freestanding shelves. To Theresa's surprise, Dillon hadn't left town, in spite of his life still being in danger.

Alice retracted her tape after making a pencil mark on the wall. "Nick tried to get him to leave, but Dillon wouldn't go. Said he'd rather die than run away from a death threat."

Alice picked up a shelf, lifting it into position. "You mind holding this so I can get a good look?"

"Sure." Theresa grabbed the shelf. "Did anyone explain to him the point of a death threat is to tell you someone is about to kill you?"

Stepping back, Alice scanned the wall, hands on her hips. "We're talking Dillon, darling. Anyway, he's still here."

"Maybe I should go talk to him."

Alice took the shelf from Theresa, putting it to one side, then picked up a cordless drill. "You sure that's wise? I don't think Nick wants you out in the field."

"You too? Look, I'm a partner in this business. If I want to go out into the field, then I'll do it."

The tool whirred as Alice drilled into the wall. "Sorry. I just know he's worried about you. Scared, really."

"He needs to get over it."

With a twist of the chuck, Alice replaced the drill bit with a Philips head. "You don't understand. He thought he lost you and when he found out what Izzy had done, he felt so

138

responsible. It's very difficult to forgive yourself when you think you've let down people who count on you. Believe me, I know."

"He doesn't love me, Alice."

"Here, hold this." She positioned a triangular wood bracket on the wall, waiting for Theresa. "I beg to differ. He's an idiot. Men are idiots. I should know, right? He loves you. He's just scared of what loving you means."

"Which is?"

Alice inserted a screw into a hole in the bracket, then with a quick whir of her drill, tightened it in place. "If he loves you, sooner or later, he'll have to let go. You know, 'til death do you part?"

"I can't spend my life in a cocoon, Alice. If he loves me then he's going to have to man up."

Moving Theresa to her side, Alice tightened the second screw. "What do you want me to tell him if he asks about you?"

"The truth. Now, I'm going to see if I can get Dillon to hide out until this blows over."

~ * ~

Theresa drove up to Dillon's single story, ranch-style house, built in the 1980s. His double dually pickup sat in the driveway. Stepping up on the porch, she noticed his front door stood open an inch. She almost shouted out his name, then thought better of it, instead drawing her M & P 9mm. She pushed the heavy wood door open. Silence. Keeping her gun low, her back to the wall, she swung into the living room. Empty. A lamp lay broken on the floor. She stepped into the dining room and then the kitchen. No sign of Dillon.

Two pops, like soft gunshots, caught her attention, then a man in black stepped through the bedroom hallway into the kitchen. He raised his gun toward her. She dove behind the kitchen island, firing twice on the way down. The intruder fired, bullets splintering cabinets. In a crouch, she moved to the side of the island, careful to keep her head down. Footsteps moved closer to her. If she let him come around on her, she'd be dead. Listening for footfalls, she created a mental picture of the room and her approaching killer. She counted silently to three, then staying low, she fired in the approximate direction she pictured him to be standing.

A grunt, the clack of metal across tile and a thump told her the shots had found their target.

She moved quickly to kick the gun away, the attacker lying in his own blood, but still breathing. "Who are you? Who sent you?"

The man looked Hispanic, in his twenties. He smiled, blood in his mouth. "Too...late."

"Too late. Too late for what?"

His head fell to one side. Dead. She walked through the rooms hoping to find Dillon, but also afraid of finding him. Then she entered the master bedroom. The shades were drawn, lights off. She could make out a mound of duvet covers and two bloody pillow cases. Dillon and Dolores.

Tires squealed outside. Heavy footsteps, the door slamming open. He has a partner? Theresa leaned against the bedroom wall by the door. She inched her way into the hallway. Better to be on offense than defense. This sonofabitch wouldn't know what hit him. Boots on tile. He was in the kitchen. Silence. Now or never. Theresa took a deep breath, letting it out slowly to calm herself. She tensed her muscles, ready to plunge into the room, firing if necessary. Something hard pressed into her back. She jumped, then stood frozen in position.

"Theresa? What the hell are you doing here?"

"Nick? I could ask you the same question. I might have killed you."

"You might have killed me? I'm the one with a gun at your back." She turned, lowering her arms, her eyes tracking to the muzzle of his 9mm. Nick lowered his gun, flipping the safety. "What are you doing here?"

"I read through your file. Alice told me Dillon refused to hide out, so I thought I'd better check in on him, talk to him."

"Theresa, something could have happened. That's why I asked you to stay away."

"Something did happen."

He looked at the feet of a dead man visible from the doorway. "Yeah, I see."

"No, not the dead guy in the kitchen. Dillon. He's dead."

"What?" Nick shook his head. "Ah, hell. Where?"

"In the bedroom."

Nick walked past Theresa, down the hall into Dillon's bedroom. With a flick of a switch Nick flooded the hallway with yellowish light from the bedroom. Laughter. He's gone over the edge. How can he look at a couple murdered in their own bed and laugh? It was sick.

"Dillon. Where are you? It's Nick. Dillon, I don't have time for this."

Theresa grabbed her gun, noticing Nick's boots sitting on the floor. That's how he snuck up me. When she got to the door, Nick stood in the middle of the room, holstering his gun. The bed, a pile of duvet covers and sheets, had two red pillows. The room had a sweet catsup odor. Next to Nick stood the deceased Dillon and Dolores.

Theresa felt truly startled. "You're alive."

"Yes, ma'am. Hope we didn't scare you. I saw that guy coming up the sidewalk, so I threw a bunch of catsup packets in our pillow cases and we hid in the closet. Pretty good thinking, eh?"

Dolores, fuming beside Dillon, exploded. "Good thinking? Good thinking?" She backhanded him across the shoulder, causing Dillon to cower a bit. "Good thinking would have been to leave town the way Nick suggested. But oh no. You're too tough a guy to run from trouble. Besides, you didn't want to miss the damned bass tournament this weekend."

"It's a big one, Dolores."

141

"Big one." She smiled at Nick and Theresa, but her eyes were fire and rage. "You kept us here like goddamned sitting ducks so you could catch a damned fish." She paced the room. "My God, I thought Harlen had issues. You're one tit short of a full udder."

"Now, Dolores, I don't even know what that means."

"You've got the IQ of a pecan that's been done over by a squirrel. If you were a cow patty, you wouldn't have the sense to stay put."

"Dolores. There's no call for this."

She stepped up to him, swinging. "You could have gotten us killed. Killed, Dillon. As in buzzard bait!"

Dillon took the blows, but Theresa stepped in, pulling Dolores back before she completed what the assassin had attempted.

Theresa kept her arms wrapped around Dolores as Dillon backed away. "Everybody calm down."

Nick glared. "I don't know, Theresa. I think Dolores is on pretty firm ground. What kind of idiot walks right into danger when she knows it's not safe? When she's been told it's not safe?"

Dolores struggled to get free, only encouraging Theresa to hold on more tightly.

"I stopped the guy. If I hadn't been here, do you think he would've been fooled by catsup packets for long?"

"Not my point."

Theresa pushed Dolores away, stepping up to Nick. "What is your point, cowboy? That I'm a frail little thing that should stay barefoot in the house while her big, strong man watches out for her?"

"I didn't say that."

"Like hell you didn't. Shit-for-brains over here," she pointed to Dillon, "doesn't have the sense to stay alive."

"Now that's more to my point."

"Which is why people like you and me protect them. We're here because in the real world, he'd be dead in five seconds."

Dillon spoke up. "Now hold on there."

Nick and Theresa in unison said, "Shut up."

Nick kept his emotions under the surface, but Theresa knew the telltale signs. His left eye squinted ever so slightly and the ring finger of his right hand tapped on his leg. No doubt he thought he loved her, but he was so afraid of losing her he had let his fear cloud over the love. The question in her mind, and today's events only fed it, was how long she'd put up with him.

"How about if we get these people somewhere safe, Nick. Not good for business to have our clients getting killed."

She glanced over at Dolores and Dillon, who, watching their rescuers bicker, now held hands. She could see it in their eyes. *Our boat might be sinking, but Nick and Theresa are on the damned Titanic.* "I'll talk to Alice. We'll get a safe house lined up for them."

Nick seemed to sense they were standing on a precipitous ledge, choosing to back away with her. "Good idea. I'm going to meet with Tex Sawyer. See what he can tell me about drones." Walking away, he paused. "And, uh, thanks for being here when it counted."

The line of her lips creased up slightly. "We're a team, Nick. Right?"

He nodded. "Yeah. Right."

UAV Shopping

Tex Sawyer's place in east Pflugerville consisted of a modest fieldstone house, a barn, two hangars each capable of holding four or five full-size airplanes, and surrounding farmland. Nick had called in advance, so Tex expected him.

A man in his fifties in jeans and a white button-down shirt answered the door. "You must be Nick Sibelius."

"Yeah. Thanks for your time, Mr. Sawyer."

He stepped outside, guiding Nick to a porch swing. "Aw, call me Tex. Roger that?"

"Right. Roger. I mean, Tex."

"You said you had some questions about UAVs. Maybe interested in purchasing one?"

"Yeah. I understand you build these birds."

"Roger that. Although my AMA brothers think I'm foxtrotting all over their parade."

"Excuse me?"

"Academy of Model Aeronautics. They think I'm fucking up their thing. But I tell 'em to shove it up their alpha-hotels."

"Why do you think they don't respect what you're doing?"

"Goddamn foxtrottin' Federalists, that's why."

"Foxtrotting?"

"Damn, boy, don't you speak the English? Foxtrottin'. You know…" He inserted an index finger into the curled fingers of the other hand with a back and forth motion. Now stay with me."

"So these Federalists don't want you to fly any birds not sanctioned by the AMA or the FAA?"

"Bingo. But I tell them the FAA is one hundred percent FUBAR. FU. BAR."

"And what you'll build for me, is it legal? I mean I'm totally with you on how the FAA has sucked those Federalists into their lies, man. Totally. But I've got a business to run, so getting afoul of the government over a livestock surveillance plane is not in my best interest."

Tex laughed. "Sure. Sure, I understand. You're not going to have any troubles with my birds. All legit. At least as far as the FAA goes. I was talking about, well, you know..." His eyes twinkled with mischievousness. "Other applications."

"What can these do beyond surveillance?"

Tex cocked his head, studying Nick, then gave him a nod, as if he'd made some kind of decision. "Hypothetically, let's say you want something to monitor your land, identify rustlers, that sort of thing."

"You build aircraft for those types of applications? Because if you do, I'd be interested. My ranch borders Mexico, so if I can ID a rustler I can get the law to prosecute them. Of course, they've probably stolen a bunch of livestock by then. But at least I'd stop them."

"Oh, I can do more for you than identify a rustler. How about blowing the motel foxtrotter away?"

"Shoot him?" Nick leaned in to let Tex know he was seriously considering the possibility. "Firepower like that would come in mighty handy. You sure it's legal?"

"He's a trespasser, ain't he?"

"Yeah, I suppose he is."

Tex put an arm across Nick's shoulders, guiding a young man through the vagaries of the world. "Son, you live in the great state of Texas. Hell, our own damn governor shoots at stuff when she jogs. Man, gotta love a woman who packs a concealed weapon on a run. And besides, the Constitution guarantees we have the right to bear arms. It don't say whether we're talking about BB guns, assault rifles or armed

UAVs. All the same in my book. If you outlaw weaponry, then only the bad guys will have rocket launchers."

Nick looked across the porch to the hangars beyond. Two men with assault rifles stood nearby. They had the look of ex-military.

"Maybe you could show me a few aircraft, while I'm here."

"I thought you'd never ask." Tex stood up, ushering Nick off his porch, toward the hangars.

"Must be some pretty sensitive stuff to have armed guards outside."

"Oh, one of my clients. A bit paranoid if you ask me. But what can you do? He wants his guys here with eyes on the prize."

They reached the first hangar. Tex punched in a code on a pad by the door.

"Client wanted the fancy lock, too?"

"Yeah, but now I don't have to worry with keys, so it's all good." He flipped a switch and the large space flooded with fluorescent light. An array of small aircraft sat on the hangar floor.

Nick took in the sight of scaled down airplanes and helicopters. Tex had his own personal air force. "Quite a selection."

"Oh, I've been building and refining my aircraft for some time. Look at this one." Tex stepped over to a small fixed wing plane with a five-foot wingspan. "One of my first commercial versions. I'd been building replicas of real planes, B-52s, B-1's, when I realized, wait, Tex. You could build yourself an original and make it pay for itself. Sure enough, I built the prototype for the Eagle Eye in my garage. She carries a digital camera and can stay on position for a couple of hours. Not bad for a first try. Of course, now I've got aircraft you can put in the air for hours circling at high altitude."

His eye caught something across the hangar. Nick followed along as they picked their way past several planes, stopping at a helicopter. "Of course, this is my pride and joy. She carries over one hundred pounds in payload, which means she can be armed. Now a police officer doesn't need to get in harm's way with a sniper on a building or someone running from the scene of a crime. Justice One comes with a public address package, miniaturized rocket propelled tear gas projectiles, and small caliber arms."

Nick looked beyond Justice One to an aircraft very similar to the plane he blew up with a Claymore. "And what about this bird, Tex?"

"Oh, that's a prototype. Codename Switchblade. She has the potential to carry payloads of fire retardant, primarily for tricky forest fire situations."

"She could be armed too, right?"

"Sure. I'm field testing several armed versions as we speak. But Nick, it's probably more firepower than you'd need for your ranch. Sure, I could sell you one, but it's a bit of an overkill, if you know what I mean."

"The border's a dangerous place." He stepped closer to Switchblade, inspecting the wing. "Can I trust you, Tex?"

"Sure you can."

"Because what I'm about to tell you carries a penalty, a severe penalty, if it ever gets repeated."

"Son, in my business, confidentially is a sacred code."

Nick lowered his voice. "I've got business interests which require, how shall I put it, covert access to the border. Some of my competitors have decided to challenge my authority and the government has also created a nuisance with their own drones in the area. Just last week a Border Patrol drone picked up on one of my mules. Lost an entire shipment."

Tex cocked his head, chuckling. "I had a feeling you were more than a rancher. I may be able to help you out. In fact, I know I can."

"Show me. I'm very interested."

"Tell you what. I don't keep the more tactical side of the business here in Pflugerville. I have a facility out in West

Texas with a private strip and no neighbors to speak of. Why don't you come out tomorrow? I'll give you the coordinates. You can see my product line and we can put together a solution for you. How's that sound?"

"Music to my ears, Tex. I look forward it."

~ * ~

Tex was standing by his hangar watching Nick leave when his phone rang. Reynolds.

"You didn't kill her, Tex. How did you not kill her?"

"I've been meaning to call you about it, Mr. Reynolds. You see, we had a bead on her but my drone got blown to bits by a bomb. A foxtrottin' Claymore to be precise. Ripped my bird to shreds. It's like she knew we were gunning for her."

"You telling me that your air attack failed because she blew you up with a land mine?"

"Well, yessir." The line went silent. "Sir?"

"What?"

"You want me to put together another assault?"

"She's in prison, so no. I'll have to use other means. Besides, I need you to keep your focus on the rise of our Republic. Clear your calendar. From now on, you're the Air General of the Republic."

"Uh, sir? I do have one more potential client to see. I just finished a meeting with him. He's coming out to West Texas tomorrow."

"Whatever you discussed, tell him it's off."

"He, uh, could be a useful member of our militia. At least, talking to him he sure sounded like he'd be a patriotic Texian. He lives in south Texas."

"I see what you mean. Could be useful, another contact near the border. What's his name?"

"Sibelius. Nick Sibelius."

"Tall, handsome fellow with gray blue eyes?"

"Yeah, sounds like him."

"He's not a patriot, Tex. He's a spy."

"Shi-I mean, sierra. I, I didn't know."

148

"It's okay. You said he's going out to the operation in West Texas tomorrow?"

"Yessir."

"Good. Make damn sure he doesn't get there. It'll be good practice for some of our pilots."

"Just to be clear, do you want me to keep him away temporarily or permanently?"

"To the end of time, Tex. The end of time."

~ * ~

Nick drove home from Tex's place as billowing cumulous clouds turned a fiery red with the setting sun. Tomorrow he'd get the evidence he needed to stop Reynolds from continuing to make attempts on Dillon's life and from selling drones to the wrong people. He pulled into the drive up to his trailer, remembering Theresa wouldn't be there. It was his fault she had left. She thought he was a jerk who couldn't commit, which was probably partially true. But he knew the full truth. He didn't want to set himself up for a fall. He had loved his wife, the surgeon. Smart, sexy, self-confident. Seeing her ride a doc on their bed still burned in his mind. It was bad enough she did an ER doc named Lester. God. How do you lose your woman to a guy named Lester? But the worst part was he hadn't had a clue. No idea whatsoever that his beloved bride spent lunchtimes banging Lester. What if he gave himself to Theresa, trusted her? How would he know if she screwed around behind his back? She could be in bed with half of Pflugerville, everyone talking behind his back, laughing, and he'd be clueless.

Being the fool would be bad enough, but she wanted to put herself in harm's way, just like today. He wouldn't be able to be there every time. One of these days, something would happen, something terrible, and he wouldn't be there. She'd be injured or dead, all because he hadn't anticipated what would happen.

Once home, he opened a bottle of Jack. Didn't bother with a glass. Sometimes you just have to drink your poison

149

straight. No, he couldn't lose Theresa. Knowing she lived, even if it ended up being with another man, would be better than living on the edge, waiting for the unthinkable to happen.

Pink Commando

Nick had been taking flying lessons off and on for over a year, but just hadn't made the time to get his certificate. Since he couldn't fly himself, he asked Alice to line up a charter flight to West Texas. She surprised him when she volunteered to fly him.

"You're a licensed pliot?"

"What kind of a sexist thing is that to say? Because I'm a girl I can't be a pilot?"

"Alice, you know I didn't mean it that way."

She gave him a devilish smile. "I know. I'm making up for lost time."

"I knew you flew helicopters for a time in the Army, but I didn't know you still flew."

"Got my civilian instrument on the islands with Johnnie. He loves island hopping by plane, so I brushed up on my fixed wing. I've got our Mooney at the Georgetown Airport. Since Johnnie isn't a pilot he insisted I keep it."

Nick gave her the coordinates, then met her at the airport the next morning. As he walked into Pilot's Choice Flight Center, a young woman sitting at a worn desk greeted him. Having taken lessons here, he knew several instructors.

"Hi, Nick. You're back. Ready to get that certificate?"

Sandy looked like she was sixteen, but he knew from their conversations during flight lessons she was a twenty-two-year-old aeronautical school grad who taught flight lessons to build her hours and get multi-engine time toward a commercial job.

"I wish, Sandy. But no, today it's business. Has Alice Coleman been in yet? She's in a Mooney."

"Alice? She's a hoot. I believe she's outside the hangar pre-flighting."

Nick walked through the hangar, past a twin Baron with its engine cowlings removed. Devil Dog, a blue B-25, stood on the far side. Alice, in a pink and white seersucker jumpsuit, screwed a wing tank cap back in place on a sleek, low-winged airplane. She looked up from her checklist.

"Hi there, Nick. Ready to go?"

"Don't you think the jumpsuit's a bit—"

"Too fashion forward? I know. Especially for West Texas. But if I don't bring civilization to the remote west, who's going to do it? Besides, the only other option is my birthday suit." She fumbled with the suit zipper by her neck.

"No, no. Pink stripes are fine."

"Seersucker."

"Excuse me?"

"The fabric. Seersucker."

Satisfied with her preflight, they both boarded the plane. She toggled switches to begin her startup, then flipped on the magneto.

"Nick, you really think this guy might be selling armed drones to the bad guys?"

"It looks like it."

"Maybe the better play here is to gracefully bow out. We're talking about illegal international arms dealing. This can get very nasty."

"I wish I could, Alice. Without me, Dillon doesn't stand a chance. Besides, whoever was behind the drone made a serious tactical error. They failed to kill me."

Alice met his gaze. "You've dodged the bullet. Walk away."

"I'd like to Alice, but the governor asked me to investigate."

"The governor?" She shook her head. "You really think she has your back?"

"No, I don't. But whatever Tex Sawyer's up to, I think it's in her best interest to stop it. And like I said, if I stop Tex, I keep Dillon alive."

~ * ~

They gradually climbed to eight thousand feet above a layer of overcast. When Nick took his flying lessons he always flew visually, below the clouds. On this day, clouds obscured the string of lakes created by damming the Colorado River, the rising office buildings of Austin, and the granite dome of Enchanted Rock to the west. Above them a perfect azure sky, below them a billowing mass of soft white cotton.

Alice put the aircraft on autopilot. "Nick, you mind if I ask you a personal question?"

"Sure, I suppose."

"What's up with you and Theresa? You love her, so why are you being such a jerk?"

Nick turned to his transgendered office manager pilot fashionista. "We're not going to talk about this."

"She loves you, too. But if you keep throwing obstacles in the way you're going to lose her."

"Obstacles? I'm not throwing obstacles in her way. I just don't want anything bad to happen to her."

"I see. Best to make her leave you so you won't be there when she does need you."

"I didn't say that. It's complicated."

"We've got time before we get to Sawyer's place. What are you saying?"

Nick did not want to have this conversation. Not so much with Alice, but with anyone. "Like I said, we're not having this conversation."

"Because, Nick, if you're going to dump her, I've got a friend who would be perfect."

"For me? No, I don't think—"

"Not you. Theresa. Someone who would appreciate everything she brings to the table."

153

Nick couldn't tell if she winked under her flight glasses, but she might as well have. "You don't think I see what you're doing? Trying to make me jealous. Make me run back to her, beg her to stay with me. Well, it's not going to work. She's a big girl and she's made her decision."

"Her decision, Nicholas, was you. But you're so afraid of losing her you lost her. Idiot."

Yes, he feared losing her, but what was he supposed to do? She didn't want him hovering around her, protecting her. So he was just supposed to stand around until something terrible happened, something he could have, should have prevented? "Call me an idiot again and you're fired."

"Yessir."

They flew in silence for another thirty minutes until Alice pulled Nick out of his thoughts. "Looks like we have some company."

Alice pointed to an aircraft at three o'clock from their position, flying at the same altitude. "I'm climbing five hundred, just to be safe. Sometimes guys get up here flying autopilot and don't pay attention to traffic."

She keyed her mic to inform air traffic control, moved her throttle to increase her power, then gradually climbed to eight thousand five hundred feet. Nick kept an eye on the aircraft, which appeared to be turning and climbing toward them.

"We've got another at ten o'clock." To her left, another aircraft appeared also in a collision course. "I think we've got trouble."

"Maybe they're an escort."

Something silver blurred past, a metallic popping following behind it. A third aircraft.

"Nick, I think whatever that was just shot at us."

They watched a small plane with a ten-foot wingspan climb away, just as the other two aircraft closed in on either side. *Tink, tink, tink.* One rushed past overhead, the other diving below.

154

"Get us on the ground, Alice. We're sitting ducks up here."

Alice dropped the flaps, slipping the plane into a steep descent. *Tink, tink, tink, tink, tink.* An explosion rocked them, the right wing bursting into flame. "Incendiary bullets. Shit! Mayday, mayday, mayday—"

Tink, tink, tink. Sparks flew as a bullet destroyed the radio. Blood spread across Alice's right arm.

"Alice. Alice, you okay?" Nick grabbed the controls.

"A scratch. But they're picking us apart."

Tink, tink, tink, tink. Nick pulled out his gun, handing it to her. "I'll keep us in a descent."

Alice took Nick's gun, flipping open a small pilot-side window. "Keep diving. You learned to land yet?"

"Not really. Just keep 'em off us."

A drone rolled into position for another pass. Flashes from a mounted gun preceded several more pings against the fuselage.

Alice took careful aim, firing. The drone rolled away. "I think I got it."

The drone reappeared to their left, this time placing several shots into the engine.

"I think you pissed him off."

The aircraft shuddered with an explosive bang. Smoke billowed into the cockpit.

Alice gave Nick his gun. "Shutting down fuel. Throttle to idle. We're going in, Nick. This is going to be rough. Gear up for this one. Seat belts. Open your door."

Ground approached quickly. Brown, rocky soil dotted with scrub. "Think I've a got a dirt track. Come on, baby. Come on."

Alice leveled off as they neared the ground, still carrying too much speed. They floated down the track littered with loose rock and yucca and mesquite. "Hold on. Here we go."

A crunch and rumble as the plane settled, then a bang as they heaved forward, the nose driving hard into the ground. Their world flipped over, then slid with metallic screeching to a halt. Nick hung upside down, the cabin filled with dust and smoke. Flames and black smoke billowed from the engine compartment. He turned to Alice, hanging unconscious by her seat belt, blood dripping from her arm. Nick struggled with his own belt, releasing the buckle, falling headfirst into the roof.

He squirmed through the door warped open from their collision with the ground. On hands and knees, he turned, unbuckling Alice, catching her as best he could, but more concerned with exiting the plane than bruises and cuts from the cabin. Getting a handhold, he dragged her out the door, and with a burst of energy, away from the plane. Black smoke rose from the wreck, then the fuel tank on the other wing exploded, a fiery rain of debris setting off small brush fires around it.

High above, a drone circled on position. They needed to get away. They needed to find some cover. Nick tore away a piece of his shirt, pressing it into her wound to stanch the bleeding. She stirred.

"Alice. You with me?"

She smiled. "That was quite a ride."

"I'll get us some help." He pulled out his cell phone. No signal.

"No worries, Nick. I had flight following. They'll come looking for us in an hour or so."

A buzzing. Cicadas? Nick stood up for a better view. In the distance a black speck rose over the scrub. Helicopter drone.

"Alice, don't move. They'll be looking for movement and I'm going to give them what they want."

"Nick."

"Don't move." Nick ran ninety degrees away from Alice and the burning aircraft.

An approaching drone picked up his movement. The craft sped toward him, spitting micro bullets, each exploding in the dirt around him. He zigzagged, then dove behind a large scrub bush. A maniacal buzz increased in volume as the helicopter drone hovered on the other side of the bush, rising to get a better view. Nick, 9mm in hand, approximated the craft's location from its sound. The drone rose up, but Nick placed three quick shots into it, bits exploding off as the bird spun wildly out of control, then crashed into the rocky ground.

A second and third drone approached. One peeled off toward Alice while the other circled back to Nick. He ran, sliding down an arroyo, tumbling in a dusty heap, then clambering up the other side. The drone, almost on him, opened fire, bullets ricocheting off rocks and exploding in the dirt. To his left, a galvanized steel water tank sat about thirty yards away. He sprinted to the tank, diving in as the drone passed overhead, bullets pinging off the steel side. Nick poked his head up through the stagnant water. The drone circled back, slowing down to find him. He took a deep breath, then squatted down under water, peering up through the muck. Even under water he could hear the drone's high pitched buzz. Then it appeared right above him, hovering.

Springing to his feet, he grabbed its skid, slamming it down to the water, blades splattering. Its engine screamed to escape, then, choked on water, went dead silent. In the distance a buzzing reminded Nick one more drone remained. He pulled himself out of the tank, running to Alice. He found the bird hovering above her.

"Alice, you okay?"

"I think they don't want to kill me quite yet."

The helicopter turned to Nick, then raced toward him.

"Nick, run. It's coming for you."

"I have had just about enough of this." Nick stood ready, holding his gun in both hands.

"Nick, run!"

Shooting down our plane, then hunting us like animals? No, this ends.

"Nick!"

Right here. Right now.

157

The drone, six feet off the ground, fired. Rounds whizzed past him. He raised his gun, aiming carefully.

"Nick. What are you doing?"

The drone closed on him. Fifty yards. Forty, Thirty.

"Nick."

He squeezed his trigger, the bullet exploding from his gun, passing incoming rounds from the drone, then smashing into the craft's rotor, flipping the bird back into an awkward and fatal dive into hard, unforgiving ground. He stood for a moment, gun at his side, a small dust devil dancing across arid land, a shattered drone only a few feet away. Nick stepped over to Alice, who sat propped up against a large rock, holding a piece of Nick's shirt across her wound.

He holstered his gun, then sat down with her. "I hate to say it, but I have to admit you may have been right."

"About?"

"The governor. Looks like Frannie set us up. 'Hey Nick, go to west Texas and investigate Tex Sawyer.' Great idea."

"You figured she was using you to stop Tex. How were you to know she was in cahoots with him?"

Nick leaned his head back, closing his eyes. "Looks like we're going to have to find a way out of this place. Did you say the FAA will come looking for us?"

"Yeah, that's what I said. Only..."

"Only what, Alice?"

"Looks like someone might beat them to it."

Nick opened his eyes. Beyond the burning Mooney, three Humvees approached. Men carrying automatic weapons stood in the open vehicles as they pulled to a stop between the plane and Nick and Alice. Four men hopped off the Humvees, their weapons trained on Nick. Then Tex Sawyer stepped out of the lead vehicle in what appeared to be a military uniform, only unlike anything belonging to the U.S. Military. He wore knee-high black riding boots, his pants blossoming out to the sides. Around his waist, a leather belt with holsters for pearl-handled chrome Colt .45s on either side. He wore a cropped, fitted jacket, the epaulets traced in silver embroidery. Medals, gold and silver with ribbons the colors of the rainbow, adorned his jacket. Dark tear-shaped flight glasses gave him a bug-like appearance. A black lacquered helmet only added to the insectoid visage.

He walked up to Nick, a lieutenant holding two pit bulls at bay to his side. Tex removed his glasses, staring at his visitors. He leaned over inspecting Alice. "What the holy foxtrot are you?"

"She's my pilot."

He turned to Nick. "I don't remember talking to you, you drone killer."

Alice spoke up. "I'm his pilot."

He returned his attention to her, squinting his eyes. "Nice outfit. Put her in the car."

Two men stepped over. Alice looked to Nick, but he shrugged. They weren't in a position to resist at the moment. The men helped Alice to her feet and then walked her to the front Humvee.

"Son, you're in a heap of difficulty." His dogs growled, baring teeth. "My, oh my. Dalihla and Jezebel don't like you very much."

"You named your dogs Dalihla and Jezebel?"

"Whiskey-tango-foxtrot, boy. You come by invitation, mind you, then destroy my property, start an illegal fire on my land, and now you insult my dogs? Goddammit. I've had just about enough of your fucking antics."

"Shouldn't that be foxtrotting antics?"

"Shut up, alpha-hotel."

~ * ~

The ride to Sawyer's facility, while only a couple of miles, took almost thirty minutes of cross country trekking through rock-strewn fields and arroyos. Once they had to turn back because the lead Humvee driver put his front end over a sheer drop-off. After they winched him back to safe ground, they sought a usable route. Nick wasn't sure what to expect from Sawyer's facility. He hadn't imagined the

159

pseudo-general had built wood barracks like something out of WWI movie, complete with Spads and Sopwith Camels. Dark green sandbags stacked four and five high protected gun emplacements. Men wore either khaki flight suits or uniforms reminiscent of the United States Calvary, complete with duck cloth fatigue jackets and riding pants.

His hands were tied behind his back. One of Sawyer's men seized him from the Humvee, then directed him at gunpoint to a desert-camouflaged hangar. Once inside, he bound Nick to a side frame along with Alice, who looked bloodied, but still alert. Sawyer's steps echoed across the hangar.

"Thought you could infiltrate our operation, did ya?"

"I don't know what—"

The man, armed with a modern-day assault rifle, planted the butt of his weapon firmly in Nick's gut. He folded over, the wind knocked out of him, his hand cut against a rough edge of the framing.

"I don't recall asking you to speak. What I said earlier is what they call a rhetorical question." He laughed. "How about you, sweetheart? How did Nick Sibelius rope you into his little escapade?"

Nick watched Alice study the enemy, searching for a weakness.

"You are a girl, ain't you?"

"Yes."

"Your whole life?"

She scowled. "Have you been a man your whole life?"

"What? What are you tryin' to say? Goddammit, if you backtalk me one more time I'll rip off your head and sierra down your throat. You hear me?"

Nick glared at Tex. "Leave her out of this. She just flew me out here. I'm the one you want."

Tex nodded to the guard, who responded with a rifle butt in Nick's back. Yes, the frame would cut his rope if given enough time.

Alice spit the word out. "Sierra?"

"Shit. It means shit, goddammit."

"Oh, then yes, I hear you."

"Good. Now why don't you two tell me who's behind your attack."

Nick slid down, keeping his bindings in contact with the sharp edge of the framing all the way to the floor.

"I don't recall giving you permission to sit, alpha-hotel. Now stand up or we'll start in on the girl."

Nick grimaced, then slowly wormed his way back up, his rope bindings cutting and tearing against the frame.

"Look, mister. Like I told you in Austin, I'm interested in purchasing some drones from you. Although now I'm not too sure. I mean what the hell are you doing? You shoot me out the sky and then sic your damn drones after me? No way to run a business."

Tex stepped up to Nick, inches from his face. Nick could have broken the last fibers, grabbed his head and ended it right there. But they'd have to contend with twenty well-armed men. Better to bide his time for the right moment.

"Listen here, Sibelius. I have it from very good authority why you're here."

"Frannie, eh?"

"Who?"

"The governor. No need to deny it."

Tex glared at Nick as if he wanted to rip out his throat, then a smile erupted across his face and he howled with mirth. He laughed so hard he had to rest his hands on his knees. His guard, caught up in the moment, laughed some, but restrained himself. Once Tex regained his composure, he stepped back over to Nick. Without a word, he punched him in the face and then the stomach. Nick slid back to the floor.

"Foxtrottin' waste of time. If you two have a maker, you better start your prayers, 'cause you're not long for this world. In fact, because of you we get to do an old-fashioned execution. Blindfolds, cigarettes, the whole shootin' match. Hey, shootin' match. That was a good one." He turned to

161

his guard. "Don't let 'em out of your sight. I'd like to shoot 'em at dawn, but we've got orders, so we'll do 'em when we've completed our mission."

Nick's head pounded from Sawyer's punch, and blood trickled down from the frame cutting his wrists.

The three of them, Nick, Alice and their guard, sat in a back corner of the hangar waiting for Sawyer's return. Over the next two hours, Nick worked the rope binding his hands across the frame's edge each time the guard looked away, until he finally broke through. He gave Alice a subtle nod. Alice sighed, then moaned. The guard, irritated and inspired by Sawyer's behavior, groused, "What's your problem, bitch?"

"I, I don't know..."

Alice sounded weakened. Broken.

Their guard, a twenty-something with a crew cut and the attitude an automatic weapon gives a young man, sounded perturbed about having to interact with his enemy. "What do you want?"

Nick chimed in. "She's just a pilot. Doesn't know anything. You need to help her."

"Shut up." He turned back to Alice. "I can't hear what you're saying. For a big girl you sure have a little voice." He stepped toward her.

"I, I..." Alice took shallow breaths, her head lolling back and forth. "I..."

He leaned further in, turning an ear to hear her weak voice, gun to his side. With an unexpected swiftness, Alice scissored her legs around the guard. At the sudden turn of events, he hesitated to cry out long enough for Nick to bolt up beside him, wrap an arm around his neck, and apply pressure until he passed out. The guard crumpled to the ground, Nick catching his assault rifle on the way down. He grabbed the man's knife off his belt, cutting Alice out of her bindings, then checked the man's pockets—some change and a cell phone. Four bars.

"We've got a signal."

"Who you going to call? Not the governor?"

"She did offer to help, if I needed it. And Tex's reaction made it pretty clear she's not involved. By the way, Oscar-worthy performance."

"Thank you." Alice toed their sleeping guard. "You should have killed the bastard."

Nick couldn't believe Alice, standing before him in pink seersucker, wanted to whack their guard. She must have seen incredulity in his eyes.

"Nothing personal, Nick. A tactical choice."

"Well, this guy is misguided and probably needs some jail time, but I'm not going to kill him for being an idiot."

"If he was just an idiot, it wouldn't be an issue. You do realize he's going to sound off as soon as he comes to?"

Nick handed her some rope. "Here, tie him up. I'll look for some tape for a gag."

Nick found electrical tape and some rags on a bench, which Alice applied with an attention to detail that led Nick to wonder what exactly she did in Iraq.

"You've got some interesting skills, Alice."

"Didn't think I'd be using them again. Just like the old days."

"Except now you're a pink commando."

She smiled, nodding in acceptance. "I like it. Alice Coleman—Pink Commando."

An Irate Governor

The arc of Tex Sawyer's life propelled him to this moment in history—the moment when the Republic of Texas would rightfully reclaim its status as a sovereign nation. But far more important in Tex's mind than a realized Republic was an honest-to-God air force under his personal command. He had wanted to join the military, the U.S. Air Force his obvious first choice, but they wouldn't have him. Their damn commie shrink said he had sociopathic tendencies. As far as Tex was concerned the Air Force and all those other bastards keeping him out of the sky could go foxtrot themselves. He could fly circles around any of them and willingly, hell, happily drop nuclear weapons on anybody stupid enough to foxtrot with him.

Then Bruce Reynolds walked into his world with the hope and promise of fulfilling his life's purpose. Not only was he now the architect and builder of the Republic's Air Force, he was its chief pilot and commanding officer, reporting directly to the self-appointed President of the Republic. He figured Reynolds would hold elections once they freed Texas from the tyranny of all those left-wing progressives, atheists, and gay people in Austin.

On the cusp of a day Texian children would surely be talking about for years to come, General Tex Sawyer, Commander in Chief of the Air Force of the Republic of Texas, stood ready behind his well-trained crew of pilots, each controlling an armed drone. He had argued for a full-on assault of Lackland Air Force Base in San Antonio. Hit the bastards where they least expect it. But Reynolds insisted on a smaller target. Something to demonstrate strength, without creating an all-out war immediately. Maybe Reynolds had a point, but he sure hoped the negotiations would get bogged down some so he'd have a chance to stick it to all those aviation assholes in every branch of the military.

His target today, Marfa Municipal Airport, stood like a gem in the desert, its hangars protecting privately owned planes and gliders. Its runways were a little overgrown and cracked, but still viable. He wondered if they should be blowing up fellow Texian property, but Reynolds insisted the good people of Marfa would understand their sacrifice would make the Republic a reality. And indeed, Tex felt ready to sacrifice some drones for the cause, so why shouldn't these Marfa people? Besides, Reynolds reminded him that Marfa residents had allowed themselves to be tarnished by liberal ideas, modern art, and open air fornication.

His twenty drones took the municipal airport completely unguarded. They strafed aircraft tied down on the tarmac, dropping incendiaries on hangars. He even took out a corporate jet before it could take off. Then his wing of warriors evaporated over the hills, flying well below radar. A single fixed wing drone at ten thousand feet shot footage of flaming destruction streamed to Reynolds for his YouTube declaration of independence. Yes, Tex Sawyer had a swagger in his step. Through his leadership and superior air power, he took down the Marfa Municipal Airport and laid the groundwork for the new Republic.

~ * ~

Recovered YouTube Script
'Republic of Texas Declaration of Independence'

Background music: illegal download of Chris Rhea singing "Texas."
I'm going to Texas... I'm going to Texas...
[A shot of a blue flag with a gold star.]

Buzzard Bait

"My fellow Texians. As you know we have longed for decades to claim our rightful place as a sovereign nation. Today, we have thrown down the gauntlet of freedom."

[Cut to Marfa Airport in flames, a corporate jet explodes on the tarmac as executives run from the wreckage]

"The Air Force of the Republic of Texas has conducted a preemptory strike against those who would illegally enter our airspace and our country. For those of you who do not recognize the Republic, live under the delusion of being a state of the United States, or who live in Austin, an island of liberal debauchery, be warned. We will no longer tolerate any defilement of our national borders. To that end, we will continue our attacks until the invaders have been removed from our land or lie dead on Texas soil."

"These are difficult times in which we live. But I am heartened by the spirit, the compassion and the strength of the Texian people."

[Shots of compassionate, anglo Texians: old guy in cowboy hat smiling, nurse pushing a grandmother in a wheelchair, a mother breast feeding]

"I am reminded of a line from William Barret Travis's heroic speech at the Alamo, later falsely attributed by the American political elite to Benjamin Franklin."

[Artist's rendition of William Travis]

"We must all hang together or surely we will all hang separately. Now is not the time to cut and run, but the time to take up arms to secure a future for ourselves, our children and our liberty. Today is the end of Federal tyranny. But more importantly, today is a new day. It is morning in Texas."

[Shot of the sun rising over the Gulf of Mexico]

"God bless you and God bless the Republic of Texas."

[Fade to black]

~ * ~

166

Gov. Adamson paced her office, a glass of bourbon in her hand, Reynolds's "Declaration of Texas Independence" video still etched on her retinas. She could not believe Bruce would go off the reservation when she had explicitly told him not to make a move without her permission. *Dammit.* He always talked a good game, but she never believed he could really mount an attack. He said "soon," which in her world meant possibly next session, but don't hold your breath. She should have drowned that bastard when she had her legs wrapped around his scheming little head. *Who does he think he's dealing with? Some powerless little woman who won't put up a fight? Goddamn him to hell.*

The heavy door to her inner office clicked open. Her personal assistant Dennis poked his head through. "Governor?"

"Did I not make myself perfectly clear? I do not want to be disturbed."

"Yes, ma'am. It's just—"

"Goddammit, son. What part of do not disturb confuses you? 'Cause if you're having trouble with the English, I'm happy to ship your sorry ass out of here. I don't care what your daddy has to say about it."

Dennis looked like a child about to poop his pants. He licked his lips. "Yes, ma'am. It's just that you said you'd take a call from Mr. Bruce Reynolds anytime, day or night."

She turned her back to hide her reaction, a wave of despair washing over her. She had allowed a clearly deranged man to trample on her beloved state under her watch. "I don't think Reynolds will be calling."

"No, Governor. He's on the line. Now."

She took a deep breath, regaining her composure. "I'll take it on line one."

Sitting behind her desk, she scanned her surroundings, taking in the power and authority of her position. She picked up the phone.

"Frannie?"

"Bruce. I thought we had an agreement. You wouldn't make a move until I gave the word."

"I know, Fran, but you see, I've made other plans."

"Other plans? What other plans?"

"You know how much I care about you, Frannie. Hell, we're good together. But I know you. When we create our Republic you're going to want to be President. You wouldn't be the woman I love if you didn't."

"What does this have to do with blowing up a municipal airport?"

"Everything, Frannie. You see, I'm a success because I never settle for second. When I buy two hospitals in a market and shut one down, it's not just good business. The one I shut down is a loser, second best. I will not be associated with mediocrity."

"Bruce, destroying property is not going to resurrect your cherished Republic."

He laughed. "It's my Republic now, is it? You know Frannie, I don't think you ever wanted Texas to have its freedom. I think you like it just the way it is."

"Listen to me, Bruce. You've had your fun. I get your point. You're serious about a Republic. But you've got to understand, no matter what I say in public, we're woven into the fabric of this country. Tearing Texas out of that whole cloth will cause irreparable damage."

Bruce shouted back so loudly Fran pulled the phone away from her ear. "The Republic of Texas is its own whole cloth, perfect and ordained."

How did she not see this coming? "You're a fucking lunatic. Why did you call anyway, if all you were going to do is spout diatribes like a middle grader on a debate team?"

"I called to offer you a hand in partnership. I will be President of our great Republic, but I had hoped you would stand at my side as my Secretary of State." He paused. "But I let my desire get in the way of my judgment."

"If you're trying to say you're a dickhead, I can't agree more."

"You will regret your treatment of me, Governor. We execute traitors to the Republic, so I would suggest you leave Texas, which will soon be my sovereign nation, in the very near future."

She considered what to say in this moment. What statesman-like words she should use to convey her moral and patriotic outrage. Something school children would learn when studying the history of the state a century from now, like "Remember the Alamo!"

She settled on two words.

"Bruce?"

"Yes?"

"Fuck you."

Escape

When Nick called the Governor's direct line she immediately picked up.

"Governor?"

"I'm assuming you need something, since you called my private line."

Nick explained what had happened, from being shot down by drones to their brief interrogation and Tex's delay due to a mission.

"Yes, I just got the news some drones flattened the municipal airport in Marfa."

"Why would anyone attack Marfa?"

The line went silent. Nick pulled the phone away, checking to be sure he still had a signal.

"Mr. Sibelius, it's time we put Mr. Sawyer out of business."

Nick gave her the coordinates and as much as he knew about the buildings, size of the force and terrain. He also asked her to let Theresa know about their status. She promised to have boots on the ground in an hour, so all they had to do was survive until they arrived.

A buzz of a thousand angry bees filled the air. The drones returning from their mission. Tex would be back before the National Guard could get to them. Nick and Alice slipped through a back door. Scanning the area, they saw two more large hangars, one on either side of them. Behind the hangar, semi-arid desert spread out as far as Nick could see. They could make a run for the desert, but Tex had men, Humvees and drones to quickly hunt them down. Alice seemed to have come to the same conclusion. Then

Nick's eyes fell on a ladder lying on the ground by the hangar. A darker shade of gray halfway up the corrugated steel wall betrayed an incomplete paint job. Nick stepped over, hauling the ladder up.

"What are you doing?"

"We'll use this to get on the roof. I'll have the advantage up there and it's the last place they'll look for us."

Alice nodded with approval. "Nice thinking."

Together they expanded the ladder as high as it would go. To reach the roof, they'd have to take it between the buildings with a lower roof line. Exposed, they quickly positioned the ladder. Nick had Alice go first. With her wounded arm, she'd be slower and Nick would be able to provide cover, if needed. Fortunately, she made it to the top and onto the roof. Nick slung his rifle over a shoulder, clambering up to join her. Two-thirds of his way to the top, voices echoed between the two adjoining hangars. Sawyer's men were back. Nick froze as the voices got louder until they were directly below him. If one of them looked up, he'd be dead.

"Hey, man. Got a cigarette?"

"Why you always bumming cigs off me, man. Jesus. I'm not a damned vending machine."

"Do you have one, or not?"

"Yeah, yeah. Here you go. But stop asking me. Okay?"

"Last time, man."

"The last time was the last time."

"Got a light?"

The voices moved away.

"Goddammit. Get your own damned lighter."

"Come on, man. What good's a smoke without a light?"

"All right. All right. Jesus."

The voices faded behind the hangar. Nick took the last few rungs, silently pulling himself up onto the roof, then rolling over beside a prone Alice.

171

She whispered to him, "We won't be able to lower the ladder without drawing any attention. Hopefully, they'll just think someone left it there when they were painting."

Nick moved to the far side, giving him a view of the entrances to the other two hangars, another building with antennas and satellite dishes he assumed must be a control room of some kind, and a row of single story Quonset huts, which were probably barracks. He could hear Tex ranting below him.

"Golf-delta. Sierra-oscar-bravo! I give you one golf-delta thing to do and I discover you've got your head so far up your alpha-hotel you couldn't be trusted to tell me if the foxtrotting sun was rising. Son, get the foxtrot out of my golf-delta sight. If I ever see you again, I will split you open like a watermelon, rip your foxtrottin' heart out, and eat it while you foxtrottin' watch. Got it, alpha-hotel? Now get away from me. Juliette and the foxtrottin' angels. Golf-delta-foxtrottin' hell."

Yeah. He was pretty pissed. His men ran this way and that, checking the hangars and each barrack. When they came up scratch, Tex deployed five helicopter drones armed with what looked like little missiles. Four flew out over the desert on the four cardinal directions. The fifth, executing a perimeter search of the facility, would be trouble. Alice had taken up a position next to Nick. Without a gun she could only watch at this point. All the helicopter drone needed to do was fly over them and they'd be spotted immediately.

Alice sighed. "This is not looking good."

"Take this and give me cover if I need it." Nick handed her his gun. "And if that helicopter comes after you, shoot it down." He crawled away.

"Where are you going?"

"I have control issues."

He made his way to the ladder, which still rested against the roof. He took each rung, careful to make as little noise as possible. Once on the ground he tipped the ladder over, walking it hand over hand until he had it resting on asphalt.

Staying near the wall, he made his way behind the building, then dashed to the next hangar. Creeping to its front corner, he spied a building bristling with antennas fifty yards from his position. The control center. Running across the tarmac in the open would be like putting a target on his back. Instead, he put hands in his pockets, strolling across. He reminded himself if he looked like he owned the place people would assume he belonged there. Once at the door, he grasped the knob, which to his surprise turned to open. Tex must feel very secure out here. Once inside, he stood in a hallway with a door on either side. He opened the door to his right. Several rows of monitors glowed over controls resembling what Dillon used to fly his RC plane. One man sat at the controls of what Nick guessed must be a helicopter drone, while another looked over the drone pilot's shoulder.

Movement to his immediate right caught Nick's attention. He turned as a gun muzzle swung up level with his head. Nick grabbed his attacker's wrist, forcing the gun up. His attacker kneed him in the gut, but Nick held on, taking the man down with him. They struggled for control, both sets of hands around the gun. Hard steel pressing into his chest, he thrust his finger behind the trigger just before his attacker squeezed with crushing force. They stared at each other, grimacing, fighting to survive, when Nick shifted his weight, wrenching the gun away. The man stunned him with a punch to the face, but Nick marshaled his strength, shoving the weapon up into the man's gut, then squeezing the trigger. His attacker's body jerked, lead tearing into him, his viscera muffling the blast.

The second man, having heard the commotion, reached for his weapon from a waist holster. Nick pivoted, keeping his attacker's gun embedded in his body. Bullets exploded out of the now dead carcass, hitting the second man in the chest and head. The force of Nick's shots took the man off his feet, slamming him into the pilot, who reached for his gun.

Nick kept a calm, menacing tone in his voice. "Fly the drone or die."

The pilot hesitated, pushing his dead colleague away, then took back control of his drone. He may have followed Nick's instruction, but he didn't sound rattled at all. "They'll find you and kill you. Why not just surrender?"

"Shut up and fly the drone."

"You know, I don't think so." He pushed away, calling Nick's bluff, his drone now flying without any direction.

Nick rushed over, keeping his gun on the pilot while grabbing the stick. He'd have to put the gun down to control the aircraft. "Get on your knees, hands behind your head."

"You're making a mistake, buddy. There's no way you get out of here alive."

"On your knees or you'll be as dead as your friends."

Nick had to look away from the pilot, only for a moment, to check his controls. A bolt of pain exploded across his shoulder as the gun flew away from him, pieces of glass and plastic raining down. The bastard had smashed him with a flat screen, then tackled him to the ground. Nick struggled to get an advantage, but every move he made, the pilot countered. Nick knew each second he didn't have control of the drone lowered their chances of surviving until the governor's forces arrived.

The two struggled to their feet, the pilot connecting a punch to Nick's face. He fell back, flipping over a table. His attacker sprung into the air to pounce on him. Nick grabbed the sharpest thing at hand, a ball point pen, impaling the pilot in his stomach, as he crashed down on him. Still fighting, the pilot grabbed Nick's throat, pressing thumbs into his trachea. Thick, warm liquid gushed over Nick's hand as he continued to jab the man's gut. His vision narrowed, a tunnel between himself and a face filled with rage, until his attacker's grasp slackened, and then his body draped limp across him. Nick pushed the man away. Drenched in blood, he took in deep breaths to get his head clear, then wiped his bloody hands on the back of the dead man's shirt. He had to get to the drone.

Back at the controls, he took a moment to regain a sense of the vertical and horizontal. Fortunately, the drone had gone into autopilot mode when the pilot stepped away. It must have been hovering in place the entire time they fought. Swinging the helicopter around, he gained a bird's-eye view of Sawyer's operation. Then he saw men gathered behind several Humvees, firing at the roof. Alice lay prone, rifle in hand. A flash from her gun, then a man below, shot in the chest, sprawled to the ground. Nick flew the helicopter behind her attackers, who he hoped would assume the drone worked for them. He had two firing options labeled one and two. He used the built-in scope to aim, then took a chance, pressing one. A rocket shot from his drone, slamming into the center Humvee. It exploded in a fireball. Sawyer's other men turned their guns on his drone, one bullet shaking it, but then a second doing serious damage. The world twirled around and around, racing to the ground, then his screen went black.

He grabbed a Glock off the dead pilot's body, then stepped back out into the hallway, cracking open a door to the outside. Alice still lay pinned on the roof. The pilots for the desert chopper drones must be through the other door. If he let those drones come back they'd easily take her out. He turned the knob. There had to be four men in this room. A suicide mission. But he couldn't let Alice die without trying to save her. He put one hand on the door knob, his other at the ready with a handgun. Outside, small arms fire rattled, then booming explosions. The Texas National Guard.

Nick threw the door open, firing. He caught the first pilot, who went down immediately. The others dove for cover, firing back with side arms. Nick retreated out the door. All he had to do was keep them busy. He hoped the guy who owned the Glock kept a full clip. Nick moved back into the room, using tables for cover. One pilot rose, firing

175

several rounds. Nick rolled to his right, catching sight of the shooter between two tables. He fired. The man groaned, followed by a clicking sound of a gun falling to the concrete floor. Two more to go. Another jumped up, firing rapidly. A back door slammed open, the men's footfalls echoing off the floor as they escaped outside. Nick followed them out, but they had already disappeared around the building.

He picked his way back to the hangar, using buildings and vehicles as cover. Men lay dead, scattered across the tarmac. Several cars and a van sat parked in the distance. Behind one of the cars he could make out Theresa. *What the hell is she doing here?* He worked his way toward her, calling out so the guardsmen wouldn't drop him where he stood.

"What are you doing here?"

"Good to see you too, Nick."

"Theresa—"

"The governor called to tell me you and Alice had gotten yourselves in a little fix. I thought I'd come out to help. Oh, and you're welcome."

"Thanks."

Nick scanned the assortment of men in a variety of jeans and hunting fatigues. Not National Guardsmen. "Who are these guys?"

"Well, the governor wanted the situation handled, but didn't want anyone to know about it. This is some kind of covert assault team of hers."

"She has a covert assault team?" Nick figured they were all law enforcement.

"All I was interested in was saving your ass, so I didn't quibble with her."

"How's it going?"

"We've got them trapped in the hangar over there. Alice is fine and getting her wound tended to."

Nick checked his clip for rounds. "The control center for the drones is disabled. So, the drones Tex sent out looking for us won't be circling back to attack."

"Great. The team's about to breach the hangar."

176

"Okay, Theresa. Let's do this."

Smoke grenades cascaded into the hangar, quickly filling it with thick, gray smoke. Sawyer's men stumbled out, coughing, tossing their weapons. One of the governor's assault team grabbed each man, binding his hands with zip ties behind his back and sitting him on the ground. A female member of the team came out last, leading Tex Sawyer away from the hangar.

She bound his hands as he ranted. "As a military leader of the sovereign Republic of Texas, I demand treatment according to the Geneva Convention. I am General Tex Sawyer, Commander in Chief of the Air Force of the Republic of Texas. You will release me or suffer the consequences."

Nick stepped up to Tex. "The Republic of Texas didn't sign the Geneva Convention, Tex. But you'll have plenty of time in prison to catch up on your Texas history." He walked away from another nut case he ended up having to stop, mumbling to himself. "How do I get these cases? Why not a divorce? A missing person? No, I have to get the whack jobs."

Theresa caught up with him. "What are you going on about?"

Nick shook his head. "I just want a normal case. Just one. Is that too much to ask?" He turned, Theresa walking beside him. "And what are you doing here? This is the very thing I wanted you to avoid."

"Don't be an ass, Nick. There's no way in hell you're in the crapper and I'm not here to help. No way."

They walked across the tarmac to a waiting van. Alice already sat in the front passenger seat. Nick opened the side door, turning to Theresa. "Thanks."

She studied him, as if her gaze could get past his barriers, his fears, his history. "No problem. This saving thing goes both ways."

~ * ~

Buzzard Bait

After the governor's team dropped them off at the airport in Georgetown, Alice went into the flight center to talk to the manager about recovering her plane. Nick and Theresa stood in the flight school parking lot.

"Thanks for coming to our rescue, Theresa. I really appreciate it."

She hesitated, as if deciphering some code in his words. "Didn't think I'd hear you say those words. You're welcome. We're business partners, and Nick, we're friends, too."

All the things getting in their way—out of control bass boats, drug-tainted sex, missed conversations—rushed through his mind. He had to sort things out with her. "About us. Theresa, I haven't had a chance to tell you. Bobbi drugged the beer you drank back at the trailer."

Her loving smile went to a straight line. "Drugged? With what?"

"A roofy."

"A date rape drug? I don't understand."

"I guess she planned on incapacitating, then killing me. Less dramatic than a Claymore, but still effective."

"How did I get it?"

"She must have switched the beers when I wasn't looking."

She sighed, looking up to the sky. "So, I didn't take a shower and go to bed, did I?"

"Not exactly. We kind of, well..."

She glared at him, her voice tinged with the sharp tones of an accusation. "What did you do?"

"Slow down. I didn't know you were drugged. I just thought you were particularly, well, passively horny."

"What did we do, Nick?"

In hindsight he realized he should have known something wasn't right. Theresa never took a completely passive role. But in the moment, his testosterone-driven mind had reasoned she was tired from a long day and enjoying the ride. He smiled weakly, more out of embarrassment than memory. "We made love."

"We made love or did you make love and I was conveniently in the room?"

"Look, you're right. I should have known something was off when you didn't take much of an active role. I just thought you were really tired. Afterward, we talked. I told you how scared I was of losing you and that I realized I had been holding on too tightly. I told you how much I love you. I do, you know, love you."

She turned her back to him. Things were bad enough between them, now this would surely deep-six them for good.

"Theresa."

Her shoulders shook. *Crap. She's crying right in the middle of the parking lot. How do I keep hurting this woman?*

"Please, Theresa. Talk to me."

She looked back, a tear rolling down one cheek, but her mouth open, laughing. "So, you had a heartfelt one-on-one with an unconscious woman?"

Nick laughed nervously. He wasn't sure if she saw humor in the whole episode or if this was some kind of trap. "Yeah, I guess so."

"Did we have a good talk?"

"I thought we did."

Her laughter faded away. "I'm sorry I missed it."

"Me too. Maybe we can try again, eyes open this time."

She put her hands on his chest. "All I've ever wanted is for you to love me as an equal. I love you, but I'm not going to be your burden."

"You're not."

She stood up on her toes, kissing him gently on his lips. "Yes, I am."

Alice's alto voice broke through the bubble they had created around them. "You two need to get a room or I'll need to turn the hose on you."

Alice had changed into shorts and a pink polo. Theresa took a step away, her mouth in a slight smile, but her eyes sad with regret. "I'll wait for you in the truck, Nick. I'll give Dillon a call with the good news."

Alice strode to Nick, her head cocked knowingly. "My, my. Looks like Nicholas and Theresa have worked things out. Excellent."

Nick ignored her comment. "Alice, you were great out there today."

"Thank you, Nick."

"But I am sorry about your plane. And the arm too."

She glanced at her sling, off-white against her pink shirt. "Oh, this? Just a few stitches. I guess I'll have to hold off on spaghetti straps for a while. And don't worry about the plane. It's insured."

"From damage caused by armed drones?"

"You're forgetting my boyfriend. Johnnie will take care of it. Which reminds me. I need a favor."

"Sure, Alice. Anything."

She put her free hand on his shoulder. "Don't tell Johnnie about me being shot in the arm. The poor dear will go crazy, probably insist on coming to Austin, then hover over me for days, if not weeks."

"Sounds like he loves you, Alice. Why not let him be here for you?"

"It's hard enough being a transgendered woman in this world. I'm not going to add being a woman who's reliant on a man."

He looked over to his truck. Theresa was on the phone in the cab. "You know he only wants to hold you close because he loves you. There's nothing wrong with that."

"You said you'd do anything."

"Yeah, I did."

"Then do what I ask. I'll tell him when the time's right, but I don't need some man to come racing over here to save me. Okay?"

"Okay. But why don't you take a few days off? I don't think getting shot is part of your job description. Take a long weekend, pamper yourself. We'll start back on Monday."

"Hmmm. I have been meaning to take a spa day." She leaned over, pecking Nick's cheek with a quick kiss. "Thank you, Nicholas. You're a sweetie."

After parting ways with Alice, Nick lifted himself into his pickup, a bit sore from his adventures. At least Tex was off the street and Dillon would be safe. Job done. If only he could get his relationship turned around. He glanced at Theresa. She sat motionless, staring at her phone.

"What's going on? Something happen?"

"It's the governor."

"What does she want? Give us a medal or something?"

"I have no idea. Sounds urgent though. She wants us in her office within the hour."

The Republic Strikes Again

Sam Westerfield left his one-room apartment in the darkness of early morning. As usual, he got in a 2006 Suburban, picked up some coffee and a couple of donuts at the HEB grocery store, then made the twelve mile commute to his work, the George W. Bush Desalination Facility. He listened to a local talk show rant about the next election, then flipped to NPR. His wife, well, ex-wife Joan, liked listening to NPR. He'd never tell her, but when he listened to "Morning Edition," he somehow still felt connected to her. It had been only six months since the divorce. He'd moved out to a crappy apartment and she'd moved on. Some guy she met at church. Damn Christians. If they aren't trying to force their religion on you, they're stealing your women. He looked at the man staring back at him in the rearview mirror. Older and sadder than he remembered. He didn't really mean all of that about Christians. He just wanted to be back home, Joanie actually loving him, Christopher and Suzie sitting on the couch with him. God, he missed the kids. He wasn't the best dad in the world, he'd admit to it. But seeing them only every other weekend made a mediocre dad worse. They'd hang out, but he felt increasingly awkward, unsure of what to say and out of touch with their teenaged lives.

Passing the security check, he pulled into his parking space, then walked to the door he went through five days a week, fifty weeks out of the year. He liked his job at the plant and he liked being an engineer, but with the divorce he found his routine monotonous. Life was increasingly short and he was pissing it away in slow motion.

R. W. Hacker

Flipping on his office lights, he scanned his little eight-by-eight domain, turning on his laptop, and noticing the files waiting for his attention. But before he sat down, he stepped back into the hallway then out a door, up some steel stairs, and along a gangway high above the plant. Cool, humid morning air buffeted his face. He sipped his coffee, the sun a reddish orange slit peeking out from the horizon. Standing on the gangplank, sipping coffee as the sun rose in the east constituted the best moment of his day. When he didn't want to get up with his alarm, he'd remind himself of his gangplank, then force himself into the shower to start the day. Always peaceful. And this morning proved no exception.

Over the din of the plant—the sounds of water rushing through pipe, pumps driving liquids, a truck delivering materials—he heard something odd. A buzz. Yes, like a thousand bees. But these looked like giant birds. The buzzing increased in intensity. He didn't think to run, mesmerized by a fleet of thirty, maybe forty winged things. Planes?

A flash, then an explosion. *Pop, pop, pop.* A fire ball rose to his left, then sharp pains stabbed into his stomach, up his chest and to his cheek. He dropped his coffee. Explosions all around him now. He looked down. Five small holes traced up his torso. A hand to his burning cheek came back bloody. His blood.

He knew he needed to move, but he felt so tired. So weary. If only Joanie were here. They'd go away. Maybe Hawaii. She always liked Hawaii. He lowered himself on the gangplank, sounds muffled, light scattered. He'd wait for her. He laid his head on the metal grating. Yes, he'd wait for her.

~ * ~

Nick and Theresa walked through the rotunda of the state capitol, then up a wide staircase, following the edge of a balcony to a large oak door which took them into the governor's offices. Nick knew things were in a crisis when

183

her personal assistant didn't have them wait for an hour, but instead led them immediately into her office.

They found Governor Adamson standing before a massive desk, a Lone Star state flag behind it. On one wall hung a large thirteen-point buck, on another, photographs of the governor with several presidents, a UN Secretary-General, some sports Hall of Famers, and a few Teddy Roosevelt-style pictures of her standing over dead animals she had slain with her high-powered rifle. Small in stature, she still filled the room with her charisma.

"Where the hell have you been?"

"Good to see you, Governor. This is my partner, Theresa Soliz."

Theresa stepped over to shake her hand.

Governor Adamson took it in both of hers. She met Theresa's eyes. "You've taken care of business?"

Theresa looked to Nick, then back to the governor. "Yes, ma'am."

She dropped Theresa's hand and walked around her desk toward her leather chair embossed in gold with the state seal. Nick figured she probably had "The Gov" stenciled on the back.

"You've taken care of our situation, eh? Don't lie to a politician, darling. We deal in lies." Before Theresa could respond, Governor Adamson continued. "You didn't answer my question, Nick. Where the hell have you been?"

Nick motioned to Theresa to sit down in one of the two chairs in front of Adamson's desk. He sat in the other. "We were keeping a crazy from setting up an air force to take over your state, Governor."

"Right. Tex. The son of a bitch." She pounded her desk with a fist. "To hell with lethal injection. I'm going to string that asshole to a tree and use him for a piñata, goddammit."

"You might get some push back, Governor. I don't think lynching is legal in the state anymore."

She leaned in, her face red with anger. "You think this is funny?"

184

"It's over, that's what it is. We got him." Nick shook his head. This woman needed to run a marathon, or get laid. Something.

Her brow furrowed, a rage just below the surface. "What?"

"I've never seen you quite so worked up. This Tex guy got to you, I take it."

She stood, pacing the room. "Tex? He's nothing. And no, Nick, we didn't stop a damned thing."

"What are you talking about? He's been arrested, the drones destroyed."

She picked up a file off her desk, tossing it to Nick. "I'm saying Tex wasn't the ringleader you made him out to be. You see those pictures?"

"Looks like a refinery fire or something."

"It's something all right. My desalination plant got blown to hell and back this morning, while you were making Texas safe from Tex."

"There are more drones? Do you know who's behind it?"

"I got this message just an hour ago." She tossed him a letter.

Nick read aloud. "Using my mighty air force to dominate Texas air space, I will destroy critical infrastructure until the state formally renounces statehood and reclaims its rightful place as a sovereign Republic of Texas declaring Bruce Reynolds as President of the Republic."

He handed the letter to Theresa, who scanned the document. "Crap."

Governor Adamson stood behind her desk, hands on her hips, waiting for Nick's reaction.

"Bruce Reynolds. The healthcare guy wants to be the president of a new republic?"

"Over my goddamned dead body!" She slammed her fists on the desk.

"Why don't you call out the National Guard? Have the Texas Rangers arrest him?"

The governor paced again, like a caged predator tormented by her captors. "Are you out of your fucking mind? What do think they'll do to me if it looks like I let some whack job almost take over the entire goddamn state? Besides, what you didn't see that accompanied the letter were photographs of me in a compromising position with our little Hitler wannabe."

"Supporting his secession plan?"

She stood in the middle of the room, her eyes aflame with rage, spittle flying with every word. "No, not supporting his secession plan. Personally compromising."

Nick stood, sighing as he absorbed the full meaning of what she said. "Oh, so you and Reynolds had a relationship." For a moment tears welled in her eyes as she massaged the back of her neck with one hand. Nick considered comforting her, but then thought better of it. "Don't you think a few nude pictures pale in the face of a statewide revolution?"

She glared. "Don't be an idiot, Nick. They'll crucify me. Every paper, radio show, and goddamn digital news outlet will be tweeting my ass right into oblivion. Can you imagine me making a second run for president when I can't even keep my bare ass out of the papers and my own damned state in the Union?"

"You're running for president again?" Theresa blurted the words.

"It doesn't goddamn matter. Maybe. I haven't decided. But I sure as hell don't like some two-bit pseudo revolutionary taking away my options." Governor Adamson walked back around to her desk chair. "I'm not sure I could get re-elected to governor, hell, city council member, with this shit happening."

Theresa dropped the letter on the governor's desk. "Plus, he's threatening the economy and the safety of the state."

"Yeah, yeah, yeah. Whatever you need to say to yourself. Bottom line, we're ending this asshole. Today."

Nick asked, "You want me to stop Reynolds?"

"Yes, I want you to stop Reynolds. What do you think I've been talking about?"

"I understand the political pressures you're under, but don't you think this is something for law enforcement to handle?"

She leaned into her desk, eyeing him.

"Sit down, Nick."

He hesitated, then lowered himself into the chair.

"I'm forming a special unit, a Governor's Task Force, to handle sensitive matters involving the security of the state. You and your business partner are the first two members of this elite group under your leadership."

"I appreciate you thinking of me, but you still need to bring in the Texas Rangers."

She chuckled. "I knew you'd say something like that. So much integrity. It's rare these days, Nick. So, here's the deal. I have substantial evidence your girlfriend..." She glanced at Theresa. "Sorry, darling. Your ex-girlfriend, MaryLou Perkins, murdered a man. Jason Black."

"You wouldn't."

"Wait for it. I also have evidence you let her go not once, but twice. And then you let a known criminal, Cherry Swenson, roam free."

"I don't believe you."

"Roam free to impale my boy's ass with her damned bicycle spokes."

Theresa turned to Nick. "Is this true?"

"Yeah, Nick." The governor challenged him with a slight smile. "Is this true? Tell her."

Nick had failed to share the whole story with Theresa, but he drew the line at outright lying. "Yeah, it's true."

"Jesus, Nick."

The governor continued. "So, the way I see it, I've got you as an accessory to murder and assault, as well as providing assistance to a felon, several times over. You're going love my prison system. All the orange jumpsuits you want to wear and a very small cell for years."

Nick shook his head, disgusted at himself and her. "You're a mean, coldhearted bitch."

"Thank you, darling. But giving me compliments isn't going to make your life better. Maybe I should put this in a different light. You can be the leader of the most elite enforcement team in the state of Texas, handling cases under the direction of the Governor's Office, or you can spend the rest of your adult life in prison."

Nick rose, anger rushing in his chest. "I should rip your damned head off."

Theresa grabbed his arm, pulling him back. "Nick, stop. You think killing a governor is going to solve anything?"

"It won't solve anything, but it'll sure feel good."

She looked at the governor. "Could Nick and I have a few moments?"

"Sure, I'll step into my side office. Mind you, if he walks out my door, I'll have my beloved Texas Rangers all over his ass in a heartbeat."

With the governor away, Theresa glared at Nick, her arms across her chest.

"You told me about MaryLou, but you forgot to mention the whole helped-her-murder-a-guy thing. Don't you think it would have been good to tell me something like that?"

"What was I supposed to do? 'Hey, by the way, you know that woman I was seeing? Well, she shot the man who killed my partner, so I let her get away with it.'"

"Yeah, that would have done it. Just a little heads up. 'I aided and abetted a felon, Theresa. Just want you to know.'"

"What good would it have done?"

"Do you have any more secrets I should know about? Any felonies outstanding? Murders committed across state lines?"

"Yeah, funny." Nick paced the room.

"I'm not joking, Nick Sibelius. If you can't tell me the truth about MaryLou, then how am I supposed to trust you?

188

We're business partners. What you do on the job impacts our business together."

"Oh, my mistake. I thought this was about us. But no, it's about the business."

"Don't you dare go there. You know how I feel about you. But the business is a different matter. I've got my life savings wrapped up in this and I just find out the governor can pretty much string you up by the balls and slap you senseless anytime she wants."

He stopped in front of a wild pig's head, eyes fierce, teeth bared. He turned back to Theresa. "I'm not going to let her do it. She's not going to force me into some special task force."

"You're not. You *want* to go to prison?"

"No, but I'm not going to let her dictate terms to me."

"Think, Nick. You go to prison and you're done. We're done, the business is done. If you do ever get out, you know you'll have to leave the state just to get a job."

"What do want me to do, Theresa? Just go along with her plan?"

"Yes."

"What?"

"Listen to me. Go along with her, form her task force, be the leader. It'll buy you time to find some leverage in this mess you're in. And you have to admit, being on an enforcement task force reporting to the governor will give you the ability to help people and not waste your time taking photographs of illicit lovers for divorce lawyers."

Nick looked at her. She had a point. Frannie would definitely put him behind bars and throw away the key. The woman could hold a grudge for years. In the task force he'd at least still be walking free and able to figure some way of getting out from under her thumb.

"Well?" Theresa's eyes pleaded him.

"Yeah, I guess I see your point. But if I do this, if we do this, job number one is to figure out how to get out from under her."

189

"Agreed."

A door to the side office opened on cue, as if, and in Nick's mind, exactly like Frannie had been listening the whole time.

"You've come to a decision, Nick? Do you work for me or do I sic the Texas Rangers on you?"

Nick stepped up to her. At five-one she looked small from his tall vantage point, but he knew from experience Frannie had more in common with a rabid badger than a cute kitten. "I'll run your task force, but what assurance do I have you won't use this against me in the future?"

She smiled, stepping behind her desk, then sitting down. "I've been studying you, Nick. A man of very high integrity, which is rare these days. Do I have your word you will serve as the director of my task force as long as I'm in office?"

He looked to Theresa, who nodded, then turned back to the governor. "Yeah, you have my word."

"Well, that's good enough for me." She pushed a thick manila envelope toward him. "Here's all the documentation of your alleged crimes. I'm giving this material to you because I know if I don't, you'll spend all your time trying to figure out how to get it. But more to the point, you're a man of your word, so I'm going to trust you."

Nick reached for the envelope.

The governor leaned across her desk, putting her hand on his. "Don't make me regret it."

He slipped the envelope out from under her hand. "Fran, you're a hard driving bitch of a woman."

"Thank you, Nick. Don't ever forget it."

Safe House

Before leaving the governor, Nick arranged to meet with Tex Sawyer, who was currently being held in a safe house outside of Austin. Quentin told him Governor Adamson had thanked him for his service to the state then requested he hand Tex over to several plainclothes DPS officers.

"What did you think?"

"I don't know, Nick. They could have been who she said they were, but I got this odd feeling around them, like they were CIA or something."

Nick figured she probably knew the CEO of a private security firm who sent agents to places like Iraq and Afghanistan and, in this case, Texas.

The house, a small two-bedroom bungalow nestled among cottonwood trees off a dirt road on 290 southwest of the city, made a difficult sniper target. A black SUV with blacked-out windows sat parked out front. A man in cowboy boots, jeans, a button-down white shirt under a bullet proof vest, and a Stetson stood by the bungalow door with an M4 assault rifle. He also carried a Glock 9mm on his hip and Nick figured he had an ankle weapon as well. This guy meant business.

Nick pulled up beside the SUV.

"Keep your hands where this guy can see them, Theresa."

They stepped out of the truck, hands raised, as the heavily armed man watched silently.

"I'm Nick Sibelius. The governor's task force. Here to see your prisoner."

He didn't lower his weapon. "We've been expecting you. I'll need to see some ID from both of you."

They both pulled out their licenses, holding them up. The man motioned them forward, examined the documents, then handed them back. "Come on through."

Entering the house, they found Tex Sawyer, still in uniform but without his gun belt, helmet and sunglasses, bound to a chair in an otherwise empty bedroom, his eyes shifting nervously. A young black man in his late twenties with a military buzz cut walked over to Nick. "We've been holding him here as instructed for your arrival. You must be very good at extracting information."

"Why do you say that?"

"Well, I volunteered to get him to talk." He smiled. "Sort of a hobby of mine. But my boss told me I needed to cool my jets. Said I made too much of a mess last time. But you know what my mama always used to say."

"What's that?"

"You gotta break a few eggs to make a cake." He laughed at his own joke, slapping Nick on the shoulder as he passed. "I'll leave you two to it."

Alone with Tex, Theresa shut the door. Nick stood in front of him, hands on his hips.

Tex stared at them, fear in his eyes. "Wh-what you going to do to me?"

"You're going away for a long time, Tex. Between the State and Federal charges, I don't imagine you'll see the outside for quite a while."

He swallowed, blood draining from his face. "You don't know what you're talking about. I want to see my lawyer."

Nick glanced over to Theresa, sharing a laugh with her. "Lawyers are for American citizens. You're not an American."

"I am too."

"I thought you were one of those Texians. That's what you call yourselves, right?"

"I demand to see my lawyer."

Theresa circled behind him. "Don't worry too much about spending time in prison, Tex. You've heard of the Diablos Tejanos?"

He twisted his head around, following her movement. "The cartel? What do they have to do with any of this?"

"Don't know how it happened, but they heard you've been supplying armed drones to their competitors on the border."

"Whoever said that is a liar, goddammit."

"Tex." Nick leaned in with a foot on Tex's chair. "It doesn't matter whether you did or didn't. All that matters when you're sitting in a tiny cell with no one to protect you is the Diablos think you crossed them."

"I just wanted to fly, you know. That's all I wanted." He looked to Nick, his voice quavering. "You gotta help me. Please."

"Here's the thing, Tex. You know how we found out about you, don't you?"

"Bobbi Shank?"

"No. Reynolds. He gave you up."

"Bruce Reynolds? You're lying."

"I'm telling you, he decided you were a liability." Nick turned to Theresa. "What was it he said? Oh, that's right, you're a stupid good ol' boy with some harebrained scheme to take over the state."

"What? No, he wouldn't."

Theresa pulled up a chair, sitting down across from Tex. "Oh, yes he would. See, we went by his office, thinking he was the leader of some crazy Republic of Texas militia, but it turned out it was you."

"He's lying. The son of a bitch. He recruited me, goddammit!"

"You're saying he's the leader and he's setting you up?"

"That's exactly what I'm saying."

Nick looked to Theresa. "I don't know, Theresa. Sounds too easy. Tex here knows how to build drones. He even had a facility where he kept them all. Called himself the

Commander in Chief of the Republic's air force. No, Tex is definitely our guy."

"I'm not your guy. Lady, what's your name?"

"Theresa."

"Theresa, you know I'm telling the truth. Bruce Reynolds recruited me into his militia and put me in charge of creating a drone air force. Well, I had to do it. Don't you see? I've spent my life barely scraping by, then suddenly I've got all the resources I need to build anything I want? But he's the mastermind. Not me. I'm just a little cog in the machinery."

She shook her head. "I want to believe you, Tex, but I've got to say, I don't think you're being totally honest with us."

He looked back and forth between Nick and Theresa. "Honest? Of course I'm being honest."

"Well, what about the other drones, the ones not at the West Texas facility?"

Tex rolled his eyes, shaking his head. "You didn't ask me about those, now did you?"

"Oh, so you're only going to answer questions we ask?" Nick stood up, motioning for Theresa to do the same.

"Whoa, where you goin'?"

"If you're not going to tell us the truth, Tex, you're just wasting our time. There's a guy out here who's been sharpening his knife just to have a chance to talk with you."

"This is America. You can't detain me and then let some crazy slice me up to get information. I've got rights."

"I thought you wanted a Republic?" Nick turned to Theresa. "What was that guy's name?"

"Are you sure, Nick? Once we go down this path, we'll have blood all over our hands."

Nick glared at Tex. "I'm up for a bloodbath if that's what it takes. And if he survives, the Diablos will finish him off."

She put a hand on his shoulder, a sadness flitting on her face. "I'll bring him in."

"Hold on, golf-delta. Hold on. I didn't say I wouldn't talk, now, did I?"

194

Theresa turned back to Tex, concern in her voice. "If you're not going to be completely forthcoming, we don't have a choice. I'm sorry."

"Forthcoming, I'll give you forthcoming. Reynolds stashed my drones in a farm southwest of San Antonio. Give me a map and I'll give you the coordinates. Nobody hangs Tex Sawyer out to dry."

~ * ~

With new intel from Tex, Nick and Theresa drove back down the dirt road to Highway 290. Nick got on the phone. "Governor. Yes, we've spoken to him. I've got the locations for the other drone base. Yes. No, I'm not giving you the coordinates. Not unless you have DPS remove him safely from the safe house. What's that? Well, that's how I'm playing it. You can either play or fold. Yes...uh, huh. Damn you to hell too, ma'am."

Theresa asked, "Do we have a problem?"

"Nope. I just asked Fran if she wouldn't mind arranging for the DPS to pick up Tex from that deranged commando in there and she said she wouldn't mind at all."

"Why do I think you're not telling me everything?"

"I'm not sure about the governor. I'd like to think she wouldn't kill someone to protect her reputation in the state, but I'm not taking any chances. This way Tex will get to a Huntsville prison cell in one living, breathing piece."

~ * ~

Tex smiled to himself when Sibelius and the woman left his interrogation room. Not only had he kept the Republic's secrets, he managed to misdirect them in the process. He wondered how long it would take them to figure out they'd been duped. The black guy stepped back in, a seriously scary smile on his face. He pulled up a chair, flipping it around to straddle it right in front of him.

"Sounds like you gave it up to Sibelius."

Tex had that puking feeling. "Yeah, yeah. I had to talk. He forced it outta me."

"Did he now." The commando pulled a fighting knife from his vest. Tex could only imagine how many blades this guy carried around on his person. He put the gleaming edge of steel on Tex's cheek, stroking it down, the edge oriented up. "I wonder if you told them everything you know."

"Oh, yessir. I did. Every last thing."

He positioned his blade behind Tex's ear. Tex felt a dribble of warm blood roll down his neck. God, he liked his ear.

"Hmmm. I don't know, Tex. I've got a feeling about you."

A *pop, pop, thud*, caught his tormentor's attention. The man slipped his blade into a slot on his vest, then pulled his handgun as he swiveled away from the chair to the door. "Don't make a sound, Tex. Or I'll come back and take both your ears off."

The man crept away, leaving Tex alone for what seemed like hours, but was probably only minutes.

Finally, overwhelmed by silence, Tex had to speak. "Hey, what's going on?"

No response.

"You gotta talk to me. It's part of the Geneva Convention."

Pop. Thud. Bang, bang. Pop. Thud.

"Shit." Tex didn't like the sound of this. Didn't like it at all. Footsteps moved toward the door of the eight-by-eight room he'd sat in for the last twelve hours. "Who's out there? I've got my rights, you know." *Who am I kidding? That Sibelius guy figured he had what he needed. Now he's taking everyone out, so there'll be no witnesses.* "You don't want to do this, whoever you are."

The door crashed open and banged against the wall. A man in black, including a full facemask, his handgun sporting a suppressor, stepped inside.

Tex, fear crawling all over him, sat tied in place. "Who are you? What do you want?"

The man pulled the nastiest blade from a sheath on his leg. God, he'd rather take a shot in the head than be stabbed to death. The masked gunman strode toward him, Tex about to throw up. Then the knife-wielding man reached behind Tex, cutting his bindings.

"I'm here for you, General. The Republic needs you."

Tex let out a deep breath and hoped his savior couldn't smell the pee dribbling down his pant leg. "Damn straight, young man." *What a relief. Jesus.*

"President Reynolds's orders are to take you to Alamo Base to lead Firebird."

Firebird. The codename for the Republic's initial assault against strategic oil refineries on the Texas coast. The planning, the engineering, the training all coming to fruition. He'd need a change of clothes. A man can't create history in piss-soaked pants. At least he'd never heard of anyone doing it. They ran out of the safe house past three dead bodies. Tex didn't like being so physically close to death. He preferred killing by remote control, then seeing the damage on a television screen. His rescuer led him to a black pickup, then they raced away into the night.

South of San Antonio

Dashing down a highway toward the site of Sawyer's drones, Nick got a call, putting it on speaker phone. "Governor. Like I told you before, I'll give you the coordinates after I check out the site we got from Tex."

"I need the coordinates, Nick."

"What you need is for me to confirm the information, Governor. You don't want to go in if he's feeding us bad intel."

"Oh, I think it's pretty good intel."

Nick and Theresa looked at each other. "You know something we don't?"

"The safe house was compromised."

"Tex escaped?"

"Yeah. Lost three men in the process. It's time to put that son of a bitch down."

"But Governor, he still may have been lying."

"The time for patience is over, Nick. I'm shutting this down. Give me the coordinates."

Nick frowned, then nodded to his partner. "Theresa's texting them now. Give us time to check this out. If I can confirm the drones are there—"

"You do what you need to do, Nick, and I'll do what I need to do. But my advice to you is to not hang around there for long."

Arriving at the site of the Republic's covert drone operation, they found themselves looking at what gave every appearance of being a farm. They parked on a shoulder down the road, then walked back, a full moon lighting their way. A long dirt track led to a white frame farmhouse, goats roaming an enclosed yard. A large barn, aged by time and Texas heat, sat further back. Beside it, a larger corrugated steel structure with six massive garage-like doors promised to be the location of the drone force. Theresa leaned with one hand on a fence post, avoiding barbed wire.

"Looks like Tex may have been telling the truth, Nick."

"Yeah, maybe. I'd like to be sure before we let the hounds loose though."

"How do you plan on being sure?" She cocked her head, then put hands on her hips. "Going in there? You want to go in there to confirm the drones? Nick, remember West Texas? He had thirty guys with automatic weapons."

"I know. But don't you think it's odd we don't see any activity around here?"

She looked back to the farm. "Yeah. I suppose. But, Nick, if you're wrong we're going to be in it deep."

"We?"

"Don't start. Yes, we."

"I don't think we both need to go. You stay back, be sure someone doesn't sneak up behind me."

"Weak. Let's go." She drew her weapon then leapt over the gate before Nick could stop her.

Splitting up, they approached the farmhouse from two sides, crouching in a cotton field to obscure their advance as much as they could. When Nick reached a chain link fence to the farmhouse yard, he scanned the area then scrambled over. Goats scattered, one protesting the intrusion. A dog barked in the distance. The first shot took him off guard.

Slamming to the ground, Nick took up a position behind a riding lawnmower. Looking to his right across the yard he could see Theresa squatting behind a chicken coop. Fortunately the shooter wasn't the best shot, at least with the first one. A second shot rang out, pinging off the lawn mower. Theresa rose, firing several rounds into a window, glass shattering. The gunman fired again, this time in

Theresa's direction. Nick used the distraction to run to the house, his back slamming up against the side. He motioned to Theresa, who rose again, firing several more rounds as Nick jumped up on the porch, then crashed through the front door. He rolled across the foyer, finding a man in jeans, a blue cowboy shirt and hat, aiming a Winchester lever action rifle outside. Nick had him dead to rights.

"Drop the gun or I *will* shoot. And I don't miss."

The man froze for a moment, as if weighing whether to swing around firing or give up his gun. He chose the latter, crouching to lay down his rifle. Then he stood, hands in the air. He had the look of a Texas rancher Nick had seen before. Quiet, determined, ready to stand up and fight for what he cared about, tough. The man glared at Nick as if assessing him.

Nick kept his gun on the rancher. "Where's everyone else?"

"There is no everyone else. Just me."

Footsteps on the porch. "You sure you're alone?"

"I'm coming in." Theresa. She passed Nick, glancing at him on her way to the kitchen. Doors opened and her footsteps pounded on old wood floors. "Clear downstairs." Gun at the ready, she went upstairs. Nick kept his gun trained on the man, while the rancher eyed the ceiling following Theresa's progress. She came back down, her gun holstered. "We're clear, Nick."

The rancher lowered his hands.

"Hold it there, buddy. Keep your hands where I can see them."

"Just thought we could all use a drink, all this shooting going on."

"A drink. You mind telling me what you know about Tex Sawyer?"

The rancher kept his position, hands behind his head. "That crazy son of a bitch?"

"You know him, then?"

"Years ago I was flying for the Civil Air Patrol. In the middle of a flight Sawyer goes ape shit and almost kills us both. You mind telling me what that nut job has to do with you trespassing on my property?"

"Drones. Where's he keeping the drones?"

The rancher shook his head, his face a question mark.

"You want to keep an eye on our friend here? I'm going to check his barn."

The rancher took a step forward, but Theresa drew her gun, leveling it at him, convincing him to stop in his tracks.

"Who are you people? What are you looking for?"

Nick stepped out of the house, crossing the yard to a large corrugated steel building. No signs of any other human beings, only goats and a cow dog now following him around. He slipped through an opening past a large sliding door. The dank odor of hay, manure, grease, and gasoline wafted over him. A tractor with a tire removed sat next to a 357 Chevy Nova on jacks. He had a sinking feeling in his gut. Tex Sawyer had given him bad information and worse, Nick had passed it on to the governor. He speed dialed her. Nothing happened. No signal. He stepped outside, holding his phone in front of him like a Geiger counter looking for radioactivity. Still no signal. They needed to leave. Now.

He ran across the yard, shouting to Theresa. She had the rancher in front of her and out the door when he reached them.

"We've got to go."

"What are you talking about, Nick?"

"Tex set us up. And I have a feeling the governor is about to drop the hammer. We've got to go."

"So, this guy isn't—"

"Don't think so."

The rancher dropped his hands, his voice filled with frustration. "Would you two please tell me what the hell's going on?"

"There'll be time to talk later, mister. Right now, we all have to get away from here."

201

"Like hell."

The helicopter came in low, its rockets hitting the barn in a thunderous roar, the structure at first imploding followed by a massive explosion of flame and debris. The concussive force of the blast knocked them to the ground.

Nick rose to his feet shouting. "Run!"

He grabbed the rancher, who was bleeding from his ears, while Theresa ran alongside them down the track to the car. A second chopper fired missiles at the house and several outbuildings. Each exploded in massive fireballs, rocking the ground beneath their feet. Nick stood at the gate in disbelief. In a matter of moments, all of the buildings had been destroyed, wreckage strewn throughout, and the surrounding fields were in flames.

~ * ~

"Governor, you blew up a farm." Nick could only hear Fran breathing on the other end of the line. "Governor. You there?"

"Yeah, I'm here."

"You just blew—"

"I heard you the first time. Dammit."

"I asked you to wait, to let me check it out first."

"If you ever breath a word of our conversation to anyone, I swear—"

"I think you have more to worry about than my talking to the press."

Silence.

"We've got to stop him, Nick. God only knows what he's got planned next."

"I'm doing everything I can, Governor. Just don't blow anything else up without a confirmation. Indiscriminate bombing does not make good campaign press."

Nick could have sworn he saw something flash over a rise to the north, maybe a reflection from the beginnings of a sunrise.

The governor laughed. "Didn't take you long to figure out how to play me like fiddle. Okay, no more bombing, but you've got to find this guy. Now."

It was a flash. Binoculars? "I'm on it."

He slipped the phone back in his pocket and kept his eyes on the ridge. "Do you see something, a flash, over there?"

Theresa, looking in the same direction, nodded her head. She glanced to the rancher who sat by the rear tire, literally shell-shocked. "Yeah. Hey, Mr. Hofstettler, what's over the ridge?"

"Just pasture land. There's a dirt track that runs from this road up along the fence line. It's a dead end, so if someone's up there, it's not because they're passing through."

Nick jumped in the car. "Stay with Mr. Hofstettler. I'll be right back." Before Theresa could answer, he gunned his engine, tires burning across asphalt. Turning onto the dirt track, he saw a pickup approaching from the other direction. Nick slammed his brakes, a dust cloud overtaking him. He opened his door, pulled out his .45, and took aim at the truck. One hundred yards. It continued to speed toward him, clearly intent on slamming into him, or more likely, swerving off at the last minute to escape him. Fifty yards. The driver peered over his steering wheel, his hands jerking as he struggled to keep on the bumpy track as he gained speed. Twenty-five yards. Nick squeezed his .45's trigger, the gun exploding in recoil, the bullet hitting its mark. The truck's passenger side front tire exploded, chunks of rubber flying off. Nick fired four more shots into the grill and the truck swerved to his left off the dirt track, its hood popping open, steam billowing out of the engine compartment, the horn blaring.

Nick dropped his spent clip, slamming another in place, as he ran toward the vehicle. Gun pointed at the driver, he pulled the door open. The young man in his twenties moaned. Blood flowed down his face from a crease in his forehead matching the arc of the steering wheel. Binoculars and a map lay on the seat beside him. Nick grabbed a fistful of shirt, dragging him out and throwing him on the ground. He rolled over on his back, lifting himself up on his elbows.

Nick stood over him, gun aimed at his heart. "Who the hell are you?"

"Republic of Texas number three-five-seven-two..."

Nick put a foot in his chest, slamming him to the ground. "I don't have time for your little game. Who are you?"

"Republic of Texas number three-five-seven—"

Stepping back, Nick fired his .45, a spray of dirt kicking up between the man's legs.

"Jesus, what are you doing? That could've shot my balls off. Are you crazy?"

"Yes. I'm crazy. And I'm very disappointed in myself for missing."

"You wouldn't."

Nick fired again, this time between the man's thumb and forefinger of his right hand on the ground.

"Dammit! Okay. Okay." He sucked on the hand, blood on his lips. "Jesus. You just had to ask."

"So?"

"Danny Wilson."

"And Danny Wilson, what are you doing on this ridge with a pair of binoculars?"

"I can't tell you. I'm dead if I say anything."

"You'll be dead if you don't."

"But you're the law. You can't just go up and kill people."

"Here's the thing, Danny. I'm not the law. Seems to me you've got a choice to make. Do you want to tell me what I want to know and live long enough to keep Tex from hunting you down or do you want to disappoint me, in which case I just kill you right now. Which is it?"

He chambered a round for effect.

"All right. No need to get violent. I'll tell you what you want to know. You're right. Tex sent me. He wanted to be sure you guys took the bait, which I have to say, you took like a catfish to stink."

"So why the sleight of hand? What did he not want us to know about?"

"Aw, man." He struggled to a seated position.

"Your choice, now or later?"

"Right. Okay. He's got a big attack planned out of the East Texas base."

"Where's the base?"

"Don't know." Nick put his gun to Danny's head. "No, I swear on my mother, I have no idea where the base is located. But I do know where they're going to attack."

"Where, Danny?"

"Texas City. Today."

~ * ~

Nick and Theresa left Danny under citizen's arrest with Mr. Hofstettler until the DPS arrived. He was more than happy to keep a gun on the man he considered partly responsible for the destruction of his farm.

Sitting in the passenger seat, Theresa glanced over to Nick. "Don't you think we should tell the governor about Texas City, Nick?"

"He might be lying to us. And from what I've seen to date, Fran would blow the city off the map and claim a terrorist attack. We'll go in, make sure he's telling us the truth, then call her."

"We're going to drive to Texas City? It'll take hours."

"I've got a friend, an ex-air force fighter pilot with a plane in San Antonio. I called her, so she's expecting us."

"Did you happen to mention we might be flying into a full-on drone attack of Texas City?"

"Yeah. She said she'd pack chutes for both of us."

Texas City

Adriana Hummingwell sat on the screened-in porch attached to her dilapidated, two-bedroom, one-bath house near the southern tip of Bolivar Island. Since Katrina tore through, she had a clear view to the refinery tank farm through what used to be a big house, but was now a concrete slab. Roger Hemphill, a crusty old bastard, had lived in the house as long as she could remember. He said he'd been through many a storm in his lifetime and he wasn't about to go turn tail for this one. Adriana, having lived through one too many tornados growing up in Oklahoma, did not like the idea of being anywhere near a hurricane. With Roger shaking his head in disgust, she had packed up her rusty Toyota Corolla with as much of her stuff as she could and had driven to Oklahoma for a brief vacation. Little did she know at the time, her vacation would go on for months.

Once she did return to her little piece of heaven on Bolivar Island, Roger's big, well-built house no longer existed. Neither did Roger. In fact, quite a few places on the island disappeared, swallowed up by a raging sea or flung into a million pieces to be found across the flatlands outside Houston. Her little place miraculously survived. Although it had been flooded and half the roof ripped off, the structure still clung to its foundation. Since her return, she had been gradually rebuilding the house, which didn't stink as bad now as it did right after the storm. She even built the enclosed patio she enjoyed at this moment.

A clear blue sky extended to the horizon, the already hot late morning air cooled by a constant Gulf breeze. Much of her reconstruction had been completed, she had a job working the ferry, and it looked like no one would be building on Roger's slab anytime soon. A barge pushed along by a tug lumbered up the channel, floating past the refineries in Texas City on its way to port in Houston. A buzzing noise interrupted her thoughts. Bees? She didn't recall seeing much in the way of bees on the island, but you never knew when those damn killer bees would swarm all over you. Fortunately, a good screen between herself and the outdoors kept away the mosquitos and would surely keep away any bees. The sound grew louder then faded to the south toward Texas City.

She had gone inside to pour another cup of coffee when the first explosion rumbled across Galveston Bay. Wrong time of day and late in the year for fireworks, and besides, only a fool would shoot off fireworks by the refineries. She sat down, the webbing of her aluminum lawn chair creaking from the strain. Through her screen, red and orange flames erupted, a bright flash followed by a delayed clap of thunder. Before she could finish her coffee most of the refineries in Texas City looked to be on fire, thick black smoke rising high into the air. Hell and damnation. First Katrina and now this. She went into her bedroom to pack. Just in case.

~ * ~

Pulling into Hondo Municipal Airport, Nick drove to a hangar at the north end of the field. A woman in a blue flight suit inspected a wing on a single engine plane, a Cessna 182. Nick parked at the end of the hangar row, waving to the woman, as Theresa came around the other side of the car.

"Who's this?"

"Our pilot. Sharee, how the hell are you?"

Their pilot, a black woman in her thirties, wrapped her arms around Nick as he hugged her.

"Nick. So good to see you." She stepped back, tapping his shoulder with one hand. "I wondered how you were doing after Houston and then all that press you got in Austin."

Buzzard Bait

"I'm fine, Sharee. How are the kids?"

"Andre is nothing but trouble and Cassie, well, she's the apple of her daddy's eye."

"And Leon?" Her husband had served two tours in Iraq and the last one in Afghanistan.

She smiled with a hint of sadness. "I'm just glad to have him with us. He misses his legs, he was quite the runner, but he'll learn to manage. I'm getting him a pair of those running blades for Christmas." She turned to Theresa. "And is this Theresa?"

Theresa looked to Nick then held out a hand. "Yes, I'm Nick's partner."

Sharee laughed softly, raising an eyebrow. "His partner. Is that what it's called nowadays?"

"All right, Sharee. Enough." Nick glanced at Theresa. "I may have mentioned we're in a relationship."

"Did you now? We are, sort of. He can't seem to figure out what he wants."

Sharee rolled her eyes at Nick. "He can't? Nick, she's beautiful. What are you doing?"

"Okay, I'm not up to being double-teamed here. Besides, we've got business to attend to."

Theresa shook Sharee's hand. "Speaking of business, Sharee, do you understand what we might be flying into?"

"I hear armed drones. No worries. I'm faster and I've flown lots of missions. And I understand from the man who can't make a commitment—"

Nick shook his head. "Sharee."

"I understand we're observers, not combatants. If it gets too hot, we'll make a run for it."

~ * ~

After completing a walkaround, Nick and Theresa boarded Sharee's plane, taking off toward the east. Two hours later they flew down the middle of Houston, over the bay toward Texas city. They descended, circling the refineries, then turned north to Bolivar Peninsula.

Theresa sat in the backseat with Nick to Sharee's right.

Theresa shook her head. "Not seeing anything. Maybe this was another of Tex's lies."

Nick surveyed the view. The Gulf of Mexico extended to the horizon on their right, the bay and Houston to their left. In front of them lay miles of coastline. "Okay. I guess it was a bit of a long shot to fly out here and find Tex and his drones."

Sharee continued scanning the horizon. "Well, people think it's easy to find something from the air, but actually...wait a second."

Nick followed Sharee's gaze. "What is it? You see something?"

"Two o'clock about two thousand feet below us."

Nick peered down. A large flock of some kind of bird, no, a group of drones.

Theresa tapped Nick's shoulder. "We better notify the governor."

"No time. We're all that's standing in the way of those drones blowing up the refineries and storage facilities in Texas City."

"I can buzz them, but I don't think we want to try to ram one of those things."

Nick drew his .45. "How about shooting them? Can you bring us up beside one?"

"Yeah. Just be sure you don't shoot us in the fuel tank. Okay?"

Sharee made a turning descent, slowing the plane with flaps to match the speed of the drones. Beside them a group of ten gray aircraft with ten-foot wingspans flew in a loose formation toward their target.

"Let's take them out from the back in case they've got a video feed. Theresa, why don't you look out the other side to be sure we don't get one of them trying to surprise us."

Nick opened the window. The force of the air held the rectangular glass up against the wing. Shooting on the ground was one thing. Hitting a moving target from a moving platform would be something completely different.

209

Especially with a handgun. He felt a tap on his shoulder from Theresa.

"You might want this. I figured we might need a little extra firepower." She passed up a tactical shotgun. "It's loaded with slugs. Good hunting."

"You are a woman of many surprises." Nick poked the shotgun's muzzle out through his window, sighting the last drone in the group. A shotgun shell would spray a wide pattern of pellets at a target like a duck or a drone, but also damage the wing. Theresa's slugs, a solid projectile like a big fat bullet, would avoid the airframe and do maximum damage to the targeted drone. He fired, the shotgun's blast audible over the din of their engine and the wind noise. Missed. "Damn."

He took aim again, exhaled, then squeezed the trigger. Hit just behind the wings, a drone's tail cleaved off, sending the bird into a spin. He found the next, blowing off a wing, and a third exploded into several large chunks. At this rate they just might stop the drones.

"Nick." Theresa spoke from the back. "We've got company. One of the drones just swung up below us."

They couldn't see it. Pop, pop, pop. A series of holes ripped through the hull to Theresa's right, the small slugs embedding into the panel.

Sharee pulled up on the yoke. "Let's see if it can follow me." The nose tilted skyward, her Cessna's engine at full throttle clawing its way. "Tighten your harnesses."

"This thing can do aerobatics?"

She gave Nick a smile. "No. But I can." She pulled the nose up and over until they hung upside down, the ground where sky should be. "There you are, you little bastard."

Nick's stomach went up into his throat, but he also saw their attacker below and just ahead of them. "Pull up beside him and I'll take him out." He pumped the action of his shotgun, hoping to God the wings held as the plane completed its loop.

210

Theresa shouted, "Nine o'clock. It's coming straight at us."

Sharee looked left. A drone approached level at their altitude on a collision course. The drone driver must have decided to take them down kamikaze style. Nick couldn't fire from his position, as they closed on the drone in front of them.

Theresa yelled into her mic, "Sharee, it's closing. It's closing!"

They raced toward the tail of the attacker in front of them. Two hundred yards, one hundred yards. The kamikaze closed in from the side. Fifty yards. Forty. Thirty.

"Hold on, kids." Sharee nosed down slightly, then barrel rolled, the kamikaze a blur flashing past. She rolled upright, the attacker drone's tail a mere plane's length away. The impact happened quickly. A rhythmic banging as the Cessna's propeller slashed the drone's tail away. Sharee banked, the drone breaking up, then falling thousands of feet to the bay below.

Nick looked to his friend. "Some wicked flying there, Sharee."

She smiled. "Can't say I didn't enjoy it. Looks like our drones have decided to call it a day."

"Yeah, but I don't think it's because of us." He pointed across the bay to Texas City. Several plumes of thick, black smoke rose from oil storage tanks.

Theresa broke into the comm. "I've got three drones heading north across Bolivar Peninsula."

They dropped down to three thousand feet, a couple thousand above the drones, following them up the peninsula. At the north end of Bolivar, the drones circled, landing on a dirt strip by two quonset huts.

"What do you want to do, Nick? I've got enough fuel to get us to Chambers, thirty miles away. We either land here or go to Chambers. Not enough fuel to stay on station."

"Land."

Theresa spoke up from the back. "You sure about this, Nick? We don't know what Tex has on the ground down there."

Nick reached over, flipping a switch on the radio to cut communications with Theresa. "I'm going in alone. You leave me on the road, then get out of here. Call the governor with the coordinates and tell her I'm on site."

"What about your partner? She's going to be seriously pissed."

"Yeah, well, I guess I don't blame her."

Theresa tapped him on his shoulders, pointing to her headset. He twisted his head back, shrugging his shoulders. Sharee lined up with the main road, flaring just before touching down on her mains, then letting the nose drop to the ground. Nick pulled off his headset and unsnapped his harness as the plane came to a stop.

Theresa slapped the seat back in front of her. "Hey, where do you think you're going?"

Nick stepped out. "Let the governor know what's going on, Sharee."

"You sure about this?"

Theresa unsnapped her harness, moving to get out.

Nick looked her in the eye. "Not on this one, Theresa."

"Nick, what the hell are you doing?"

I can either keep you safe or keep you near. I choose safe. "What I should have done before."

"Nick, goddammit." She pushed on the seatback, but Nick straight-armed it firmly in place. "This is the very thing I'm talking about. Sharee, stop this plane."

"Sorry, honey. I just met you. Nick and I go way back. Better buckle up."

He shut the door, Theresa banging on the window as he ran behind the plane. The Cessna's engine revved up, the plane taxiing, then gaining speed until it climbed into the air, away from the very danger Nick now rushed toward.

~ * ~

212

Nick was done with Tex Sawyer. He'd been shot down, tied up, threatened with execution, attacked countless times by Republic mercenaries, almost shot down again, and worst of all, the son of a bitch had managed to hit Texas City. He didn't know what he would be up against, but he did know this had to end. Now.

The governor would apply overwhelming lethal force to not only destroy Tex, but obliterate him. No evidence. No tracks back to Reynolds. No inconvenient ties to her. He could have flown on to Chambers, letting Fran do her worst. But Nick had an aversion to keeping things in the dark when it came to the safety and security of a community or a state or a nation. Tex needed to be captured and put on trial for terrorism, and Reynolds and anyone else involved in this deadly game exposed to the light.

Making his way from the two-lane road, he crossed over sandy scrub, keeping low as he approached the Quonset huts. Across the makeshift airstrip, a black limo sat parked outside one of the huts, then a suit stepped out with Tex at his side. Nick knew the suit. Reynolds. They shook hands, then Reynolds got into his limo and drove away. The distinctive thump, thump, thump of helicopters rumbled up behind him. Three in all. Probably more of Fran's covert team. If he was going to get Tex, he'd have to act quickly.

Nick moved to flank the huts, staying as low as he could in knee-high brush. Small arms fire coming from the huts forced him to the ground. He fired a few rounds in their direction, but his .45 was no match for their automatic weapons. The shooting paused. A bullhorn came to life with Tex's voice.

"Whoever you are, you might as well surrender to the Republic of Texas. You've got ten seconds to throw down your weapon and walk toward us, or I'll have my boys put you down."

Nick shouted to Tex. "You hear those helicopters, Tex? They're coming for you. Let me bring you in. You'll get a fair trial."

"Trial? For what? For being a patriotic Texian? Call your birds off or we'll take them out too."

"Tex, those aren't my helicopters. I'm telling you, surrender to me or you don't stand a chance."

"Surrender? Son, I have the legacy of the Alamo behind me. I don't surrender. And I think your time's up."

Nick took a deep breath. Why won't people just do what I ask? "Okay. I surrender. I'm coming out."

He rose from the scrub, his gun dangling from its trigger guard on one finger.

"I'm surrendering. Do you see those helicopters? They're not mine. They're here to kill you."

Two men ran toward Nick as Tex continued his banter on the bullhorn. "Well, I don't think they want to kill you. So, we'll just use you for a shield. You see, that's why I'm the leader of our air force. Strategic thinking. It's the key to success."

The three choppers roared over Nick, firing missiles and .50 caliber machine guns. Nick hit the ground, covering his head with both hands. Several massive explosions thundered through the ground. When he looked up, the quonset huts and everything nearby, including Tex, his drones and his men were consumed by a massive, fiery explosion. The three helicopters hovered over their work, then turned back south, flying low across the peninsula.

The two Republic gunmen who had been running toward Nick lay sprawled on the ground. When he got to them, he found one dead, impaled with a twelve inch shard of galvanized metal, and the other dead from the concussive force of the blast. He realized he must have been only feet from the kill zone. He sat down amidst the destruction. One thing was for certain. His new employer definitely had a sting in her tail.

I See You

The next morning Nick sat in front of his Airstream, a cup of coffee in one hand, reading the news on his cell phone with the other. He looked up from Middle Eastern wars when Theresa rolled up in her MGB. On the phone last night, he had wanted to explain, to help her understand why keeping her out of the fray with Tex was the right thing to do, but she hung up on him somewhere between "Hi" and "Theresa."

"Morning, Nick." All business. "Mind if I get a cup of coffee?"

He picked up a thermos. "I've got it right here, along with an extra cup. After our brief conversation last night, I wasn't expecting you."

"Did you see the news?"

"Yeah. The paper made it sound like a terrorist bomb assembly gone terribly wrong."

"You think the governor took Tex out?"

"I think Fran is a conniving, power hungry politician who will go to almost any length to secure her goals."

"I'll bet Reynolds didn't anticipate a covert team of gubernatorial helicopters armed with Sidewinders. I suppose she wants us to track Reynolds down, put an end to this nonsense?"

"I spoke to her a few minutes ago. Looks like Fran's distancing herself from the whole sordid mess. She told me she'll be passing Reynolds to Homeland Security."

"She's giving him to the feds? He blew up an entire desalination plant and several oil storage tanks and left quite a few dead bodies in his wake. She doesn't strike me as the type to step away."

"I guess the whole thing's too hot. She's more worried about her reputation than getting justice. All she wants is to keep her distance."

"So, we're officially done then."

"Yeah. The first case for the Governor's Special Emergency Operations Team has come full circle."

Nick's phone rang and Dillon's number flashed on the screen. "Looks like our client is calling. Time to give him the good news about coming back to Texas without looking over his shoulder."

He put the phone on speaker so Theresa could share in the celebration of saving their client's life. "Dillon, glad you called."

"Ah, Nick Sibelius." It wasn't Dillon.

"Who is this?" The man sounded like Reynolds.

"Is that really important? What is important is that you do a certain task for me."

"What are you talking about? Put Dillon on the line."

"You will do this task within certain time parameters. If you do, I will give you Dillon, safe and sound. If, however, you don't complete the task, or, you fail to complete it within my time parameters, I will put a bullet in Dillon's head. I'll admit, there's not much to damage in his head, but trust me, he'll be dead all the same. And his blood will be on your hands."

Nick and Theresa looked at each other. Moments ago everything seemed tied up nicely with a bow. It had all turned to shit with one phone call.

"You still there, Nick, or do I need to get your attention by shooting off one of Dillon's fingers?"

"No, no, I'm here. There's no need to shoot off a finger. I'm right—" A loud bang interrupted him.

Dillon screamed out in the background. "Jesus. Oh God, you shot me. Jesus!"

Nick shouted into his phone. "Reynolds, stop! I'm here. I'm listening. There's no need to shoot."

Reynolds voice sounded far away, like he had his head turned from the phone. "Here, just put pressure on it. And quit whining. It was only a finger." His voice got much louder. "Where were we, Nick?"

"You have a task for me and you want it done within a certain time limit."

"Very good. My, you're a good listener. Here's the deal. I'd love to run you all over town to phone booths, like in the movies, or maybe some kind of crazy scavenger hunt, so I know you're not being followed. But you and I both know you could easily conceal a GPS and have someone tracking your every move. So, I'm going to send you to a new location where you'll find your first clue. If you're late, Dillon's dead. If I see anyone follow you, Dillon's dead. If I see anyone approaching our meeting location at any time, Dillon's dead. If I see a cop or someone acting like a cop, Dillon's dead. Are you getting the picture?"

"Yeah. Do what you say, or Dillon's dead."

"Excellent. You have twenty-five minutes to get to Taylor Municipal Airport, Hangar A 16."

Theresa tapped on her cell phone, then whispered to Nick. "My map says its thirty minutes away."

"Who do you have with you, Nick?"

"My business partner. She says it'll take thirty minutes to get there."

"Then you better hurry up, since you've just wasted thirty seconds. Goodbye."

The line went dead. Nick and Theresa ran to his truck, slamming doors shut. He threw it into reverse, speeding backwards down the track and into the road. A horn blared. A car, its tires screeching, rushed past them. He put his truck in drive, accelerating as fast as he dared go. As he overtook the car, its driver leaned out, yelling obscenities.

"Left here."

Nick followed Theresa's direction, the rear end sliding out from under them. Regaining control, he accelerated again, climbing an incline, then flying through the air at its apex, slamming hard to the asphalt. When he got to Highway 79, he turned onto the nearly straight stretch of road, speeding over 100 mph. Cars blurred, telephone poles racing past and behind them. He looked in the rear view mirror. No police. Good. They couldn't afford to slow down or be stopped. Twenty-four minutes later he turned left into the airport, racing through the gate and across the tarmac to a set of hangars.

"It's A. Look for A."

He drove past parked airplanes to one side.

"There it is, Nick. There." Theresa pointed to hangar A 16. He slammed on the brakes, jumped out of the truck and ran to the hangar. Now what? His phone rang.

"Very good. Just wanted to be sure you weren't followed. And besides, I had fun. Didn't you?"

Nick looked around. Reynolds had to be there somewhere. How else would he know? Then a small security camera on the top corner of the hangar caught his eye. Damn.

"What now, Reynolds?"

"You will have Bobbi released, then bring her, along with her phone, to me."

"She's locked up in the Pflugerville Justice Center jail. How am I supposed to get her out?"

"I understand you have a special relationship with the governor of the illegal state of Texas. I'd use her influence or poor Dillon will need someone to hold his coffee cup. You have two hours before I call. If you don't have her, I'll shoot off a finger every ten minutes."

"Two hours? I can't get the governor to release Bobbi in two hours."

He waited for a response, but the line went dead.

~ * ~

218

Theresa got on the phone with Quentin to make sure the Pflugerville PD still had Bobbi in custody at the Justice Center, while Nick spoke to Governor Adamson.

"I'm sorry, Nick, but there's no way I'm letting a killer go free for some crazy who thinks the Republic still lives. I will not be dictated to by revolutionaries and terrorists."

Nick heard echoes of her presidential campaign. "Look, Governor. If you don't release Bobbi, one of your largest campaign contributors will continue to maim and then kill an innocent man."

"All Americans, and especially Texans with a heritage of the Alamo, know blood must be spilled and treasure spent for freedom."

"Get off your damned stump speech and talk to me like a normal human being. I'm telling you, Reynolds will kill him." Nick heard only some static on the line. "Governor."

"If you're going to be the Director of my Special Ops Team, then you need to grow a pair."

"How about this, Fran. If you let that bastard kill Dillon, I will call a press conference outlining how you coordinated covert violent attacks on citizens without necessary cause and then failed to save Dillon because you didn't want to upset your largest contributor."

"You won't do it. You don't have the balls for it, Sibelius. So just be a good little boy and tootle back to your trailer. Let the adults handle this."

"I'm going to put you on speaker, Fran."

"It's Governor, to you."

Nick turned to Theresa. "We're going to call the local stations of all the major networks. And don't forget Univision."

"Where do you want me to start, Nick?"

"You know someone at KVUE, don't you? Let's start there. You listening, Fran?"

"You wouldn't dare. If you take me down, you'll go down with me. How are you going to explain your actions

219

as the Director of the team? I don't recall giving you the go ahead to attack Sawyer's compound."

"Fran, after running for President you should know better than to think anybody gives a shit about the truth. They want to hear what they want to hear. And I'm betting there's lots of people in this state up for lynching you."

Theresa spoke into her phone. "Lisa, yeah it's Theresa. I've got a big story for you. Uh-huh. Yes, and it involves the governor."

"Nick, don't do this. It will destroy us both."

"Your choice, Fran."

Theresa glanced at Nick with a mischievous smile. "It's huge, Lisa. Yes...you want to get your editor in for this? I completely understand. I'll hold."

"Goddammit, Nick. Okay. Okay. I'll check into releasing Bobbi."

"Not good enough."

"I'll get her released today."

"The editor should be on the line any moment."

"Dammit. Okay. I'll get her released to your custody immediately."

"And I'll stay on the line with you, so I'll hear the conversation with the Pflugerville Police Chief."

"Fine."

Theresa gave Nick a wink, then concluded her call. "Hey, Lisa. I do have a story for you, but I'll need to wait a day or two. Yes, you'll have an exclusive. Bye."

After arranging for Bobbi's release into Nick's custody, Governor Adamson offered a few choice words for Nick.

"You're still the Director of my Ops Team."

"Really? I'd think you wouldn't trust me enough."

"Trust you? Hell, you're an open book. I trust you to do the right thing, which is pretty unheard of these days and usually puts you on the losing side. But at least you're predictable. Besides, it took some cojones to be willing to throw us both under the bus. I like a man with balls."

"Thank you, I think."

"You want me to call in the DPS to hunt Reynolds down?"

"I think the only chance Dillon has of surviving is if I give Reynolds what he wants. Once Dillon's out of the line of fire, do whatever you want."

"Nick, I always do whatever I want. Except, it seems, with you. But I'll find a way."

"Good luck with that, Governor."

The line went silent as Nick turned into the Justice Center parking lot. He looked at Theresa. "We dodged a bullet there. I thought Fran wasn't going to budge and we'd end up on the evening news."

"Wouldn't happen."

"Why? Sounded like your friend Lisa could see her Pulitzer moment coming to fruition."

"Yeah, about that. Lisa's a lifestyle reporter for the station."

"But she called in the Editor."

"Actually, her cameraman."

"You faked it?"

Theresa flashed a wicked smile. "I can be very convincing when I need to be."

Nick's phone rang. Reynolds.

"Nick, I'm very disappointed."

"Reynolds, I'm at the Justice Center. The governor has released Bobbi into my custody. I just need to walk in and get her."

"Ah, Nick. All of these excuses. I didn't make a fortune in healthcare by listening to nurses or administrators whine about losing their jobs. I walked my talk. Always."

"Reynolds, I'm walking in the door. Just hold on."

"Would you like to talk to Dillon?"

"Yeah, sure."

Theresa ran to the chief's office, hoping to explain their situation to her past boss. After a brief conversation, the chief led her into an interrogation room. Nick stood in the hallway, phone in hand. Dillon came on the line.

"Nick? Nick?"

"I'm here, Dillon. I've got you. We have what Reynolds wants and I'm coming to get you."

"He's going to shoot me again. Jesus. He blew off my middle finger. Clean, fucking off."

"It's going to be okay—"

"Nick! Jesus. Please. No, no." The explosive discharge of a gun forced Nick to pull the phone away from his ear. Pressing it to the other ear, he heard Dillon moaning and weeping. Then Reynolds got back on the phone.

"In ten minutes I will call. If you do not have Bobbi with you, I will remove another finger. Please hurry Nick. You've only got an hour and twenty minutes before we'll be calling him Stubby."

Nick ended the call. "Crap."

Theresa had Bobbi out of the interrogation room and moving to the front door of the Center. She glanced at Nick. "What?"

"Another finger."

The Chief handed Nick an evidence bag. "Figured you'd probably need something in here. Be careful with her, Nick. She's a piece of work."

Nick opened the bag to be sure he had Bobbi's phone. "Thanks, but I always use extra precautions with women who try to kill me with land mines."

"So there's more than one, eh? You need to settle down." He winked at Theresa. "Stop hanging around dangerous women."

They raced back to Nick's truck. Theresa put Bobbi between them.

Bobbi looked to either side of her. "What's this about? You two feeling sorry for me? Decided I'd like a nice drive in the country?"

Nick cocked his head, Bobbi glaring back. "How did you get tangled up with a guy like Reynolds?"

222

An exasperated breath exploded from Theresa. "Nick, she's a psychopathic serial killer. She doesn't need a reason for anything."

Bobbi snorted at Theresa, then stared straight ahead. "There's nothing wrong with being a serial killer. Especially if it gives me peace of mind. Some people abuse alcohol, some use drugs. I kill band directors."

Theresa shook her head. "Nick, I know we're trying to save Dillon, but do you really think letting this nut case on the street again is in the best interest of anyone?"

Bobbi turned on Theresa. "What do you mean, save Dillon?"

Nick rolled down his window, letting some fresh air into the cab. "Your buddy Reynolds is shooting off Dillon's fingers one at a time until we get you to him. He seems to have a real need to see you."

"You're taking me to Reynolds? Damn." She shifted her eyes, a trapped animal scanning for some route of escape.

"I thought you two were buddies?"

"Reynolds? He's just like Lenny." She shook her head, staring forward.

"Who?"

"My daddy. Thought he could take advantage of me, and so does Reynolds. Like I'm his personal property."

"Well, he does have you running illegal financial schemes and killing people."

"Yeah, all for the sake of his damn destiny."

Nick glanced at her. "The Republic?"

"Yeah. He has a harebrained idea to secede from the Union, bringing the Republic of Texas back in all of its glory."

"Tex was ranting on about it. What do you think he's planning?"

She chuckled. "Why should I tell you anything? You're going to let him kill me to save Dillon."

"I do have to make Reynolds think I'm giving you to him, but only long enough to get Dillon out of harm's way."

223

He nodded to Theresa. "We won't let anything happen to you." Bobbi rolled her eyes. "Besides, you say Reynolds thinks you're his property. Sounds like we have a common enemy. He's going to a lot of trouble to bring you back and I'm guessing he doesn't have the best of intentions. Explain to me what's going on. Let me help."

Bobbi eyed Nick, pursing her lips in thought. "Okay, I'll tell you what I know, as long as I have your word you'll let me walk after we've stopped him."

"I'm not a cop, Bobbi. It's not my job to arrest you."

"What about her?" Bobbi nodded to Theresa.

"She's not a cop either, right, Theresa?"

"This is a mistake, Nick. Girlfriend here is nuts."

"Theresa."

"Okay. I'm not a cop."

Bobbi studied Nick, then settled back. "In the beginning I just thought he was a crooked businessman. Wouldn't be the first, right? But he started acting weird. I took pictures of his plans, so I'd have some leverage against the guy. Which is why I had those documents on my phone."

"When Dillon caught sight of them, you were worried he either had discovered Reynolds's plan or would let him know you had his documents."

"Yeah, maybe. Okay, yes. I had stolen the documents, then headed to Fort Worth to put some distance between us. I kind of drink under pressure and believe me, I felt under the gun. I woke up to Dillon. God, do you have any idea what it's like to wake up to that guy snoring beside you, naked with drool rolling down his cheek?"

"I don't even want to imagine. So, you woke up and there was our boy, Dillon."

"Yeah, I got out of there as quickly and quietly as I could. Only I left my damn phone. By the time I realized what I had done, Dillon had left. I spent the week waiting for the other shoe to drop, but Reynolds never called. I went to a gun show in Austin, just on the off-chance Dillon would show. And sure enough, he did, with my phone in hand."

"You had your phone with the documents. What made you think Dillon, of all people would break your encryption?"

"I sometimes shout stuff in the middle of sex."

"Do me, guapo, do me?"

Bobbi winced. "He told, huh?"

"Dillon mentioned something about it."

"Well, I suppose he also told you it's my password. Dillon picked drunk sex as the time to actually remember something. He told me he saw the documents. I couldn't risk it."

"But Dillon's pretty harmless, don't you think?"

"You don't know Reynolds." She stared out the window. "I figured if he knew I let Dillon see sensitive documents about his plans to start up a Republic, well, I wouldn't last a day."

"You hired a two-bit con, Harry Crenshaw, to kill Dillon. Only Harry planted his boat in a cliff instead. Then you hired someone else to kill him at the RC airfield."

She chuckled, shaking her head. "Let me give you some advice. Never ask a band director to kill someone for you. He outsourced to Crenshaw."

"Band director? You must mean Andy. You killed him with the tuba?"

"He got what he deserved. They all do."

"You had him naked, duct taped to a tuba with a water hose shoved down his throat."

"Judge all you want. I needed closure."

Nick looked at Bobbi. She appeared to be a normal woman. Some might call her intelligent and attractive. But the stuff coming out of her addled mind left him almost speechless.

"Okay. He hired Crenshaw, who missed, and then he hired someone else?"

"He did it himself. Or should I say, didn't do it. He couldn't hit a longhorn at point blank range with a howitzer."

"After he came up short again you decided you needed your closure?"

"Yeah." She dropped her head back, taking in a deep breath. "God, it felt good."

Nick's phone rang again. "Okay, I've got Bobbi and her phone."

"Good. Otherwise Dillon here would only be able to point with one finger on his left hand. You will now go to Kitty Hill Medical Center."

"Kitty Hill? It's closed."

"Of course it's closed. I'm the one who bought it, fired everyone, and then shut it down. I'll meet you in the ICU. You have forty minutes."

~ * ~

Theresa tapped the location into her phone. "Forty minutes? Nick, if you go full out, we're barely going to make it."

Speeding down backroads, she directed him as they tried to buy some time.

"Right here, Nick."

He turned onto a small two-lane road, the high crown occasionally dinging against the underside of his truck.

"Look out!"

A tractor pulled out of a dirt lane, leaving Nick no time to stop. He slammed on his brakes, swerving to miss the tractor, but crashing through a barbed wire fence and down a ditch, slamming into the embankment. Airbags deployed with a loud bang.

With seat belts and airbags they all walked away, but as the farmer shouted at him for almost destroying his tractor, Nick feared Dillon wouldn't fare so well. He called Reynolds.

"What are you doing calling me?"

"We had an accident. The truck is totaled. I need more time."

"That's such a tragedy. Oh, and, not...my...problem."

226

"Come on. It was an accident. I've got to get another vehicle."

Reynolds spoke in a creepy, calm voice. "Stop screaming, Dillon. I know. I told them, but they failed you."

Dillon screamed and begged in the background. Nick tried to reason with Reynolds. "What are you doing? It's my fault, not his. We just..." Another loud bang, followed by a scream and then Dillon moaning. "Stop! I'll get a car."

"You better, Nick. If you're late, he loses another finger. And if you try to stall again, I'll blow off his whole damned hand. Got it?"

"Yeah, yeah, I've got it. I'll be there."

He shut off his phone, running out in the road. A young man in his early twenties, blocked by the tractor, waited in his Audi for the farmer to move out of the way. Nick banged on his window, but he shook his head no. Nick tried the door handle. Locked. He pounded again. The man raised his middle finger. Nick looked to Theresa to see if she had any ideas, then took out his .45, pulled back on the slide and fired into the Audi's rear window. Grabbing a rag off the farmer's tractor he smashed out the remaining glass while the driver sat paralyzed in shock.

Nick reached in, unlocking the driver door. "Get out. Now." The man, his face pale with fear, did as he was told. Nick nodded to Theresa who had Bobbi at her side. "We've got to go."

Nick pulled around the tractor, past his abandoned pickup, then accelerated down the road. At the hospital they didn't bother trying to unlock doors. Nick fired at the glass doors, then kicked through. He hoped they'd make it in time, but then he heard a distant shot and a scream. They'd missed the deadline. Following signs through empty hallways, they made it to the ICU, to Reynolds and to Dillon. Reynolds stood at a half circle desk which must have been the unit nursing station. He had Dillon, both hands bandaged with bloody rags, tied to a wheelchair, a gun to his head.

227

"We're here, Reynolds."

"You made it. Good. Dillon's such a baby about getting his fingers shot off. I see you've got Bobbi and the phone."

"Just like we agreed."

"Good. Lay the phone on the counter and let Bobbi go."

"What about Dillon? Why don't you let him go and then I'll give you Bobbi and the phone."

"How about I shoot him in the kneecap, then you give me Bobbi and the phone?"

Dillon begged. "Please, Nick. Please. Do what he says. He'll shoot me. You know he'll shoot me."

Nick stepped toward the counter, pulled Bobbi's phone out of his hip pocket and placed it on the countertop. He nodded to Theresa, who cut Bobbi's bindings, guiding her towards Reynolds.

"Let me have Dillon. We've given you what you want."

"Bobbi dear, why don't you roll Dillon over to our friends."

Bobbi stepped over to Reynolds, then got behind Dillon's wheelchair, rolling him toward Nick and Theresa. "Bruce, don't you think this has gone a bit too far?"

"No, I don't. I think I've made a lasting statement for the glory of our great Republic."

"What are you talking about?"

"They thought destroying my air force would destroy the dream. But they don't understand. The Republic of Texas will never die. The Mexicans tried and failed. The Americans tried and failed. No, the Republic will last forever."

"But Bruce, there's nothing left."

"I'm left. And I will be a martyr to the Republic. With my death, our great Republic will live in the hearts and minds of the people forever." He smiled. "But I don't expect any of you to understand."

Theresa took the wheelchair from Bobbi, who stayed beside them. Nick didn't want Reynolds to commit suicide, but he also didn't want to stand around a lunatic too long for fear he'd decide everyone had to die with him. "You do what you have to do, Bruce. We won't stop you."

Bruce laughed. "Of course you won't stop me. You can't. In two minutes this building will implode, burying us in its rubble. But don't despair. You too will be martyrs for the cause. Long live the Republic of Texas."

"If you don't mind, we're going to pass on your offer." He turned to Theresa and Bobbi. "Run."

Nick, with Theresa pushing Dillon, ran down a hallway, shots ricocheting off tile walls. Bobbi followed close behind. Left, right, through the lobby and crashing through the front doors. Nick shouted to them, urging them on. "Keep going!"

They ran out into the parking lot. Two minutes had passed, but no explosion. Then Nick's phone rang. Reynolds.

"Bobbi, help Theresa get Dillon in the car." Nick put the phone to his ear. Reynolds was laughing.

"What's so funny, Reynolds?"

"It was priceless. I'm a martyr for the cause." He howled into the phone. "Do you really think I'd blow myself up? Nick, Nick. You're not too bright."

"What was the point, Reynolds?" Nick opened the driver's side door. "I'm sure you want to tell me."

"The point is—you're dead."

A high-powered rifle fired from the roof. Bobbi, having helped get Dillon into the truck, had run past Nick to freedom. The round hit her square in the back, slamming her to the ground mid stride. Blood gushed from a gaping wound.

"Down!" Nick dove for Dillon, dragging him out the opposite door and onto the pavement with the car providing cover.

Another blast as a bullet just missed, hitting asphalt behind him. Bobbi lay still in a pool of her own blood, her eyes open, but life draining away. He rose, firing his .45, giving Theresa cover to huddle behind the car with him.

Not the best defense against a shooter with a sniper rifle. He looked to Theresa. The fear in her eyes softened, her lips curving into a wistful smile. All the time they'd wasted talking about how overprotective he was with her and now they were all going to die from a sniper's bullets.

Inching her way to the back fender she fired several rounds toward the roof. *Tink. Tink.* Two successive sniper rounds tore holes through the car's trunk lid inches from her, forcing her back behind the rear tire. Nick looked around for an escape route, but they'd never be able to move Dillon from this position without a sniper getting a clean shot. He pulled out his phone, hoping Fran would not leave them hanging.

Nick felt the blast more than he heard it.

A deep rumble of explosives, vaporizing everything in their immediate path, brick, mortar, concrete disintegrating into millions of particles, large chunks of stone and brick flying in all directions, a ball of fire consuming the oxygen in a hellacious flash, then a shock wave rolling out, knocking down everything in its path. Dirt and dust and gravel-sized chunks of hospital rained down on them for thirty seconds, though it seemed like three hours.

When the roar subsided and debris rested over the entire parking lot, Nick lay still, listening for any sound of gun fire or movement. To his right, Dillon lay on his side, his chest rising. To his left, Theresa sat upright, coated in dust, but alive. Bobbi lay dead twenty feet away, covered in debris and blood. Nick and Theresa stood up to see a radically altered Kitty Hill Medical Center. The building, the snipers, and Bruce Reynolds no longer existed.

R. W. Hacker

Loose Ends

A day after Bruce Reynolds and his vision for a new Republic disintegrated into dust, Nick dropped in on his client, Dillon, at home. They reclined on the back deck, sipping iced tea and eating some of Dolores's oatmeal cookies. She sat beside Dillon on a lounge chair, rubbing his leg with one hand. The doctor had bandaged over his two missing fingers on each hand with the index and pinky fingers exposed. Dolores had rigged up his beer hat to work with iced tea, two containers on either side of a construction hat with tubes falling to his shoulders. He took a long pull from one of the plastic straws. Nick felt horrible. His client lived, but he had lost four fingers in the process.

Dolores tilted her head, looking to Nick. "You look a little down, Nick. This is supposed to be a celebration."

"I know, Dolores. Sorry. I just, well, I feel bad, Dillon. Feel like I let you down."

"Let me down? Hell, that Reynolds guy would've killed me if you hadn't shown up in time." He waved a bandaged hand. "Yeah, maybe it would've been nice if you had shown up a bit earlier."

Dolores glared. "Now, Dillon. You should be thanking the Lord you're still walking this earth."

"No, no, you're right, darling. Sorry, Nick."

"I understand, Dillon. You lost four fingers."

"Better than his life, if you ask me." She patted his leg again.

"Besides, I can still fish and when I go to a UT game, I'm a natural." He raised both arms up in a hook 'em horns

231

salute, his forefinger and pinky of each hand pointing to the sky. He turned to Dolores. "Dolores, dear. Will you get me that envelope?"

She leaned over to a table beside her, picking up a letter sized envelope, handing it to Dillon. He held it with a thumb and a forefinger, and then reached over to Nick, presenting it to him.

Nick took the envelope, turning it over in his hands. "What's this?"

"Your fee, of course."

He shoved it back to Dillon. "No. No way."

"You saved my life, Nick. Besides, it was a business deal."

"Please, Nick." Dolores leaned over, pushing Nick's hand away. "We want you to have it. You saved my smootchykins."

"Your smootchykins?"

Dillon rolled his eyes, his face flushing. "That's her little name for me. But really, Nick. We want you to have it."

Even though they thought he had saved Dillon, and maybe he had, he certainly couldn't claim any success. Having your client lose four fingers does not constitute a win. "I'm very grateful for your commitment to our business arrangement, but here's the thing. While all of this was going on, the governor made me the Director of the Special Emergency Operations Team. I'd love to take the fee, but I'm prohibited by state law from receiving any remuneration while in office." He had no idea if he spoke the truth, but he could at least keep them from spending money they'd need for Dillon's recovery.

Dillon took the envelope back from Nick. "Well, if it's state law, I guess we don't want you to do nothing unethical."

"Thanks for understanding."

~ * ~

When Nick got back to his office, Theresa's MGB was parked by the front door. They hadn't spoken at any length

232

about their relationship, but given her absence from his bed, he concluded the news couldn't be good. Alice backed out of the entryway, one arm in a silk tangerine sling to complement her white and tangerine sundress, the other arm wrapped around a box.

"You're not leaving me again, are you Alice?"

She swiveled around, successfully navigating the door, her lips, also tangerine, curved into a smile.

"No, dear. Just thought I'd take some of our old coffee mugs to Goodwill on my way to the spa."

"Glad to hear you're taking a long weekend. You deserve it." He peered into her box, scanning for any favorite mugs.

"Well, it's an extra special weekend."

"Really?" A cream-colored mug with a worn gold rim and the burnt orange coffee-stained logo of the University of Texas sat in one corner. He reached for it.

Alice pulled the box away. "What are you doing?"

"My mug. The UT mug. You can't give it away."

"It's all stained and nasty." She scrunched up her nose in disgust. "I'll buy you a new one."

"You don't toss something out because he's not shiny and new anymore."

"Are we still talking about a coffee mug?"

Nick reached over, grabbing his mug. "Of course we are. It's just a special mug."

"Please tell me you won't use it around clients. Nothing worse than trying to bring in new business and you make them puke when they see you drinking out of that thing."

"The mug stays." He didn't know why a damned mug was so important.

"All right. The mug stays."

He shifted the conversation away from his prized possession. "You were saying your long weekend's going to be special?"

"Oh, yes. Johnnie's in town. We're going to make the weekend of it."

233

"I thought you wanted distance, to do your own thing, to be free—"

"I know what I said." She had a silly grin on her face, like a schoolgirl who's just been kissed by the quarterback. "I suppose love trumps everything else."

"I'm happy for you, Alice. I really am."

"I know you are. Now, why don't you go in there and make nice with your love."

"Yeah, well, we're business partners. That's all."

"Just go in and tell her how you feel. It baffles me how you manage to deal with all kinds of crazies, but can't seem to handle normal relationships."

"Quentin and I have a great relationship."

"Normal women, Nick. Normal women."

"Point taken." Nick tipped an imaginary hat to Alice, then stepped into the reception area.

Theresa called out from her office. "Is that you, Alice?"

"No, it's, uh, Nick."

She came out of her doorway. "How'd it go with Dillon?"

He fumbled with a stapler on Alice's desk. "Fine. They tried to pay me, but I just couldn't take money from a guy I should have saved who now has four missing fingers."

"He's alive, Nick. It could have been much worse."

"You think I should've taken the money?"

"No, I think you should cut yourself some slack. Sometimes surviving is enough of a prize. I imagine Dillon will miss his fingers, but he's damned happy to be able to miss them in Dolores's arms."

He put down the stapler, turning to Theresa. After everything they'd been through together, Nick couldn't imagine another woman who could understand him as well as Theresa. He did feel protective, maybe overly protective of her, but only because he loved her. They needed to get out of this quicksand they'd been in lately. They needed to commit.

"Theresa, I've been thinking about us."

234

"I've been thinking about us, too, Nick. I know you love me. I love you, too."

"That's exactly how I feel."

"But—"

"But what?"

"We're stuck in a holding pattern. I need to be an equal in this business and in our personal life."

"I agree."

"Yes, I think you do agree intellectually. But when the bullets start flying you revert to protection mode, taking complete responsibility not only for the job at hand, but for my personal safety."

"Yes, but—"

"I don't want you to spend the rest of your life afraid you're going to lose me. I need you here, in the present."

"I can be here, in the present."

"I want to believe you, but you and I both know you can't. You've got too much baggage with your ex, with MaryLou, and with me. We're business partners, so I'm not going away. But if I stay, then we can't be in a relationship with each other."

Nick expected to tumble into a dark well of depression when Theresa finally put an end to it. However, a sense of relief came over him, a burden lifting off his shoulders. "You're right, Theresa."

"I am?"

"Yeah, I couldn't have said it better. I do love you, but being in a relationship with someone who enjoys dealing with psychopaths and killers as much as we do is probably not healthy for either one of us."

"Yeah, I agree. So, we're business partners and friends?" She stretched out a hand to him, which he took in his own.

"Yes. Business partners and friends."

Shooting Skeet

Nick dropped by the Balcones Trap and Skeet Club for an appointment with his new boss. He'd have to find a way out from under her thumb, but at least in the meantime, he had a steady paycheck, which covered Theresa and Alice. The club, deserted for the Governor's private use, sat next to a lake. He followed gunshot blasts to a trap field where Fran shot at clays. Two men in suits and sunglasses stood nearby scanning the area. Seeing him approach, she paused. Governor Adamson was decked out in a shooting vest, hat and glasses, a shotgun broken over her arm.

"Good to see you, Nick."

"Really?"

"Of course. You and I are going to become great friends. I can feel it."

"I don't see it happening."

She frowned. "Where's your gun?"

He reached back for his .45. Both suits also reached under their jackets.

"It's okay, boys. He's not going to shoot me. At least not today."

Nick lifted his hands chest high in mock surrender. "Probably not what you have in mind anyway."

"No worries. I'm shooting a matched set of Holland & Holland shotguns." She nodded to one of the suits. "Chuck, would you hand Mr. Sibelius the shotgun over there and some shells?"

Gun in hand, Nick followed the governor over to the range. "We're shooting skeet, Nick." She loaded her gun with two shells, then closed the breach with a click of the latch.

"Haven't shot skeet before, but I'll give it try."

"The clays will come across the field left to right, right to left. You'll get the hang of it." She looked across the field. "Pull."

Two clay disks flew, which she tracked from her left. She fired. The first clay shattered, then another blast as the second crumbled midair.

"Nice shot, Governor."

Nick took his turn, missing both clays. He didn't expect to hit, but it did sting to miss in front of the governor.

"Two to zip, Nick."

"We're keeping score?"

"I always keep score. First one to twenty-five wins." She fired, once again hitting both clays. "Make that four to zip."

They continued shooting. Nick picked up more clays, but with Adamson rarely missing, he couldn't even the score. At twenty to sixteen, Nick took his position to shoot. "I'm assuming you brought me here for a better reason than beating me at skeet?" The clays flew. He shot them both. "Twenty to eighteen."

"Well, well. Performs well under pressure."

"I do my best. So, what are we meeting about?"

"I wanted to get an update from the director of my new special ops team on the whole Bruce Reynolds affair." She stepped to the line, gun at the ready.

"Interesting how your largest campaign contributor also promoted your desire for secession."

"Pull." Firing twice, only one clay shattered. "Shit." She turned back to him. "My desire for secession?"

Nick took his place. "Pull." Both clays exploded with two clean shots. "Twenty-one to twenty, Governor."

"Are you accusing me of colluding with Reynolds to create a Republic?"

"Your shot, Governor."

She moved into position.

237

"Six months ago at a press conference you chastise the Federal government about Medicaid, then suggest Texas should secede."

"Politics, Nick."

"The press figures you're just blowing smoke. But in the meantime, you get Reynolds to front your movement, keeping your distance in case things didn't work out."

"Pull." Adamson's gun fired twice, hitting one clay. "Twenty-two to twenty."

"And if things do work out, you're the president of the Republic of Texas. Pull." Both clays fell shattered. "Twenty-two all."

She stepped up to Nick, her eyes fierce, her voice a hissing whisper. "Listen, Sibelius. Say what you want to here, but if you share your little fantasy with the outside world, you will be living very dangerously."

"I believe it's your shot again."

She glared, then turned on a heel to the range, dropping two shells into her gun. "Pull." She fired twice, but hit only one again.

"A miss. Too bad. So, when did you know Reynolds had gone off the deep end?" Nick fired twice, hitting both clays. "Let's see. You're twenty-three and I'm twenty-four."

"You're about to see why I'm the governor and Reynolds is out of the picture. Pull." Her first shot hit its mark, but when she squeezed her trigger the second time, nothing happened. "Damn it. Who the hell loaded these damned shells?"

"Some things don't turn out the way we want them to, Governor. I'm guessing Reynolds got a whiff of his potential power and decided he didn't need you. In fact, you're a liability. Part of the old guard, not the new Republic. Pull." Both clays shattered under his fire. "Looks like I win, Governor."

She glared at him. "Congratulations, Nick. Good to know my new director can shoot skeet, as well as bullshit."

238

They walked over to a table, placing the guns back in their case.

"You blew the building, didn't you? Reynolds got out of control, so you put him down."

She laughed. "Reynolds was a big contributor and did a lot of good for business in the state. But when he let this whole Republic of Texas thing worm its way into his soul, he became a threat, not only to Texas, but given our border with Mexico, the security of this country. So no, I wasn't standing behind the curtain waiting to become President of the Republic. My only focus was to protect the state and the country I so dearly love."

Usually he could read people, sense if they told the truth. But with Adamson, the picture blurred. He couldn't tell if she actually tried to create a new country or if her professed love for Texas and America rang true.

"You didn't have anything to do with a vacant hospital building exploding just as Reynolds's snipers were trying to kill us?"

"You want a confession?" She walked away, her bodyguards flanking her. Then she turned back, a sly smile cutting across her face. "I will tell you this. Bruce learned an important lesson about my beloved Texas."

"What's that?"

"When we say, 'Don't mess with Texas', honey, we damn well mean it."

Buzzard Bait

240

R. W. Hacker

ABOUT THE AUTHOR

Richard Hacker, after living many years in Texas, moved to Seattle, Washington. He may be wanted by authorities for transporting Texas BBQ across state lines. His writing has been recognized by the Writer's League of Texas and the Pacific Northwest Writers Association.

www.richardhacker.com

Follow the author on Facebook:
www.facebook.com/RWHacker

Buzzard Bait

R. W. Hacker

ALSO BY THE AUTHOR

Other Books in the Nick Sibelius Series

KILL'T DEAD OR WORSE is a full-flavored Texas novel worthy of your attention!
Hacker masterfully weaves his plot through the cultural fabric of the Lone Star State. A smart novel chocked full of great characters.
Brian Braden, *Underground Book Reviews*

KILL'T DEAD OR WORSE

After a murdered partner, a cheating wife, and a lost job in Houston, Nick Sibelius sets up a private investigation business in a small Texas town hoping to find some peace and maybe himself. When two lovers disappear and a fisherman turns up dead, he finds himself drawn into a web of crime and deceit involving MaryLou, a beautiful woman with a mysterious past; Junior, a failed farmer whose best intentions seem to always result in a dead body; and Barry, a sociopathic dentist turned illegal toxic waste entrepreneur with a violent right-wing agenda. When the felon who killed Nick's partner in Houston joins forces with Barry, Nick must not only stop the toxic waste dumping while finding his client's missing daughter, but keep from being killed in the process. In the end, MaryLou's dark secret will either save him or kill him -- whichever comes first.

ALL HAT AND NO CATTLE

One thing Nick Sibelius knows for sure—his wealthy new client, Texas entrepreneur Dan Hoyt, is 'all hat and no cattle'. When an open and shut case of vandalism leaves more questions than answers, Nick must untangle a knot of egomania, desire, and greed. Unknown to Nick, his client, having made a deal with virtual gaming icon, Izzy Zydeco, to partner in a desalination project, is already counting his money. And unknown to Hoyt, his new partner has bigger and more insidious plans requiring the betrayal of a major drug cartel and contaminating the Austin water supply for the next century. Working with covert Homeland Security agent and past love, MaryLou, and his new colleague, Theresa, Nick must thwart Izzy and ultimately choose between justice and saving Theresa's life. H_2O is up for grabs and Nick discovers in Texas, water is a deadly business.

www.ingramcontent.com/pod-product-compliance
Lightning Source LLC
Chambersburg PA
CBHW050924120626
46552CB00001B/32